SLAY RIDE

he knows where you live

CHRIS
GRABENSTEIN

CARROLL & GRAF PUBLISHERS
NEW YORK

SLAY RIDE
Carroll & Graf Publishers
An Imprint of Avalon Publishing Group, Inc.
245 West 17th Street, 11th Floor
New York, NY 10011

AVALON
publishing group incorporated

"SANTA CLAUS IS COMING TO TOWN"
Words by HAVEN GILLESPIE, music by J. FRED COOTS
© 1934 (Renewed) EMI FEIST CATALOG, INC.
Rights for the Extended Renewal Term in the United States Controlled
All Rights Controlled outside the United States Controlled by EMI FEIST CAT-
ALOG INC. (Publishing) and ALFRED PUBLISHING CO., INC. (Print)
All Rights Reserved. Used by Permission.

"LITTLE BRIGHT STAR"
Words and Music by Mary Dean-Lauria and Allan Capps
© 1965 (Renewed 1993) JOBETE MUSIC CO., INC.
All Rights Controlled and Administered by EMI BLACKWOOD MUSIC, INC. on
behalf of STONE AGATE MUSIC (A Division of JOBETE MUSIC CO, INC.)
All Rights Reserved International Copyright Secured. Used by Permission.

Library of Congress Cataloging-in-Publication Data is available.

Cloth edition ISBN-13: 978-0-78671-820-7
Cloth edition ISBN-10: 0-7867-1820-X

Trade paperback edition ISBN-13: 978-0-78671-877-1
Trade paperback edition ISBN-10: 0-7867-1877-3

9 8 7 6 5 4 3 2 1

Printed in the United States of America
Interior Design by Maria E. Torres
Distributed by Publishers Group West

To J. J.

Sometimes a wife's paranoia is a writer's greatest muse.

PROLOGUE

Christopher Miller is running.

He cradles the child in his arms and feels the sting of a bullet biting into the back of his thigh.

He is sweating. The field of waist-high weeds whips against his hips as he plows forward. Dust swirls in the haze surrounding the sun.

Now the sweat blinds him. He can no longer see where he is running. He only knows he must charge ahead, keep his legs churning

Another sting. His thigh burns with pain.

The child in his arms shrieks. She is terrified.

So is he. If he drops the girl she will surely die.

So Miller keeps running. When his left leg collapses, he doesn't fall. He grimaces, strains forward, leaves his feet. He flies across the field. His wounded thigh is on fire but he is soaring like a hawk headed for the treetops. He looks down at the girl.

She is gone. Did he drop her? Did she slip away? It no longer matters: she is forever lost in the whirlpool of weeds swirling below.

Christopher Miller sat up, breathing hard. Trying not to wake his wife.

He knew this wasn't how it went down.

He had saved that girl.

He knew the truth, the facts. But that never altered the dream's last scene: he always lost the girl, always let her slip away. Lately the dream had been feeling less like a nightmare, more like a premonition.

Christopher Miller feared there was another run still to come.

1

It was 7:01 A.M. and Scott Wilkinson wondered if the limo driver was purposely trying to ruin his life.

He had specifically instructed the car service that he needed to be picked up at seven or he'd miss his flight out of Newark. And if he missed his flight out of Newark he would also miss the presentation in Dallas. And if he missed the presentation in Dallas, six months and three hundred thousand dollars worth of advertising research would be wasted.

He had made this clear when he set up his reservation last night. He had made it even clearer when he called at six thirty to double-triple confirm his pickup time and car number. He knew it would take at least half an hour for even the best driver from 777-CARS to find the Wilkinson home in Northridge, New Jersey. Scott had previously clocked the car service's vehicles in similar situations. Thirty minutes was the norm.

7:02 A.M.

He stood in his driveway and jabbed numbers into his cell phone with his thumb: 7-7-7, C-A-R-S. He never liked spelling out words on a keypad, found it inefficient, found it difficult to locate the appropriate letters since they were clustered together in sequential clumps of threes and four.

"Lucky Seven. Please hold . . ."

"No, sorry. I cannot hold. My car is late. I specifically requested a seven A.M. pickup."

"It's just seven now, sir."

"It's seven-oh-three."

"Do you have a car number, sir?"

"Yes. Seven-one-six." Scott could hear the operator clacking computer keys. She was definitely a hunt-and-pecker. Another thirty seconds might be wasted while she attempted to enter his number.

"Mr. Wilkinson?"

"Yes."

"Forty-four Canterbury Lane?"

"That is correct. Can you please advise me as to the current status of my car?"

"He should be there."

"I agree. He *should* be here, *should* being the operative word . . ."

"Car number Seven-one-six. A black Lincoln Town Car . . ."

"Actually, he *should*'ve been here at seven A.M. since that was what I requested when I made my reservation . . ."

"Yes, sir. He should be there."

"You keep saying that."

"Just give him another minute, okay?"

"Actually, it's not okay." Scott had his MBA. Gross inefficiency annoyed him. He always planned his travel itinerary with detailed precision. With a flight scheduled to depart at nine thirty A.M., the airline wanted him there no later than eight. It was a thirty-minute drive from his house. Theoretically, he could leave as late as seven thirty, but that would entail giving up his thirty-minute buffer, the one he always counted on having to cover unforeseen contingencies: traffic, accidents, weather, Acts of God. Without it, he was subject to the capricious whims of the universe. "May I please speak to your supervisor?"

"Sir, she'll just tell you what I'm telling you."

"Let me talk to your supervisor."

"Please hold."

Scott pressed the cell phone closer to his ear, as if burrowing the plastic earpiece into his auditory canal might speed things up. He tapped his toe, drumming in time to a hummingbird's heartbeat. The morning was chilly but his ear was red hot, a furnace fueled by anger, which only intensified as he listened to a professionally soothing recorded voice telling him how much his business meant to Lucky Seven Limousines and how much they appreciated his patience while he continued to hold.

"Honey?" His wife came out on the front porch. She wore a red flannel bathrobe. "Is everything okay?"

"The car's late. Again."

"Would you like coffee? I just brewed some."

Melissa Wilkinson's robe was decorated with jolly snowmen—their faces as cute and perky as hers. She was also sporting something of a snowman's belly: the Wilkinsons were expecting their first child in less than a month.

"Missy, you should go back inside," Scott said. "It's freezing out here."

"I know, but . . ."

"Uh-uh-uh," Scott said playfully. "You better not pout. I'll tell Santa."

It was December fourteenth. Sugary snow dusted the resin sculptures standing in the Wilkinsons' front lawn. A six-foot Santa conducting a choir of roly-poly snowmen.

"Really, honey. Go back inside. You'll catch a cold."

"You want me to call the car company?" she asked.

Scott wiggle-waggled the phone next to his ear.

"Oh. Is that them?"

"Yes."

Melissa didn't have her MBA. In fact, Scott liked to joke that at college, Melissa "majored in Greek—she was president of her sorority." She was twenty-six, her husband thirty. She was sweet and beautiful and blonde and cuddly and the main reason Scott Wilkinson worked so hard. Soon, the baby would come and he'd have to work even harder. Eighteen years from now, college would cost a fortune. Scott had already run the numbers.

"Here it comes!" Melissa bounced up on her toes and pointed. "Over there."

Scott saw a black Lincoln Town Car crawling up the street.

"Looks like it."

"Have a good one, hon!" She threw her arms around Scott's neck and kissed him. "I really only came out so I could do that again."

"Well, I'm glad you did," he said, squeezing her tight. He flicked his wrist and read his watch over her shoulder. "I better scoot. We're five minutes behind schedule."

"Fly safe, sweetie. Hurry home."

"Will do."

Scott grabbed his rolling suitcase and hoisted it off the ground so he'd be ready to fling it into the trunk as soon as the driver popped open the lid. He figured he might pick up a few seconds that way.

7:06 A.M.

Everything was back under control. He still had a twenty-four-minute buffer.

2

Christopher Miller tore another chunk out of the coconut pastry.

It was homemade and tasted even better than the caramel-covered custard and fried johnnycakes Mrs. Melo had already insisted he eat. Miller knew this wasn't what his neighbor had for breakfast every morning, that these were special Dominican treats, normally served for dessert. He also knew if he ate many breakfasts like this one he'd be hauling around more than his typical two hundred pounds on his six-foot frame. It wouldn't be solid muscle anymore, either.

He was stuffed.

"That was good," Miller said. "Delicious. Everything."

"Would you like more?"

Miller sensed Mrs. Melo wasn't yet ready to talk so he took another chomp to give her some time. "Coconut, right?"

"*Sí.*"

"I thought so. Thought I tasted it."

Her kitchen looked like his across the street. Small. Cozy. Linoleum table about three feet away from the stove so the oven could warm you on the outside while the food kept you comfy on the inside.

The two-story houses up and down the block were what they called "working-class homes" and that was fine with Miller. He didn't mind working hard and liked living around folks who felt the same way. Besides, his mother used to say, "the smallest houses hold the most love."

True. But, a second bathroom upstairs might be nice, too.

Miller's Jersey City neighbors were new immigrants mixed with longtime residents. Dominicans like Mrs. Melo. Filipinos. Indians. Black folk like Miller. You could count on them, and knowing this made him feel lucky. Whenever a blizzard hit, for example, every able-bodied resident on the block would trudge out to the sidewalks, snow shovels, and ice picks in hand, ready to dig out anyone needing assistance. Miller usually led the shovel brigade. He liked attacking the snow, liked battling the mountainous snowbanks left behind to block the driveways after the city's plows cleared the street.

Miller liked restoring order to chaos.

Besides, the exercise helped him stay fit—even though most of the old ladies he dug out usually rewarded him with big loaves of banana bread.

Miller pushed back from the table.

"Have more. Please."

"No, thank you, Mrs. Melo. I'm good."

The old woman's eyes were rimmed with red. Miller could tell she'd been crying, probably for weeks, probably since it had happened. He wiped his hands on the cloth napkin his hostess set out whenever distinguished guests like her neighbor, FBI Special Agent Christopher Miller, came over at seven A.M. for the breakfast buffet.

"This is Victor." Mrs. Melo pulled a fading photograph out of a folded envelope. Miller could see smudges and stains on the glossy surface. Tear drops. Worn edges from where the old woman had rubbed and rubbed and tried to touch her grandson one last time, tried to hug him with her hands.

"Handsome."

"He was going to be a doctor. The taxi job? That was only to help me. To buy heating oil and food . . ."

"He was a good man . . ."

"Yes. Very good." Mrs. Melo used her own napkin to dab at her eyes. "Please forgive me."

Her grandson's story and picture had been in all the papers back in late November. "PRE-MED STUDENT SHOT BY 'MAN IN THE MOON' KILLER." Not a very happy Thanksgiving for anybody on the block. Hard to be grateful for everything you had when you knew the woman across the street had just lost everything that made her life worth living.

"Ever since my husband die, Victor help me. He help his *abuela*."

Victor Melo had been found slumped inside his idling taxicab near the corner of Boyd and Oxford in Jersey City with a fatal bullet wound to the back of his head. He had started his shift after classes at UMDNJ, about five P.M., and reported picking up his last fare at New Jersey Transit's Journal Square train station at one forty-five A.M. Detectives found one casing from a

25mm semiautomatic handgun in the back seat of the cab, but no gun.

It had been the same with the Man in the Moon's first two victims. Both were cabbies and both had been shot in the back of the head with a 25mm handgun. Ballistic tests showed the same weapon had been fired in all three killings. When the cops did the math, checked their calendars, they realized Victor had been killed exactly twenty-eight days after the cabbie killed in October who had been murdered exactly twenty-eight days after the gypsy-cab driver slain in September.

The newspapers crunched the same numbers and tagged the killer "The Man in the Moon" because his twenty-eight day pattern followed that of the typical lunar cycle.

Victor Melo's pockets had been picked clean, so the official conclusion was that the motive was robbery, the way it was most times in such cases. Cabbies were a junkie's favorite ATM. Conveniently located. Always open.

"He was afraid to drive the cab at night," Mrs. Melo said, "but he did it for me."

"Don't go blaming yourself."

"He was going to be married. Next summer."

"I know."

"Why don't the police catch this Man in the Moon?"

"They're working on it."

"Why doesn't the FBI help?"

Miller rubbed his beefy hand around his mouth and cheeks. He could tell Mrs. Melo about jurisdictional boundaries and the Bureau's current focus on anti-terrorist initiatives. He could try to tell this grieving grandmother why the United States Justice Department's main investigatory agency couldn't really get involved in what, for the time being, was considered a matter for the local authorities.

He could've given any number of officially approved responses.

Instead he said, "We're going to look into it."

Mrs. Melo put both hands over her heart.

"We're gonna look into it starting tonight."

She dried her eyes.

"*Usted es una bendición al Dios!*" she said, fighting back the tears. Miller understood enough Spanish to know what she was saying. "You are a blessing to God."

Miller only hoped his bosses at the Bureau would think the same thing when they found out he was running an unauthorized, after-hours investigation.

He also hoped God was listening to Mrs. Melo's kind words this morning.

It was December fourteenth.

Exactly twenty-eight days since her grandson had been killed. Miller knew: The Man in the Moon would be coming out again that night.

3

"I hit traffic on the turnpike," the driver said.

"My plane leaves at nine thirty-two."

"No problem."

"I need to be at the airport ninety minutes before my flight. Eight-oh-two."

"No problem."

The big car, a Lincoln Executive L, rumbled down Canterbury Lane, headed, Scott Wilkinson assumed, for downtown Northridge and the turnpike entrance ramp. That's the route he would take, the route he always took.

Scott was back on track. They'd make up the lost time—unless, of course, there were more unexpected delays. He noticed the digital radio was set to 1010 WINS—the all-news station most drivers listened to because the station updated traffic conditions every ten minutes "on the ones."

The car seemed brand-new. The pillowy leather seat cushions crinkled when Scott shifted his weight. There were adjustable reading lamps and a silver Kleenex box. The tissue box was full. Lucky Seven Limousines might have been late, but at least they sent clean cars with copies of *Business Week* neatly tucked into the webbed seat pouches. Everything was as it should be.

Until he smelled cigarettes.

"Has somebody been smoking in here?"

The driver glanced up into the rearview mirror.

"I specifically requested a nonsmoking vehicle."

"My last passenger? He smoke." The driver had an accent. Scott figured Russian or Israeli, maybe Greek. Probably a nuclear physicist or brain surgeon in the old country, reduced in his new life to driving a cab to make ends meet. "I tell him not to, but some people no listen. They smoke anyhow."

"Yes. I suppose they do."

They reached Main Street. The driver adjusted what looked like a thick wick soaking inside a jewel-cut perfume jar glued to his dashboard.

"Air freshener make better."

The sickly-sweet scent of artificial pine trees filled the car.

"That's okay," Scott said. "I'm fine. Thanks."

"Okay."

"Careful!"

An old woman teetered on the curb. She'd almost stepped into the crosswalk because she had the green light and the Lincoln did not.

"Stupid woman," the driver muttered.

"She had the light."

"No. Light was yellow." The driver jiggled the air freshener wick.

"The light was red. Just watch where you're going, okay?"

The driver said nothing.

Scott shook his head and opened his briefcase. He needed to make some phone calls, mark up memos, make certain he had the Contact Report from the last meeting in Dallas and the Advertising Strategy and . . .

"We take Twenty-two to Nine," the driver said. "Better than turnpike."

"Really? I usually take the turnpike."

"Twenty-two to Nine is faster. Twenty-three minutes."

"Excuse me?"

"We will be at airport in twenty-three minutes. No problem."

Scott glanced at his watch. 7:15.

"Fine," he said and returned to the stack of papers in his lap.

"Which airline?"

"American."

The driver nodded. "Terminal A."

"I think so. We can double-check when . . ."

"Is Terminal A. This I know."

Scott smiled. He wouldn't argue, he'd just check the signs when they reached the airport. He pulled out his phone and pressed the speed-dial button to access his own voicemail. Once connected, he selected the option for changing his outgoing message.

"Hi. This is Scott Wilkinson. I will be in Dallas on business December fourteenth and fifteenth. At the tone, please leave a message. If it's urgent, press pound nine and you will be connected to my administrative assistant, Kim Hammond. Thank you. Have a good day." He pressed the keys to activate his new personal greeting.

Scott glanced at the glowing green digits in the dash-board: 55 mph. A good speed. He'd be at the airport in plenty of time to wend his way through security, even if they made him slip off his shoes, which they always did. Scott flew so often, he knew to wear loafers and a good pair of socks.

He glanced at his watch again. 7:17 A.M.—an excellent time to leave a voicemail message for his boss, Kent Stafford.

"Hey, Kent. Scott here. It's a little after seven and I'm in the car, on my way to Dallas to show our friends at Taco John what folks really think about their advertising and who they should target in the first quarter. I'll touch base later, let you know how it goes. If you need anything, you can reach me on my cell. Have a good one, Kent—or should I call you Mr. Stafford now that you're officially our new CEO? Hey—I owe you a lunch, buddy. Let's coordinate calendars when I get back."

He snapped the phone shut.

When he looked up, the driver's fist was reaching into the back seat.

"You want candy?"

The driver opened his palm to reveal a small tube of waxy paper.

"Is Russian. Is good. Cherry candy."

"No thanks. Maybe you should keep your eyes on the road?"

"Sure, sure. No problem."

The hand disappeared. Scott looked at the papers in his lap, cross-referenced the call list he had printed out from his BlackBerry, pulled out his pen, clicked and reclicked the point into place. He heard paper crinkling. He looked up.

The driver had both hands off the steering wheel so he could unwrap his candy. He seemed to be steering with his thighs. The car drifted to the side.

"Sir?" Scott's left hand gripped the edge of his seat cushion. "Could you please concentrate on driving?"

"Sure." The driver popped the little red log into his mouth. It was so intensely cherry that now the whole car reeked of kids' cough syrup.

Scott powered down his window a crack to let in some fresh air. He was familiar with this stretch of Route 22 East. The used-car lots with the gigantic American flags out front. The strip malls and dinette showrooms and McDonald'ses. The buildings began to blur, to race by at a clip, rolling along like the repeating background in a Saturday morning cartoon. The Lincoln was picking up speed. Scott heard wind whistling through the slit at the top of his window, the blare of a car horn.

"*Zalupa!*" the driver hissed. "Dickhead!"

Scott turned forward and stared through the windshield.

A BMW was less than twelve inches in front of them. Scott glanced at the speedometer. It read 75 and rising.

The driver yanked his steering wheel hard, slid into the right-hand lane.

"Jesus!" Scott yelped. "Easy."

The driver sped up. The car surged forward until it was blocked by the back end of a bus belching black smoke. Scott began to think the driver might be trying to go under the bus in order to get in front of it.

"Do you really need to tailgate like that?"

"*Zalupa!*" Another jerk of the wheel and they were back in the left-hand lane—playing bumper cars with the rear end of a rumbling dump truck. Out the driver-side window, Scott saw the blur of a concrete barrier, the short wall separating the eastbound lanes of Route 22 from the westbound.

"Whoa! Slow down. I'm not in that big of a hurry."

"The truck cut me off."

"Slow down."

"Fucking truck."

"Slow down!"

The driver sped up, narrowed the gap between the nose of his car and the rear wheels of the truck. He inched closer until the chrome Lincoln logo at the tip of his hood looked like a gunner's sight targeting its next victim. The sectional white concrete wall hurtled past—its craggy joints clipping along like a sideways sidewalk. The wall seemed close enough to scrape away the Lincoln's sideview mirror and sand down the door handles.

"Slow down! Please! Now!"

"Fucking truck cut me off!"

The driver yanked the wheel and they screeched back into the right-hand lane. Scott heard a horn blast—the car they'd almost sideswiped.

He fumbled in the crack between the cushions searching for a seat belt.

He wanted to be wearing one when they crashed.

4

Christopher Miller said good-bye to Mrs. Melo.

He walked down the cracked concrete path that led from her front steps to the sidewalk. Miller was heading home to eat another breakfast, this time with his wife and five-year-old daughter. He wasn't hungry, but he wouldn't miss breakfast with his girls for anything in the world.

He saw Mrs. Melo's newspaper lying in its plastic wrapper in the patchy snow. The headline was visible: MAN IN THE MOON TO STRIKE AGAIN TONIGHT?

Her grandson Victor, the killer's most recent victim, was pictured in a black box beneath the screaming headline.

Miller picked up the paper, tucked it under his arm.

He didn't think Mrs. Melo needed to see it, not this morning, maybe not ever.

He chucked the paper into a dented garbage can standing at the curb.

5

"This is fine," Scott said when they reached the departure area for American Airlines.

The driver draped an arm over his seat. "Was Terminal A, no?" He smiled. For the first time, Scott noticed the guy's face—a sharp nose and black, piercing eyes. Hair close-cropped in a quarter-inch buzz cut showing off a symmetrically receding hairline. "American Airlines is always Terminal A, Newark."

"Right," said Scott. "Terminal A."

"Twenty-three minutes. Door to door. Just as I say."

"Congratulations. And, as an added bonus, you didn't get me killed. Almost, but not quite." Scott slid out of the Lincoln.

"Would you like a receipt?" the driver asked.

Scott ripped the slip of paper out of the man's hand. Fortunately, he wasn't required to tip him. He only had to sign the voucher, something he'd already done. His company would take care of all payments to Lucky Seven Limos. Scott would never have to deal with this idiot again.

"You drive like a moron," he said as he slammed his door shut.

The driver smiled.

"Have a safe trip," he said. "Happy Holidays, Mr. Wilkinson!"

6

Nicolai Kyznetsoff took another long drag on his Marlboro and flicked the cigarette's glowing head at the crack of air near the top of his window.

He didn't want ashes in his ashtray. All Lucky Seven cars were "guaranteed smoke free."

He cruised the roadways linking the terminals at Newark-Liberty Airport, waiting for the mobile data terminal on his dash to squeak and assign him his next job, probably an airport pickup, preferably somebody landing at Terminal A.

He knew he would get a good ride. Julie was working the dispatch desk this morning. She was fat and ugly and nobody was ever nice to her because she was so disgusting. Nobody except Nicolai. He even gave her candy from time to time: jumbo bags of Solidarnosc Trufle from the shop in Brighton Beach where they sold all the really good food from home, not the cheap Romanian imitations.

Kyznetsoff's cell phone rang. He tossed what was left of his cigarette out the window.

"Hello?" He drove with one hand, talked with the other.

"Nicolai?"

"Julie! So good to be hearing your voice." He could also hear her sucking on a chocolate. "Do you have special assignment for your very best driver? Is this why you call on phone?"

"No, listen, Nick . . ."

Nicolai Kyznetsoff only let Julie call him Nick because it suited his purposes.

"Ruth Ramirez? In Customer Service? Do you know her?"

"*Da.* I know Miss Ramirez." Kyznetsoff could speak English better than most Americans, especially many of those who worked for Lucky Seven. But, he knew an occasional slip into the mother tongue made him seem more exotic and, therefore, more enticing to lonely girls such as Julie. "I know of this woman."

"She just got another complaint."

"What about?"

"You. Again."

"Impossible. No way."

"She needs to see you."

"Who makes this complaining?"

"I dunno. Ramirez said the call came in like two minutes ago but I don't have any, you know, specifics or whatever."

"*Da.* Of course. No problem."

"I'm really sorry, Nick."

"Hey—is no big deal."

Kyznetsoff heard Julie crinkle the foil off another candy and work it into her mouth. He could almost see her big fat lips over the phone—bright pink lipstick smeared around the edges, clumps of it clinging to dangling bits of lip skin.

"Oh, Nick?" she said. "One more thing—can you do me a double today? I'm short on drivers and there's all these Wall Street holiday parties and . . ."

"Sorry. I am very busy this evening."

"Really? But you always . . ."

"Sorry. Not tonight."

"If you do me this favor, I'll make sure Ramirez hears about it. It might help you with your, you know—situation."

"Thank you, Julie. However, this evening I have the prior commitments." He paused for an instant as he composed his lie. "My cousin. He is visiting from Moscow. His plane arrives this evening."

"Which airport?"

That startled him. What business was it of hers? He wove some more fabric into his fable. "JFK. He will be on Aeroflot."

"Good. As long as it's not Newark or anywhere in New Jersey. The Man in the Moon? He's going to kill somebody in Jersey tonight. The *Post* says so. Be careful, okay, Nicky?"

Kyznetsoff grimaced. *Nicky?* That was a new one. It was also insulting. *Nicky.* Like some little boy with *kakashka* in his trousers, stinking poo-poo in his pants.

"I will see you when I come see Miss Ramirez, *da?*"

"Sure. Maybe we could grab a cup of coffee or something."

"Coffee would be nice. I catch you later, okay?"

"Okay."

Kyznetsoff closed his phone and headed toward the airport exit.

He glanced up to the miniature security camera mounted on the windshield. It used infrared lighting to capture a digital image of the passenger area of the car and automatically took a photograph of every passenger who climbed into the back seat just in case one of them caused any trouble. A glowing LED told Kyznetsoff the camera was up and operational.

Good.

He'd print out an image of his first passenger, this whining asshole Scott Wilkinson of 44 Canterbury Lane, Northridge, New Jersey.

Mr. Wilkinson had no idea who he was dealing with when he called Lucky Seven Limousines to complain.

No idea at all.

7

"You sure you want to do this?"

"I'm sure. You sure you trust me with one of your cabs?"

"Of course. Besides—nobody wants to drive tonight. Everybody call in sick. They have the 'flu.' The Yellow Flu. They are afraid."

Christopher Miller followed Yousseff Awadallah out the front door of the Jersey City Cab Company. It was a drizzly night, but not actually raining—more like they were walking around inside a dark cloud. Misty air sparkled in the funnel of light cast by the parking lot's single overhead lamp.

"We all appreciate what you are doing very much," Awadallah said.

"Hey, she's my neighbor."

The bald owner of the cab company nodded to show he understood. "We will never forget your courage."

Miller would never forget what he'd promised his neighbor this morning. That's why he volunteered to drive one of Awadallah's cabs, to cruise the seedier sections of the city, to put himself out on the street as Man-in-the-Moon bait.

Of course, Miller hadn't told his bosses about his plan. If anybody from the Bureau saw him behind the wheel tonight, he'd tell them he was moonlighting. Since they all got by on government pay-grade salaries maybe they'd buy it. Maybe.

He did tell his wife, Natalie, which caused her to remind him of their wedding vows. Not the bit about forsaking all others and fidelity. Natalie, who was thirty-four and the sexiest mother Miller had ever seen, didn't worry about her husband straying. She worried about their private vows, the ones they'd made to each other before she would agree to marry this big man she so completely adored.

"If kids come along," she had said, "you promise you'll take it easy? On the job?"

Miller had said, "I do."

If he wasn't breaking that vow tonight, he was certainly stretching it.

Miller opened the door of a bright red taxicab.

"So, do I get to keep my tips?" Miller asked.

"You can keep it all, my friend." Awadallah clasped Miller's hand. "What you do is a *khayer*, for it is right and good. May Allah bless you."

Miller shook his new friend's hand and slipped into the cab. He half wished Allah could come along and ride shotgun.

"You had your bath already? Good. Let me talk to your mother again. I love you too, little angel."

Miller had parked in front of a 99 CENTS & UP shop to call home before his daughter went to bed. He flicked the wipers in another futile attempt to clean away some of the gritty swirl clouding his view. It was pointless. Like so many taxicab wipers, this set had run out of good rubber long ago, now accomplishing little besides streaking the gunk around and making the windshield murkier.

Miller glanced up at the sun visor. The regular driver of this particular cab had pictures of his kids rubberbanded to the shade. Two girls and a boy. Miller thought he recognized one of the kids. The girl. She was in Angela's pre-K class at the Horace Abercrombie School.

Miller only had the one child, and doted on her. He had been forty-five when Angela had come along and he looked at children the way he figured most grandparents must—with a keener appreciation of just how precious life is, a feeling that only comes when you're sitting on the far side of forty. Miller was grateful his wife was younger; she could do most of the chasing and corralling. He'd do the diapers. He also liked the tuck-in rituals at night. Enjoyed reading the storybooks, fluffing up pillows, and finding runaway stuffed tigers. Liked knowing his angel was safe for another day.

Natalie picked up the phone at the other end.

"Hey, old man."

"Hey, doc." Natalie had recently completed her PhD in Forensic Psychology, doing most of the coursework in night school.

"You staying safe?" she asked.

"Don't worry, okay?"

"I stopped worrying ages ago." Natalie had been

working at the FBI's local field office when they met. She'd known what she was getting into when she fell in love with the guy everybody called Saint Christopher.

"In fact, I've moved way past worrying," she said. "You can call me Cleopatra."

Miller laughed at the corny pun. "So you're the Queen of Denial, hunh?"

"Uhm-hmm. Do you know where my husband is right now? He's busy over at Toys R Us?"

"Really? I was wondering where he might be."

"Check the Barbie department. That's where you'll find him."

"Damn, doc," Miller laughed. "Don't send me over there. That's dangerous territory . . . all that pink plastic . . ."

"Sorry, old man. You have a baby girl, you're sentenced to at least five years of hard time in Barbieland."

"Don't I know it." Miller chuckled and it covered the silence, covered it for a while, anyway.

"Chris?"

"Yeah?"

"You're happy doing the job you've been doing, right?"

"Sure."

Since Angela came along, Miller had kept his vow. He had dialed it down a notch and spent most of his time managing Critical Incident Response Group teams. He still went out into the field, but nowadays, he was the general in the tent, the wise old sage looking at the big picture while other, younger agents grabbed guns and chased after the bad guys. Miller had mellowed. He wasn't the crazy fullback charging up the middle with two automatic handguns blazing away like that knucklehead in *The Matrix* anymore.

"Be careful, okay?"

"I'll probably just sit on my butt all night."

"No superhero stuff. Your little girl needs her old man. I don't mind having you around, either."

"Well, aren't you sweet to say so."

"Remember your wedding vows."

"Good night, doc. I love you."

"I love you, too. But you know what?"

"What?"

"We really do need to get Angela some Barbie stuff."

"I'll get on it tomorrow."

"Promise?"

"Yeah. I promise. Tomorrow."

First, of course, he had to make it through tonight.

8

Miller drove the cab over to Journal Square, where Victor Melo had picked up his final fare on the night he was shot in the back of the head with a 25mm handgun.

It was one A.M.

A man in a blue windbreaker flagged Miller down. He couldn't see a face—the windshield was blurrier than ever. The drizzle was thicker and mixed with fog. He pulled over to the curb. The guy didn't open the passenger door, just walked around to the front of the cab and motioned for Miller to roll down his window. The rubber squeaked as the wet glass slid down into the door.

"You lookin' to buy yourself a four-bagger?" the man said. "Or are you running your own private little thing to grab some beach time?"

The man was a silhouette, backlit by bright street lamps. Miller squinted.

"Tony?"

"Yeah."

It was Tony Cimino, a detective with the Jersey City Police. Cimino was using FBI slang to bust Miller's chops. "Beach time" meant suspension. A "four-bagger" was the worst kind of disciplinary action the Bureau could dish out: censure, transfer, suspension, *and* probation. Running your own unofficial investigation into a case? Definitely a four-bag offense.

"I'm moonlighting," Miller said. "You know what comes after Christmas: credit card bills."

"Ain't that the truth. You seen anything?" Cimino asked.

"No. Nothing unusual. Just folks in a hurry to head home."

"Thanks for helping out," Cimino said. "We appreciate it. But I promise—I won't write any letters of commendation to your bosses at the Bureau."

"Thanks. Where you guys running light?"

"Over in the Heights. We got Journal Square covered but only two units over that way."

"The Heights, hunh?"

"Yeah. That's where our doer popped the first guy."

"Maybe I'll head in that direction. See what I can see."

"Thanks, Chris."

"Tony?"

"Yeah?"

"You got any daughters?"

"Three."

"Which do they like better? The Barbie Airplane or the Talking Kitchen?"

"The Airplane. Definitely."

"All right. Thanks. Appreciate it."

"Get that Dazzling Date dress-up deal, too. That was a big hit last year."

"All right, man. Thanks, Tony."

"No, man. Thank *you.*"

Miller squeaked his window back up and started for the Heights, over to the dark shadows where very few children went outside to play with their Barbies because the mothers all knew the deal: it was just too damn dangerous.

9

Miller cruised streets he knew inside out.

He had grown up in Jersey City, spent his glory days as the star fullback for Saint Peter's Prep over on Grand. Saint Peter's was a Jesuit high school that prided itself on educating "men of competence, conscience, and compassion." His friends used to tease Miller, said he could've been St. Pete's poster child.

The teachers, the Jesuit priests in particular, didn't much care whether you were black or white or purple as long as you studied hard and turned your homework in on time. Miller always did. The consequences of failing to do so seemed far too grim.

After graduation, he'd picked up a full-ride scholarship to play football for Notre Dame. Once again, he was a star, making All-American. He majored in pre-Law and graduated with a 3.75 GPA. After South Bend, he headed to Quantico for seventeen more weeks of education and training—this time at the FBI Academy.

After the Jesuits, Miller liked to joke, Quantico was a piece of cake.

• • •

He circled the raggedy streets of the Heights.

Some of the houses were, as the real estate people liked to say, real bargains—mostly because they were burned out and currently overrun with drug dealers and street gangs.

He eased past a small park overlooking the Hudson River. Its perimeter was lined with a spear-tipped fence that snagged random pieces of garbage—a plastic grocery bag fluttered on top of one picket like a tattered flag. A car parked at the curb had its rear window smashed out. Some dude would be driving to work without his radio.

It was almost two A.M.

Miller was glad he wasn't riding alone. His Glock M22 was snug inside a paddle holster strapped to the small of his back. Miller used a Fobus brand holster—the kind specifically designed for the Israeli security service, which would allow him to whip out his .40 caliber handgun in a nanosecond if he had to. Miller was quick on the draw, worked at it all the time, and not just because he'd watched too many cowboy shows when he was a kid.

He turned the corner and looped up Ogden Avenue for the umpteenth time.

Miller wasn't used to hunting muggers. His area of expertise at the FBI involved tracking down a specific and particularly unpleasant breed of criminal: The Kidnapper. It was a specialization that started way back in 1989—on what everybody else called "The St. Christopher Case."

It was a case that earned him a medal and several months of fame and glory.

Seems this Hispanic woman had shown up at a boarding school and told the people running the place that she was eight-year-old Kathryn G. Johnson's nanny and needed to pick the girl up early because both parents had been unexpectedly called away—death in the family. The woman, of course, was lying. She wasn't a nanny. She was part of a nasty gang that wanted a ton of money from Kathryn's father.

Mr. Johnson paid the million-dollar ransom, met all the kidnappers' demands.

They, however, skipped town without giving him back his little girl.

Miller was the one who figured out where the kidnappers had taken Kathryn when the agent in charge, a by-the-book, stick-in-the-mud named Leon Owens, couldn't buy a clue. Miller did it by hiding a radio transmitter in the lining of the moneybag, tracking its signal, tracing it to a dilapidated tobacco barn near an overgrown hay field in rural West Virginia. Miller was also the one who stormed the barn, grabbed the girl, and carried her out before the shit heels inside could slit her throat.

Miller had taken two slugs in his left hamstring on that little touchdown run. Fortunately, his Kevlar vest took the other six rounds that smacked into his back while he raced for the treeline. A single FBI sharpshooter wound up taking out the four bad guys, performing his job with extreme prejudice once the sons-of-bitches opened fire on Miller.

The story of Miller's "Run to Daylight" was then splashed all over the papers, and everybody at the Bureau was glad to see Miller receive his fifteen minutes of fame. Everybody except Leon Owens, the boss who thought *he* should have been the one getting the face time because, after all, he'd been The Agent in Charge. Miller didn't get too worked up—either by Owens or by all the publicity.

He was, however, seriously touched when Kathryn Johnson handed him his medal. It was a Saint Christopher. A stainless-steel oval depicting the burly saint ferrying the Christ child on his back across a raging river. "Saint Christopher Protect Us" was inscribed on it. And so the nickname stuck.

Miller still wore it on a simple chain around his neck. He liked remembering what the medal stood for, what it said about the job.

"Saint Christopher Protect Us."

He touched it now and turned left, headed back up the block alongside the park.

He wondered if his quarry might be taking a month off. Maybe he closed up shop for the holidays. Maybe the Man in the Moon knew the cops would be out looking for him, tonight. Maybe somebody else had already nabbed him.

Or maybe he was just out there waiting.

Miller flicked on the radio to see if he could catch the news. The sound snapped in on one of his favorites: "Santa Claus Is Comin' to Town" as done by The Temps. Miller knew The Temptations were "old school," but so was he. Hell, he was old. Fifty later this year. If he couldn't be old school, who could? Besides, old school was cool, way cooler than rap or hip-hop or any of that crap they sang on *American Idol*. The Temps moved Miller. Moved his soul. He did a few shoulder dips to one side, then the other, made the backup singer moves he remembered from *Soul Train*. Car dancing. That's what his wife called it whenever Miller started groovin' while movin'. Car dancing.

"You better watch out, you better not cry, you better not pout, I'm tellin' you why . . ."

He saw a baby carriage stranded on the sidewalk, bumped up against a telephone pole

It hadn't been there the last time he circled this block.

Miller pulled over to the curb, opened the door, stepped out.

He quickly surveyed the scene, looked for the mother or father, saw nobody.

"Hello?" he called to the darkness. "Anybody here?"

No answer.

He heard noises. The crunch of twigs. The stumble of heavy feet. Somebody running away?

He moved closer to the carriage, decided the baby was more important than its fleeing parents. Instinctively, he touched the small of his back, felt the bulge, the Glock nestled in its holster. He stepped over a puddle where the sidewalk had crumbled down into a crater.

"Hello?" No answer. Just the faint whoosh of cars and trucks speeding down some distant roadway. "Hello?"

Miller half expected the baby to answer his cries with a plaintive wail of its own. He knew that's what he'd do if his parents had ever been stupid enough to park him all alone in his baby buggy on a cold street at two in the morning. But the baby didn't cry.

Miller feared the worst.

He couldn't see inside the stroller because it had one of those ruffled hoods. He needed to come at it from the front.

He swung around the telephone pole.

The baby carriage was stuffed with a black trash bag and it was lumpy.

"Jesus," Miller whispered—more a prayer than a curse.

Quickly, hoping the child hadn't suffocated, Miller tore open the twist-tied top.

The bag was half full of bottles and cans. Beer, Coke, Pepsi, Sprite. Each one worth a nickel.

He had to laugh.

This was just the set of wheels some homeless person was using to roll their deposit bottles around town.

"It's cool!" Miller yelled to the shadows, down to where he thought he had heard someone running earlier. He didn't want to deprive anyone of their income, even if it only dribbled in five cents at a time. "I'm leaving. It's cool. We're cool."

Miller shook his head, headed back to the street.

"You abailable?"

A young man in a hooded sweatshirt was standing near his taxicab.

10

Miller didn't answer.

"Yo—you abailable?"

The kid seemed nervous. Jittery. Both hands were stuffed inside the front of the sweatshirt—like he was freezing and had forgotten to pack his mittens.

"Yeah," Miller said. "Where you headed?"

The kid hesitated as if he didn't know where he was going, like he wasn't expecting to go that far in the conversation.

That's when Miller knew.

"The city," the kid finally blurted.

"New York?" Miller bought time.

"Yeah. East Village. You abailable or what?"

"Yeah," Miller said. "I'm available." He didn't move toward the cab.

"Then let's go, old man."

"Okay."

The kid sniffed. Shivered. He was worse than jittery. He was jumpy and his hands weren't leaving those front pockets.

Miller was ten feet from the taxi.

"Come on," the kid said. "I'm late."

"Sure. Sure. I can dig it." Miller strolled over to the cab. Casual. Like he picked up fares and hauled them into the city at two in the morning all the time. "You goin' into town to party hearty?" If the boy was going to call him an old man, Miller decided he'd at least try to sound like one. "Gonna shake your groove thing? I can dig it."

"Come on, pops. Let's book."

"What's her name, bro?"

"Hunh?"

"Must be one fine lady for you to haul your butt outta bed at two A.M. Must be mighty fine, indeed."

The kid thought about that. Good. He was distracted.

"Yeah. She a'ight."

"So, what's her name, bro?" Miller went to open the rear door for his passenger. The kid squinted. Wracked his brain. Needed time to think up a name.

"She . . . you know . . . she just some bitch . . ."

Miller reached for the door handle.

"She just some ho I know . . ."

Miller heard the click of metal. A pistol hammer cocking back.

"Shit, pops—I know me a lot of ho's . . ."

Miller spun around, grabbed the kid's elbow.

"What the fuck?"

He ripped the boy's right hand out of the front flap but it was the other hand that came out with the gun.

The kid was a lefty.

"Be cool, old—"

Miller tightened his grip on the right wrist. He pivoted

and slipped behind the boy, grabbed around for the gun hand, wrenching it backwards.

"Shit . . ."

Miller twisted both wrists, yanked up hard on the arms, heard shoulder tendons tear.

"Fuck!"

He kneed the kid in the back.

"Motherfucker!"

The pistol clattered to the pavement.

Miller saw it: definitely a 25. He kicked the gun up the gutter and forced him down to his knees so he could slap on the cuffs.

"Yo! Take it easy, old man!"

Miller strapped the boy's hands together with plastic FlexiCuffs. He tugged hard to make certain they were tight.

"Shit! That hurts!"

"You want a word of advice, son?"

"What, motherfucker?"

"Never call any woman a 'bitch' or a 'ho.' Especially not in front of some 'old man.' He might just be some little girl's father."

11

Nicolai Kyznetsoff strolled up the boardwalk smoking a cigarette, letting the bright morning sun go ahead and warm his face.

Yesterday's drizzle had been pushed out to sea by a blast of cold air. The morning sky was sharp blue against an even bluer ocean. Kyznetsoff knew he'd been supposed to pay a visit to Ruth Ramirez in Customer Service yesterday but he hadn't felt like it. Maybe he'd go see her today. Maybe. Maybe not.

Up ahead, he could see the Coney Island Parachute Jump, a towering steel structure sticking up like a rusty Eiffel Tower about a mile south of Brighton Beach. Kyznetsoff sucked on his cigarette and shook his head.

Americans were such sissies, with their imitation thrill rides. If they wanted to know what it feels like to parachute they should join the fucking army. They should jump out of a plane and piss their fucking panties.

People called this part of Brooklyn Little Odessa because it reminded them of the Black Sea resort in Russia, because it was full of knishes and borscht and sturgeon, and Jews who emigrated from the old country.

Kyznetsoff had come to Brighton Beach because it was easy for a Russian to disappear here, and that was what he had needed to do. Become invisible.

It was also comfortable. Familiar. He could go into a bar, sit at the marble counter and order fifty different kinds of vodka, and when he was finished, he could go across the street for his favorite candies. He could even snatch them out of the bin and stuff them into his pockets before the stupid clerks behind the cash registers knew he was robbing them blind.

Kyznetsoff wore his black Adidas jogging suit and a black leather driver's cap. It was all he needed to keep warm, to look cool. At age fifty, he kept himself physically fit, just as he had done since childhood when the Soviet state stressed physical education as one of the most important means of preparing the nation for the defense of the motherland. He still weighed 157 pounds, could still make women swoon—the young ones, not just the thick-ankled babushkas, the plump matrons who shambled up and down the boardwalk in their fur coats and headscarves, whose knees went weak whenever they saw a man such as he.

He flicked away his cigarette butt and left the boardwalk for The Avenue, up to where the B train rumbled overhead on ancient trestles, up to where he could grab a shot of horseradish vodka and another pack of Marlboros.

Then maybe he'd go see Ruth Ramirez at Lucky Seven Limousines. Maybe.

The sight of Brighton Beach's chintzy Christmas and Chanukah ornaments sickened Kyznetsoff. Cheap green-and-white tinsel, shabby with street soot, was draped off rust-coated girders and dangled across the street. It was all crap. Dime-store garlands and dirty strips of glitter bent to resemble menorahs.

Menya eto ne eb'et, he thought. I don't give a fuck about any of it.

He cared little for Grandfather Frost—the Santa Claus of Soviet Russia. He especially despised the old man's cute little granddaughter: Snegurochk. The Snow Maiden. She of the baby-blue coat, white fur boots, and golden braids, she who made friends with all the little birdies and bunnies in the forest and rode along in her grandpapa's sleigh as it was pulled through the snow by three charging steeds.

Kyznetsoff crossed the street, not waiting for the WALK sign; he just stepped into traffic and yelled at anybody who dared honk their horn.

"Eb tvoju mat!"

It was the worst way he could think of to say, "fuck you" because it literally meant, "I have fucked your mother!"

Two other drivers were smoking on the sidewalk in front of the Lucky Seven offices. Maksim was in his sixties, with greasy white hair that smelled of burnt tobacco mixed with sardines, as if he slicked it back with fish oil straight from the tin. Kostya was twenty-six and very fat. Kyznetsoff often wondered how he ever found his prick when it came time to piss.

"My friends," Kyznetsoff said and stuck out his hand. "Good to see you."

He pumped Maksim's hand. Maksim clasped his elbow and pumped back.

"Kostya. You look good." Kyznetsoff took the fat boy's hand, shook it, all the while marveling at how much like a big balloon he looked. No. A girl. He looked like a fucking girl, all soft and pudgy with curling eyelashes.

"I hear she's going to kick your ass," the fat driver joked.

"Who? My wife?"

"No," said Kostya. "Ramirez. I hear you had another complaint. Your third strike."

Kyznetsoff shrugged, sucked down some more smoke.

"Where did you hear this bullshit?"

"Around."

"It's a lie. Big fucking lie."

"Then why are you here," the older driver asked. "Why aren't you working?"

"I don't need to work. I have money coming out my ass."

"So why come by the office?"

Kyznetsoff looked around, leaned forward. "The girls. They all want me to take them to the holiday party."

"Bullshit!" Kostya jammed his hands into his leather coat looking for his cigarette pack and cheap disposable lighter.

Kyznetsoff wondered if the kid ever zipped his leather coat shut. Probably not. He was too huge—the zipper would rip off its seams before he tugged it halfway up his belly. Kostya should wear a tent. A circus tent.

"You want I should get you a girl, Kostya? I can't handle them all myself. Would you like a whore for Chanukah? Maybe eight different girls, one to light your lamp each night?"

The men laughed.

Kyznetsoff shook their hands again and strolled into the office.

"You were supposed to come by yesterday," Julie whispered.

Kyznetsoff could see that the bag of chocolates was crumpled and empty. Spent foil wrappers littered the dispatcher's desk. Brown fingerprints smudged her telephone.

"I did come yesterday but Miss Ramirez was gone."

"Really? She told me she was here until seven last night . . ."

"I worked until seven thirty."

"She's in there now."

"*Spaceebo.*"

"That means, 'thank you,' right?"

"*Da.*"

"I'm learning. See?"

"*Da.* You learn so much I bet you could teach me a thing or two, yes?" He winked to let Julie think he was flirting with her. "Are you going to the party next week?"

"I was kind of sort of thinking about it."

"You like the holidays, yes?"

"I *love* Christmas!"

"Oh, in my country, we have many wonderful traditions. Grandfather Frost. Snow Maiden. She is so sweet. You, Julie, you remind me of Snow Maiden."

"Really?"

"She has blonde hair, like you. She is kind to all God's creatures—even the lonely and the lost."

Julie blushed.

"You better go see Miss Ramirez before she gets even angrier," she reminded him.

"*Da*. And I will see *you* at the holiday party."

Kyznetsoff knocked on a door with a paper sign taped at eye level: Customer Service Department.

"Miss Ramirez?"

The door opened.

"Mr. Kyznetsoff. I thought you were coming by yesterday."

"Yesterday? Julie said you wished to see me today. I am so sorry for the miscommunication. Is this a bad time?"

"No. Come in. Take a seat."

"Thank you."

Kyznetsoff scraped a metal chair across the hard floor. Ramirez searched for a folder in the piles cluttering her desk. She found it and frowned. "This is your third complaint in under ninety days."

"No way," Kyznetsoff flashed her his smile. "Impossible. I have been here so long? Time flies when you are enjoying yourself, no?"

"The client called from the airport and said . . ."

"Mr. Wilkinson?"

"The client. We don't use names."

"Really? Okay. Is good. No names."

"The client reported . . ."

"He told me to drive faster because he was late. When I go pick him up? He was still inside—"

"Mr. Kyznetsoff?"

"*Da?*"

"We expect you to observe all of the rules of the road, including posted speed limits. It doesn't matter what someone tells you."

"I know, but when the client, he say, 'Hurry, step on the gas,' what am I supposed to do?"

"Let me just read from my notes."

"If he miss his airplane, he file even bigger complaint. He say, 'That asshole Kyznetsoff! He make me miss my airplane!'"

"He claims you drove recklessly."

"He ordered me to drive this way! 'Change lanes! Quick. Hurry. Pass this truck!'"

"Well, be that as it may—"

"Motherfucker."

"Excuse me?"

"The man is a son of a bitch, motherfucker."

"Look, Mr. Kyznetsoff—PP&W Advertising is a very important client."

"Pee-pee?"

"PP&W."

"The motherfucker—he want me to lose my job?"

"No. The client just said—"

"Fucking asshole son-of-a-bitch chicken-shit coward. Is not my fault he was late! He was in the house, fucking his wife, fucking her up the ass!"

"Careful, Mr. Kyznetsoff—"

"You are the boss's bitch, *da?*"

"Say what?"

"You give him blow jobs underneath his desk."

"What?"

"Everybody knows this, everybody say, 'Ramirez? She give boss blow job.'"

Ramirez slapped the folder shut.

"Okay. That's it. We are done here, Mr. Kyznetsoff. You are finished. Fired. Turn in your book and any outstanding vouchers and get the hell out of here. Now!"

Kyznetsoff stood up slowly, smiled, and leaned on the desk.

"Eb tvoju mat!"

He said it even though it was doubtful he had ever met Miss Ramirez's mother.

12

"Almost set, hon?"

Scott Wilkinson checked his watch. Six fifty P.M. The car service was coming at seven to drive them into the city. Melissa still couldn't decide which dress to wear.

"I look horrible," she said, turning in front of the foyer's full-length mirror. "I think I'll try the tuxedo jacket thing from Mommy Chic again."

She headed up the steps.

"Missy?" Scott called after her. "The car will be here in ten minutes."

"Maybe we'll get lucky. Maybe he'll be late again!"

She sounded so perky.

She didn't get it.

This was a very important evening. The advertising agency's annual holiday dinner with the Taco John Franchisees and Marketing Executives, very important people who only came to New York once a year, in December, so they could see the tree at Rockefeller Center and shop on Fifth Avenue and look at all the holiday windows. Scott had made a fantastic presentation down in Dallas. Now, it was time to bask in the glow of the client's accolades in front of his boss. Kent Stafford,

PP&W's new CEO, would be at the dinner. Well, he'd be at the cocktail reception—there were a half dozen other client parties in town this week and Mr. Stafford had to attend them all. If Scott wanted quality face time, he and Melissa needed to be at Tavern on the Green for cocktails, promptly at eight.

Scott heard a horn toot.

He looked out the front door's sidelight window. A Lincoln Town Car was parked in the driveway.

Six fifty-two.

Great. The car from Lucky Seven Limousines was actually early.

Scott opened the door, waved at the driver.

"We'll be right out!" he said. "Just need another minute."

The driver, a shadowy figure edged by the glow of dashboard lights, waved back: no problem.

Scott closed the door. Headed up the steps.

"Honey?"

He thought Melissa was being unreasonable. Yes, she was nearly nine months along in her pregnancy and, yes, she had gained a good deal of weight. But surely it shouldn't take this long to decide which dress to put on. She'd spent all week at high-end maternity boutiques wearing out her credit cards, coming home with at least five different outfits, each with matching shoes and handbag.

"Missy, I'm certain that whichever dress you wear will be—"

He stepped into the bedroom.

Melissa was sitting on the floor in a sea of discarded dresses, crying.

"Honey? Is everything all right?" He went to her.

"Look at me," Melissa blubbered. "I am so fat and ugly."

"No you aren't."

"I'm enormous."

Scott glanced at his watch.

"Go without me," she said, her face streaked with tears. "Tell everybody I wasn't feeling well. Tell them that I caught the flu."

Scott knelt down next to her.

"You know what, Missy?"

"What?"

"I think you look beautiful."

"I do not. I'm fat and puffy—"

"And gorgeous." He stroked her hair. "You still have that red snowman robe?"

Melissa sniffled. "Yes. Why?"

"Put it on. And those slippers."

Melissa smiled. She had cute slippers that looked like snowmen, too: fluffy white with carrot-orange noses.

"I can't wear my bathrobe and slippers to Tavern on the Green."

"Really?"

"Of course not."

"Oh. Then, I guess we can't go."

"We have to. Mr. Stafford and the clients and—"

"Nope. We can't go. I forgot, *It's A Wonderful Life* is on TV tonight."

"No it's not. They only show it on Christmas Eve."

"True. But we have the DVD! Remember?" He kissed her.

"What about—?"

"You're absolutely right. I should pop some corn, too!"

He took Melissa's hand and helped her up off the floor.

"Scott?"

"Don't worry. I'll call Kent. He'll explain things to the clients."

"Are you sure?"

"Positive."

Melissa smiled. Stared up into her husband's eyes.

"I love you, Mr. Wilkinson," she whispered.

"Really?"

"Yep."

"Well, what a coincidence. You see, I love this beautiful blonde and you know what her name is?"

"What?"

"*Mrs.* Wilkinson."

Scott went down the driveway to talk to the driver.

He still couldn't see the man sitting behind the wheel. He gestured for him to roll down his window.

When the glass slid down, Scott saw an enormously fat young man with a baby face. He was eating a thick wedge of layer cake.

"I am so sorry—we won't be needing you tonight."

"No?"

The driver had a thick Russian accent. Scott figured it must be a job requirement at Lucky Seven. Their drivers all seemed to be Russians. He handed him a signed voucher.

"Of course, you'll be paid in full. Maybe you can pick up another fare. Newark airport isn't too far away."

"Sure. Is no problem." He used a napkin to wipe the frosting off his fingers. "Is everything okay?"

"Never better. Oh, here." He gave the driver a Baggie filled with Christmas cookies. Iced snowmen. "My wife made them. They're actually quite good. You might want to stop at the 7-Eleven in town, grab a carton of milk . . ."

The man's eyes sparkled as he took the cookies.

"I thank you," he said. "I hope you and your wife have the very merry Christmas and the most happy of New Years."

"Thank you," said Scott. "And you know what? I think we will."

13

On Saturday afternoon, folks in Jersey City were still trying to buy Christopher Miller lunch.

"You the cop who caught that kid?" a stranger asked. "The Man in the Moon?"

Miller had been out shopping with everybody else the final weekend before Christmas. He had picked up the Barbie gear at Toys "R" Us and was sitting at the steel-topped counter inside the diner where U.S. routes 1 and 9 intersect.

"I saw you on TV," the man said. "Let me buy you a burger."

Miller smiled. "Thank you, but I'm fine."

The stranger shook Miller's hand and headed out the door, probably to buy a Christmas tree or some cartons of eggnog over at the A&P. It was that kind of weekend. Miller checked his watch. He still had stocking-stuffers on his list; he'd swing by Walgreen's on the way home.

It had been a few days since Miller had nabbed Marcus Ghent before he could kill another taxi driver. Ghent, the alleged Man in the Moon, looked more like a boy to Miller. The kid was sixteen and told police he had no idea he had been conducting his homicides on such a regular basis until he read about it in the newspaper. But he thought it was pretty cool to have a tag so he went out on December fourteenth because he didn't want to disappoint the media.

"Hey, Saint Chris." Tony Cimino approached the counter. "I figured I'd find you here."

"That's why you're such a good detective."

The Jersey City cop sat down on an empty stool.

"Can I buy you a burger?" he asked.

"No, thanks," said Miller. "One's my limit."

"Really? I buy 'em by the sack."

"You're young."

"Yeah. And my stomach's lined with asbestos. So—you hear the latest? When our boy wasn't popping cabbies, he was beating up on his two aunts."

Miller put his burger back on its plate.

"He's a crack freak," Cimino continued. "Made the old ladies hit the street every morning and hustle spare change. If they came home empty-handed, he knocked them around some. Busted up their faces. Broke noses, broke bones."

"Jesus." Miller shook his head. Half his burger sat on his plate. He wouldn't be finishing it.

"I thought you should know," Cimino said.

Miller leaned back on his stool.

"Why?" he said. "Why did you think I should know?"

"What you did up in the Heights was a good thing."

"My neighbor was hurting."

Cimino nodded. "I hear you."

Silence.

"You gonna order?" Miller asked.

"Nah. I already ate. You know—earlier."

Miller understood his friend was trying to find the right words to say something he really didn't want to say.

"What's going down?" Miller asked.

"You know we tried to keep your name out of this thing."

"Yeah."

"But that schmuck at the *Post* . . ."

"Yeah."

"Anyhow, I need to be out front with you here, Chris. This guy from Washington's been hocking me."

"Washington?"

"Justice Department. Must read the wrong papers. Anyways, he's up here. Nosing around. I tried to shine him on . . ."

"This guy—does he have a name?"

"Yeah. Douchebag."

"Is that what his momma calls him?"

"No. She probably calls him Leon. Leon Owens. Name ring a bell?"

"Yeah. I knew him back in the day."

"He still look the same?" Cimino tilted his head toward the front door.

Miller swiveled on his stool.

He hadn't seen Leon Owens in over fifteen years, not since the last time he'd made the headlines. The man was actually wearing a trench coat like G-men do in the movies. Outside, it was sunny and unseasonably warm, so Owens had the flaps open wide, the better for everybody to see his natty suit.

"You sure I can't buy you a burger?" asked Cimino. "Because that hardass at the door? He isn't gonna buy you jack."

14

Cimino got up, walked to the door, where he purposely blocked the newcomer's path into the diner.

"'Scuse me, pal." Cimino said and flashed the G-man his badge. "You're blocking a fire exit here. That's a Jersey City municipal code violation."

Owens moved left.

"Sorry," he said, sounding like he wasn't.

Cimino pushed through the door and out into the parking lot.

Owens jammed his fists into his coat pockets and sauntered toward the counter.

"Christopher."

"Leon."

Owens pursed his lips, nodded his head, looked around.

"Good burgers?"

"Yeah," Miller said. "Good and greasy. But I'm sure you have some just as good down in D.C."

"Mind if I sit?" Owens took the empty stool before Miller could express an opinion on the matter. "So—I hear you've been busy."

"Yeah. Holiday shopping. My daughter wants that Barbie Airplane. It's been hard to find."

"They make a black Barbie?"

Miller looked at Owens hard. The bastard didn't blink. His eyebrows were arched in a smug, my-you-learn-something-new-every-day kind of way.

"What are you doing in Jersey?" Miller asked. "You hear about these burgers from someone in the Hoover Building?"

"We both know why I'm here, Agent Miller."

"Yeah. You came up to suspend me in person?"

"You mean suspend you for running an unauthorized investigation while off-duty? It certainly constitutes a serious offense."

While Miller had been busy working with the Critical Incident Response Group out of Newark, Leon Owens had played politics and brown-nosed his way up the ranks, landing in Washington. Despite the fact that he was currently some kind of executive assistant director, most people still found it hard to take him seriously. They all remembered his Big Bust.

Five years ago, Owens had been investigating a national chain of jewelry shops suspected of moving stolen goods through its back rooms. After two years and countless agent-hours, nothing went down. Nobody got busted. No stolen merchandise was recovered. The whole operation just sort of disappeared.

A Big Bust.

"What can I get you?" the counterman asked, wiping his hands on his apron to give it a few fresh stains.

"Diet Coke," said Owens. "If you please."

The counterman gave his "if you please" a "what-the-fuck" head snap and headed off to the drink cooler.

"You used to play football if I remember correctly," Owens said to Miller. "Notre Dame?"

"I ran the ball a few times," said Miller. "Slipped by a couple tacklers who thought they had me all wrapped up."

"The way I see it, the Bureau is like a team. And, as you know, there's no 'I' in team."

"True. But there's a 'me.'"

"What?"

"There's an M and an E. So there's a 'me' in team."

That stopped Owens. But only for a second.

"Yes. Fine. I suppose there is. However, be that as it may, we cannot allow rogue individuals to take the focus off the Agency's primary mission. The time for hotdogging heroics, for breaking the rules—those days are over."

"Yeah. I guess they are."

"The Office of Professional Responsibility will be looking into your unauthorized actions. Some agents from other divisions—"

"Rent-a-Goons?"

"Colleagues from outside your immediate circle of associates. You will be put on desk duty until the OPR's task is complete."

"I see."

Miller was as good as suspended.

It could take four months for OPR to run their investigation, another four or more for the bosses to determine Chris Miller's punishment. He'd be pushing paper until this time next year. No more field commands. No more CIRG assignments.

"Anything else?" said Miller. "I need to finish my Christmas shopping."

"Yes. Don't talk to the press."

Miller said nothing.

"No more articles in the *New York Post*," Owens added. "Word to the wise? Find a rock. Crawl under it. Disappear. Understand?"

"No problem."

"Good. Nice seeing you again, Christopher."

Miller didn't return the lie.

Owens left.

The counterman came back with the can of Diet Coke.

"Hey?" he called to Owens who was halfway out the door. "Jerk. Didn't pay for his soda."

For a second, Miller wondered if he could have OPR investigate Owens for theft of services. Then, he reached into his pocket, laid some bills on the counter.

"My treat."

"Forget about it. You finished?" The counterman nodded at Miller's half-eaten hamburger.

"Yeah. Stick a fork in me, I'm done."

And for the first time in his career, Christopher Miller actually meant it.

15

Nicolai Kyznetsoff slipped into the back room of the crowded nightclub where Lucky Seven was throwing its annual holiday party.

He was wearing a red Santa cap trimmed with real fur. Mink. He saw Julie, the pudgy dispatcher, leaning against the far wall, her gold lamé blouse blending in with the glitzy wallpaper. No one was talking to her. She sipped a pink cocktail and looked miserable.

"Julie!" Kyznetsoff threw open his arms.

"Nicky? What are you doing here?"

"You look beautiful! Like a Hollywood movie star! Julia Roberts! This is what I should call you, *da*?"

Kyznetsoff actually thought Julie looked like an underdone sausage stuffed into gold foil. She should know better than to wear a midriff-baring blouse when her exposed belly button looked like a doughy thumb dimple in a lump of unbaked bread.

"You like this outfit?" she asked.

"No. I like *you* inside this outfit—"

"Nicky! Stop!"

Kyznetsoff smacked the cherry candy he was sucking and leered at Julie's obese body. "Perhaps I would like it even better if you were *outside* this outfit."

"Nicolai?"

"What? What did I say? Is Christmas party! I make merry."

Julie looked around to make sure no one was watching. Waiters passed carrying platters of food.

"What are you doing here, Nicky?"

"Making merry. Ho-ho-ho."

"But Ramirez fired you."

"*Da*. Is no big deal."

"You can't come to a holiday party for a company you don't work for anymore."

"I know. I come for *you*." He bent forward, took her hand, gave it a regal kiss. Julie's breath quickened. He could smell the hot vodka on her breath, see the gold glitter she had sprinkled on the fish-white flesh above her enormous breasts.

"You want me?"

"*Da*. I ask Grandfather Frost to put you under my tree. Naked."

She was giggling. "Nicky? Stop!"

But Kyznetsoff would not stop. He would let Julie take him home tonight. Afterward, she would owe him a huge favor. Exactly what that favor might be, Kyznetsoff did not yet know but he assumed that one day he would need access to the passenger information Julie kept stored in her computer.

"What do you want Grandfather Frost to bring you?" he asked, pointing to his red cap.

"Is that mink?" Julie couldn't resist reaching up and rubbing the fur ball.

"*Da*."

"I wondered why it was brownish instead of white."

"Is real fur. So what do you wish for Christmas, Julie?"

She moved closer. He felt her heat.

"The same thing you do. And—a picture." She dug inside her sequined purse and pulled out a disposable camera. "Sharon?"

Her friend Sharon came over, eyeing Kyznetsoff suspiciously.

"What's he doing here?"

"Just take our picture, okay?"

Kyznetsoff put on his best puppy-dog face for Sharon's benefit. "I will be leaving very soon. Do not worry."

Julie hooked her flabby arm under his. "But first, we need a picture! Me and Grandfather Frost!"

"Ho, ho, ho." Kyznetsoff played along and posed. "Have you been naughty or nice, little girl?"

The camera flashed.

"I've been nice," she said when Sharon handed back the camera. Then she squeezed Kyznetsoff's arm. "Now, I'm ready to get nasty!"

They left the party, slipped out the side door undetected by Ruth Ramirez and of no interest to the nightclub's so-called security guards. In any event, such men were no match for a former Spetsgruppa Commando such as Nicolai Kyznetsoff.

Neither, of course, was Scott Wilkinson, a young man who would have quite a few surprises coming his way in the new year.

Grandfather Frost would make sure of it.

ELEVEN MONTHS LATER

16

On the Monday before Thanksgiving, Elena Bizanko sat with a cluster of other women basking in the afternoon sunshine that streamed into Tilyou Playground.

The playground was actually a small park near the Oceana Condominium Complex in Brighton Beach. The old ladies, all Russian emigrants, sat bundled in coats and mittens and ski caps and gloves and scarves and tried to soak up as much November sun as they could before it disappeared. They gossiped in the language of their homeland, caught up on the pettiest news of the neighborhood.

Elena Bizanko was dressed in a leopard-print sweater-jacket, which she wore layered on top of three other sweaters, all in differing patterns of plaid and animal print. On her head, she wore a light brown ski cap trimmed with snowflakes. The knit cap was pulled down snugly over her ears and hid every strand of her hair. Her hands, buried inside plaid mittens, rested on top of her ample belly. She sat like a czarina.

"If I was home," she said, "I would be in clover. I would be in my villa and the maids would lay a fire in the marble fireplace."

The other old ladies groaned. They had heard it all before. They listened to Elena Bizanko say the same things almost every day.

She curled out her lower lip. She had a pudgy face with eyebrows perpetually slanting down into her frown. She looked like an angry, heavyset man—a disgruntled steelworker who knows the bosses are cheating him.

"My nephew?" Elena brayed. "He is very important man!"

"So you have said. Over and over and over . . ."

The babushkas all laughed.

"You laugh? My nephew will hear of this." Elena Bizanko flipped her mittened fist at the women. "You will all pay when he hears of it. This I can promise you!" She stood and gripped the handles on her rolling walker. Two white plastic grocery bags stuffed with farmer's cheese, sausages, and yogurt dangled off the handles.

"Elena? Sit down. We were only making merry with you."

"Pah!" Mrs. Bizanko spat out. "I am going home!"

"Don't be so stubborn."

"I am not stubborn! My nephew is a very important man."

"Perhaps so," the joker replied. "In the twenty-seventh kingdom! In a fairy-tale land, far, far away!"

"Pah!"

She pushed her walker up the footpath that would lead her out of the sun, out of the park.

"Elena—do not have a hundred rubles, have a hundred friends," one of the wiser ladies advised.

"Pah!" This time, Elena Bizanko spat on the ground.

17

The two of them sat inside Palace Fried Chicken eating hot wings sticky with red sauce. Their names were Omar and Stephann.

"Check it out."

"Yeah. I see."

"Yo. Don't be starin' at her like that."

"A'ight, a'ight."

"See them bags? Means she been to the store."

"Yeah."

"Means she been to the bank, too. They all go to the bank 'fo' they go to the store."

"A'ight."

The angry old Russian lady shuffled past the restaurant's front window, pushing her walker.

The two boys swiped their hands against their quilted North Face coats. One worked a chunk of chicken meat out from between his teeth with his tongue. The other handed him a napkin.

"Wipe your hands, dog. Don't want to leave no greasy-ass fingerprints all up in there."

"A'ight."

There was a white plastic Christmas tree set up on the

counter of the chicken restaurant. The holidays were coming.

The two boys needed cash.

Fast.

18

Thirty forty-five First Avenue was a dull brick apartment building with ratty strips of weeds running alongside the brick walkway to its front door. Trash was snared by the tangles of dead bushes that passed for landscaping.

Elena Bizanko scuffled up the makeshift ramp covering one half of the two entry steps. She unlocked the glass door and moved into the lobby.

Before the door swung shut, she heard somebody enter behind her. She looked over her shoulder and saw two young black boys in the puffy ski jackets all the black children seemed to wear. One had a nylon skullcap stretched over the top of his head. The other had on a hooded sweatshirt.

"You live here?" Mrs. Bizanko glared at the boys.

"Yeah. You got some problem with that?"

Mrs. Bizanko mumbled her reply in Russian because she knew they wouldn't understand what she called them.

"*Chernye.*"

"What you say?"

"I say nothing."

"I heard you say somethin'."

"Pah." She moved into the lobby, pushed the call button for the elevator and heard its engine whirr. She waited. The boys waited behind her. She could smell them. They smelled like chicken grease and hot pepper sauce. Paprika. The door opened and the two boys waited for her to shuffle on board. They stepped in after her. She pressed five. One of the boys pressed four.

The elevator shuddered and started its ascent.

Mrs. Bizanko lived alone in a one-bedroom apartment with her two cats. One Siamese. One Russian Blue. Her husband had died three years back. Drank too much vodka. Smoked too many unfiltered cigarettes.

"This is us," one of the boys announced. The two of them stepped off at the fourth floor.

The doors closed and Mrs. Bizanko let out a gush of air and touched her chest. Her heart was pounding beneath her thick blanket of sweaters. She leaned against her walker.

"*Chernye*," she muttered. She hated black Americans more than all the other Americans. "Niggers." It was the first English word she had ever learned.

The elevator lurched up to five. The doors slid open. She moved into the narrow hallway and fumbled again for keys in the pocket of her sweater-coat. Her neighbors were all out for the day—either at work or at the park. She opened her door. A cat meowed.

"Misha!"

Elena Bizanko was home.

She could smell the scent of wet cat litter mingling with that of vinyl slipcovers. She looked to the corner nearest the door and saw the *matryoshka* doll collection lined up in tidy rows behind the curved glass of a curio cabinet. Everything was as it should be. She rolled through the door and came into her home.

The two boys came in behind her.

One kicked the walker out of her hands.

The other shoved her down to the floor.

19

Christopher Miller had been on restricted desk duty for eleven months, almost a full year.

As a result, he had become quite skilled at computer solitaire.

And Snood.

He liked shooting the funny Snood faces at each other, making the stacks tumble down. Sometimes, he imagined the ugly gray guys, the ones with the big buggy eyes, were little Leon Owenses. Miller enjoyed knocking down those ugly gray Snood dudes the best.

It was the Monday before Thanksgiving. His phone rang.

"This is Miller."

The caller was one of Owens's flunkies down in Washington.

"I understand you're quite good with little old ladies," the young man said in a clipped voice.

"Where'd you hear that?"

"Deputy Director Owens."

It was only two P.M. Three hours until quitting time. So Miller had to listen to Owens's stooge. With the phone pressed to his ear, he used his free hand to absentmindedly slide a jack over the ten of spades on his computer screen and thought about the sweet potato pie Natalie would bake for Thanksgiving dinner the way she did every year.

"How can I be of assistance?" he said lazily. It almost came out as a yawn.

"We have an incident in Brooklyn. Brighton Beach."

"Did Mr. Owens also tell you I'm in the Newark field office? That's way over here in Jersey."

"I know where you are stationed, Agent Miller."

"Special Agent."

"Excuse me?"

"Special Agent Miller."

"Of course. Mr. Owens specifically requested I contact you in regards to this matter."

Miller moved the jack on top of the queen. He had already beaten the computer twice since lunch. It was probably time to move on to Snood.

"Go ahead," he said.

"Elena Bizanko, age seventy-nine, residing at Three-oh-four-five First Avenue in Brighton Beach, Brooklyn, was accosted in her home today at approximately one P.M. by two unknown assailants."

"And you're not talking to the NYPD because . . . ?"

"We are. But Mrs. Bizanko's nephew is Alexei Bizanko."

"Oh. I see. Alexei."

"You know of Mr. Bizanko?"

"No. But, you know, the way you said it—*Alexei Bizanko*. He sure sounds like he must be one damn important man."

Miller clicked on the nine of diamonds, dragged it up to the diamond pile.

"Indeed," said the voice from Washington. "Bizanko is the vice premier in charge of the Russian Interior Ministry."

"You mean he runs their national parks?"

"Perhaps. But, more important, he manages the country's natural resources."

"Like their minerals?"

"And oil."

"I see."

"We wish to be seen as proactive in this matter. We want Mr. Bizanko to rest assured that the United States government will make certain justice is served, that his aunt's stolen property will be recovered and returned. You need to go visit the woman."

"Okay. When?"

"Now."

Miller didn't like the sound of that. Over the past eleven months, he'd grown accustomed to punching in at nine, punching out at five. He hadn't missed a dance recital all year. A drive out to Brooklyn might mean he'd be home late for dinner.

"You want me to find out who did this to her?"

"No—and Director Owens asked me to stress this point—you are simply to introduce yourself, show your credentials, and assure Mrs. Bizanko that the United States government cares deeply about what happened— et cetera, et cetera. Let the NYPD handle the robbery."

"You cleared this with my boss?"

"Of course."

"I'm supposed to become some kind of goodwill ambassador?"

"Exactly. A team of NYPD investigators will meet you on scene. You should leave for Brooklyn ASAP."

ASAP.

That meant Miller still had time to find the missing kings and finish out his hand.

20

"Go out and buy the biggest turkey you can find!" Scott told his wife when he called home from the office on Monday afternoon.

"How come?" Melissa asked.

"Because we have so much to be thankful for this year."

"Honey—Tyler can't eat turkey."

"Okay. Pick him up a jar of gourmet turkey baby food! Organic turkey puree."

"Scott? What's going on?"

"Nothing. I'm just grateful for all I've got. A fantastic new son. The sexiest, most beautiful wife in the world . . ."

"I still need to lose five pounds."

"No, you don't. You need to eat a big slice of pumpkin pie! You need to sip champagne—"

"Scott? Did you?"

"Yep. The memo just came out."

"Really?"

"Would I tell a lie to the sexiest woman in the world?"

"Kent promoted you?"

"Mrs. Wilkinson, you are currently talking to the new Head of Strategic Planning for all of PP&W Worldwide."

"Awesome!"

"Totally. There's only one hitch."

"What?"

"I promised Kent we would absolutely, positively attend the Taco John Christmas party this year."

Melissa laughed, remembering how awful she'd felt a year ago.

"I've already picked out the dress," she said.

"Awesome. The party's at Rockefeller Center this year. The Sea Grill. Downstairs by the rink."

"I'll bring my skates."

"Hey, maybe we should hire one of those huge limos to haul us into the city. One of those megahuge Hummers!"

"Scott?"

"Okay. You're right. A good leader remains humble in front of his troops. We'll call Lucky Seven. No—we'll take the train. And the subway!"

Melissa laughed. Scott smiled. He really did have a lot to be thankful for. And with the new promotion, the big bump in salary, no one could ever take it away.

No one.

21

Miller showed his ID to the two uniformed cops stationed out front at 3045 First Avenue.

"The robbery guys are upstairs," one of the cops said.

"They call in the Feds?" asked the other.

Miller shook his head. "I'm just here to hold the old lady's hand."

"The vic?"

"Yeah."

"Some guys catch all the luck, hunh?"

"What do you mean?"

"You'll see. She's up on five."

"Thanks, guys. Stay warm."

It was cold for November. Miller knew the two uniforms would be stomping their heavy shoes on the sidewalk soon, trying to figure out how to keep the blood circulating to their toes after standing still for so long. He knew it because he'd done it often enough himself.

He entered the apartment building and decided to take the steps instead of the elevator. Before he'd left Newark, the 61st Precinct in Brooklyn faxed him what they had on the robbery. The cops figured the two black youths entered the staircase on the fourth floor after stepping off the elevator pretending to be tenants. It was a classic ploy meant to make the mark drop her guard, make her believe all danger had left her immediate vicinity when the two boys did.

Miller reached the fifth floor. Of course the stairwell door wasn't locked. Anybody could use the steps, come into the hall, and sneak up behind any old lady they wanted to. He walked up the dimly lit corridor and was hit with the stench of old world cooking. Smelled like boiled cabbage. Cabbage and fishhead stew.

A pair of detectives was inside the apartment. One was on his phone but gave a "Hey, there" nod to Miller when he flashed his badge. The other detective wore a hat. Indoors. One of those Donegal tweed deals. He stopped writing in a small notebook and glanced up at Miller, tilting his head toward the couch.

A heavy-set elderly woman sat on the ugliest couch Miller had ever seen. It was wrapped in clear vinyl to protect the fabric—a checkerboard of chocolate and tan squares.

"Mrs. Bizanko?"

"Who are you?" the old lady said.

Miller was familiar with her sour facial expression: it said, "Stay away, nigger" in about a thousand different languages.

"My name is Christopher Miller. I'm with the FBI."

"*You* are Christopher Miller?"

"Yes, ma'am."

"You are black," she said disgustedly. "The two boys who did this? They were black. Like you."

"Ma'am, I'm sorry for your . . ."

She folded herself back into the cushions.

"Meet Mrs. Elena Bizanko," said the detective in the

Irish cap, rolling his eyes. "You here on account of the big-shot nephew?"

"Yeah."

"My nephew is very important man," Mrs. Bizanko said.

"So, I've heard," said the detective. "About fifty billion times. I'm Magruder. That's Norbert."

The detective with the phone nodded.

"What've you got?" Miller asked.

"Same old same-old. Two black youths. Male. Sixteen. Maybe seventeen. Dressed like half the kids in all five boroughs: North Face jackets, baggy jeans dragging off their butts. They come up behind Mrs. Bizanko here, shove her face-first to the floor."

"They hurt her?"

"No. They just wanted to rob her."

"They get much?"

"Her jewelry, mostly costume stuff. TV. Clock radio. Some silver she kept in the kitchen and a stack of cash. She'd just been to the bank."

"What about the bookcase there?" Miller pointed at the empty curio cabinet near the front door.

"What do you mean?"

"It's empty. You don't have a fancy display case like that unless you have something you want to show off."

Miller went to the curio case.

"Mrs. Bizanko?" Magruder said.

"What?"

"What was in that cabinet there? The one near the door."

"They take it! This is why Alexei is so worried! The black boys take his dolls! They stuff them into pillowcases they steal off my bed!"

"His dolls?" Miller asked.

"Very important cultural artifacts."

"Why didn't you tell us earlier?" asked Magruder.

"I did not know if I should tell New York police."

"You should tell us everything, ma'am."

"She had them lined up in rows," Miller said, studying the dust patterns on the shelves. "Something with round bottoms."

"Okay, what kind of dolls are we looking for here, Mrs. Bizanko?" asked Magruder. "Hummel figurines? Russian folk dancers? Barbie and Ken?"

"*Matryoshka.*"

"Russian nesting dolls?"

"*Da.*"

Magruder turned to Miller. "The Russians sell these *matryoshka* in all the tourist shops. You know, you open the top of one, there's another doll inside. You open that one . . ."

Miller nodded. "You find a smaller doll. My daughter has one painted like a penguin." Miller finished counting dust circles. "Looks like Mrs. Bizanko had about three or four dozen."

"My nephew send them from Russia. I keep them because he tell me to."

Detective Magruder cracked a smile, probably just to see if it would work. "Souvenirs from the old country, hunh? My grandmother? She has these ceramic leprechaun dolls."

"*Da.* Souvenir." The old woman's face curdled. "Russian relics."

"Yeah. Okay. We'll add it to the list of missing property."

"Mrs. Bizanko," Miller said, moving toward the couch, thinking about sitting down in a chair, thinking better of it when he saw the way the old lady stared at him. "On behalf of the United States government and the Federal Bureau of Investigation, I want you to know that you're in good hands here."

"I will tell Alexei," the old woman snarled. "I will tell him I spoke to Christopher Miller. Now leave my house. Why does the FBI send to me this black man? Why they send a *chernye*?"

"*Chernye*? Now, I know you don't mean that, Mrs. Bizanko. It'd be like me calling you a dirty Russki."

The old woman seemed shocked he had understood what she said.

Miller was ready to leave. "I'm certain the police will catch the two boys who did this, might even get you back your dolls."

The detective named Norbert snapped his phone shut. "Stephann and Omar Hawkins."

Miller was impressed. "How'd you work it so fast?"

"Before they boosted it, the two assailants stopped to watch TV. Bragged to Mrs. Bizanko here that they had a friend being arraigned on murder charges and wanted to catch his perp walk."

Miller shook his head, marveling at the stupidity of so many crooks.

Norbert gave an easy-as-pie shrug. "So, I make a few calls, see who put in an appearance downtown today, see who got their face on lunchtime TV—badabing, badaboom. Mr. Delroy Hawkins. And Delroy? He has these two younger brothers with rap sheets suggesting they might like to knock down old ladies and steal their lunch money."

"Stephann and Omar?"

"Yep. Big day for the Hawkins family, hunh?"

22

Nicolai Kyznetsoff followed the two black youths down an alley behind a dark cluster of apartment buildings.

He had been casing the old lady's apartment when the two boys went in and did the job he had been planning to do for months. No problem. All he needed to do was take from them what they had taken from her.

They'd lain low for a day but were now headed where Kyznetsoff had known they would eventually go: Seymour Rosen's.

Rosen was a fence who worked out of a coin-operated laundromat squeezed between two tenements. The idea was to slip in the back door and head down into the cellar, where Rosen kept his warehouse of DVD players, computers, jewelry, and designer clothes. Kyznetsoff knew because he had employed Mr. Rosen's services in the past himself.

It was easy to see that the kids who had broken into Mrs. Bizanko's apartment were complete amateurs. They were lugging two heavy pillowcases stuffed with pilfered treasure, dragging the sacks through puddles and mud.

Kyznetsoff only wanted what was in one of the bags.

The *matryoshka* dolls.

He understood from reliable sources, former comrades back home whom he would reward handsomely, that the little old lady kept a very interesting collection. He wondered if the two boys had similar intelligence or friends in Moscow. Doubtful. The boys were stupid. The boys were black. *Chernye*. They had no idea what treasure they possessed.

The boys turned down a connecting alleyway, its sides flanked by fencing topped with curling concertina wire. Kyznetsoff congratulated himself. He had found the boys before the police. Before anyone else.

Now they entered a stretch of alley where there was no light. Even as he kept them in sight, he picked up his pace, drew closer.

He gripped the claw hammer tight in his fist. A cold weapon, it was an improvised solution, and traceable only to the construction site where he had stolen it.

23

On Wednesday, Miller sat in his office writing up the report on Monday's liaison work with Mrs. Elena Bizanko of 3045 First Avenue, Brighton Beach, Brooklyn.

He wanted to finish the paperwork fast because his four-day Thanksgiving holiday could start as soon as it was done. He was already thinking about tomorrow's feast: turkey, ham, collard greens, candied yams, corn bread, mac and cheese, peach cobbler and sweet potato pie. It was a good thing he still hit the gym most mornings—even though he hated entering his age to program the treadmill. The default setting was always 20. Miller had to scroll up thirty digits, one by one, his life flashing before his eyes every time the little green numbers clicked over another year.

His phone chirped. He hoped it would be Natalie calling to say hurry home because she'd just baked the first pie and needed him to taste-test it.

"This is Miller."

"Yeah. Agent Miller? This is Detective Magruder. We met Monday."

"Sure. Everything okay with you?"

"Not bad. Not bad. Better than Stephann and Omar Hawkins, that's for sure."

"You've got them?"

"Not exactly."

"What do you mean?"

"Just that they won't be terrorizing any more little old ladies. We found 'em in an alley behind this wash 'n' dry joint that doubles as the local fence's showroom. And they weren't a pretty sight. Looked like Freddy Krueger, Part Nine. What's weird, though, is that we recovered everything they took off Mrs. Bizanko except, of course, the cash. The doll collection, the costume jewelry, even her TV. Everything. So think about it: why kill these two punks if you're not after their swag? The crap was still stuffed inside the pillow cases."

"So what do *you* think went down?"

Magruder hesitated.

"Can I ask you a question?"

"Shoot."

"Why'd you come out to Brooklyn? Why'd the FBI send one of its top guys all the way from Newark to nose around in my neck of the woods?"

"I'm not one of the top—"

"You're the same Miller who saved that little kid down in West Virginia, right? I read about it."

"Ancient history. These days, I work indoors. Desk duty."

"So, tell me—why'd you leave your cushy desk job and come see me?"

"Because somebody down in D.C. wanted to let a Russian bigwig know we were looking out for his elderly aunt. I drew the short straw."

"That all?"

"That's all I know."

"And you'd tell me if you knew more, right?"

"If I could. Sure."

"If you could. See, that's what I figured. If you could. But maybe you can't. Maybe you guys are setting up something really big, and Mrs. Bizanko figures into it somehow."

"How do you mean?"

"Oh, I don't know. Let's say you Fibbies are on some kind of Russian mafia hunt. Some sort of organized crime task force. You ever heard of the 'thieves-in-law?'"

Miller recognized the term. Among the criminals locked away in the vast prison system run by the old Soviet Union, there'd been a legendary network of hardcases, career sociopaths able to extract respect from even the toughest of their fellow inmates. They were known as the "thieves-in-law." After the collapse of the USSR, when they were released into a society unable to protect itself, they formed a loose confederation and launched themselves into all the lucrative rackets: protection, prostitution, extortion, gambling, drugs, murder for hire. They were too vicious for anyone to stand in their way. Maybe they were expanding. Going global. Maybe Brighton Beach was becoming a new center for their international operations.

"You fellows running some kind of mob sting out here you don't want to tell me about, Agent Miller?"

"If we are, nobody told me."

There was a pause.

Miller figured Magruder was trying to decide whether he was playing straight. He couldn't blame him. Some federal agents always attempted to end-run any outside interference, tried to keep the local guys out of the loop.

Miller hesitated, then said, "I could make some calls."

"Yeah. Okay. I can't say it wouldn't help me out." He paused, long enough for Miller to wonder what he was holding back on.

"Anything else you're not telling me?"

"Well, these kids, Omar and Stephann, they were just a little deader than they needed to be."

"What do you mean?"

"For starters, someone took Stephann out with a collar choke. You know—you grab the vic's shirt collar with a cross-hand hold, twist, and use your knuckles to press in against the neck until there's no more circulation up to the brain. For good measure, while you're choking him to death, you're simultaneously making mincemeat of the guy's esophagus. Pretty slick stuff."

"So, whoever did this was a professional assassin?"

"More like a KGB-trained ambassador of bad will. My sources tell me the collar choke is one of their favorite techniques."

"And Omar?"

"A claw hammer buried in the back of his skull. Thrown from at least ten yards. You know, when the Soviet Union closed up shop, a lot of ex-KGB agents joined forces with the new bosses running the show. The mobsters. I guess you could say their KGB was sort of like our army. It didn't give 'em money for college but it sure as shit taught 'em valuable job skills."

24

United Flight 650 out of Chicago touched down on schedule at LaGuardia at 9:04 P.M. on Friday, December fifteenth.

Scott Wilkinson pulled out his phone as soon he exited the jetway.

"Hi, sweetie. Santa Claus has come to town."

"You've landed?"

"Yep. The reindeer found a runway instead of a rooftop."

"I baked cookies all day. The whole neighborhood smells like cinnamon."

"In that case, I'll tell my driver to step on it!"

"See you soon," she told him, her voice sweetly sexy, as if dusted with some of the powdered sugar she'd been sprinkling on the cookies.

Scott wove his way through the hordes of holiday travelers. He followed the crowd up the corridor and moved into position for the escalator down to baggage claim.

Scott had arranged for a meet-and-greet inside the airport. A driver from Lucky Seven Limousines should already be downstairs, bored and holding a sign with Scott's name scrawled across it.

It had been a good meeting in Chicago. A one-on-one with the chairman of Standard Foods, the huge conglomerate that ranked as PP&W's top client. Scott had proved why, at such a young age, he'd been promoted to the head of strategic planning. An extremely talented data miner, he could listen to focus groups, sift through reams of numbers, grind and filter statistics on his laptop, and then tell you why people who bought chainsaws also bought more mattresses.

Scott saw his fellow passengers swarming around the baggage carousel, the amateurs waiting for suitcases that hadn't even been sent up the conveyor belt yet. Then he saw his name: Wilkinson. The Lucky Seven guy was on time and waiting in a cluster of about two dozen other drivers. He held up the sign so Scott could spot it more easily. It blocked his face from view. All Scott could see was the tip of his driver's Santa hat.

He walked up to him.

"Lucky Seven?"

"Yes, sir. Mr. Wilkinson?"

"Yep."

The driver lowered his sign while he turned around to take the handle on Scott's rolling bag.

"Do we need to wait for more bags?"

"Nope," Scott said proudly. "Just my carry-ons."

"Shall I carry briefcase, too?"

"No, thank you. Oh, by the way—I like your hat. Nice touch for the holidays."

"Ho, ho, ho." The driver gestured toward the exit doors. "I park in lot across the way. Will you want to wait while I swing around?"

"No. I've been sitting for a couple hours. The walk'll do me good."

"Okay."

"Tell me," Scott asked, "are you all Russians?"

"Excuse me, please?"

"Your accent. Is it Russian?"

"No. I am Czech."

"Oh."

They walked out to the sidewalk. Cold air slapped Scott in the face. So did a cloud of nicotine from the frenzied fliers who raced outdoors as quickly as they could to fire up their post-flight cigarettes.

"Sorry about the smoke," the driver said.

"Not your fault."

He led Scott across the roadway, into the parking lot behind a green tubular fence bent to look like apples because New York City was, after all, the Big Apple. The lot was full of black cars all waiting for pickups.

His driver pulled out a key-ring remote. Scott heard a car chirp-chirp to his right. Red taillights flickered.

It was a stretch limo. Black with dark tinted windows. Kind of ridiculous, really, but Scott couldn't help feeling pleased.

"I get a stretch? A real limo?"

The driver shrugged.

"We are very busy tonight. Holiday parties on Wall Street. I was at airport, had opening in my schedule. You, of course, will only be charged for regular sedan."

"So, this is my lucky day with Lucky Seven?"

"Yes. I think perhaps so. May I put briefcase in trunk with suit bag?"

"No. I'll hang on to it. Might need my cell."

The driver held open the door. Scott looked inside.

"Awesome. Smells brand-new." He ducked down and climbed inside. The leather interior was classy. Rope lights edging the carpeted floor. A wood-paneled wet bar with crystal glasses cuddled in custom-built cubbyholes. An ice bucket chilling champagne. Scott heard the driver climb into the front seat. The tinted divider scrolled down.

"What's with the champagne?" Scott asked.

"Compliments of your business associates in Chicago. They request we have bottle chilled and waiting for you upon arrival. I took liberty of pouring you a glass."

"The guys at Standard Foods set this up?"

"Yes, sir. I am instructed to say, 'Happy Holidays from your friends at Standard Foods.'"

"Guess they liked the Brand Asset Builder I showed them, hunh?"

"Yes, sir."

Scott heard Christmas music. A snappy, swing-a-ding-ding version of *Santa Claus Is Coming to Town,* done by Cyndi Lauper and . . . *Frank Sinatra?*

"The music is all right?" the driver asked.

"It's awesome. Is that Sinatra?"

"Yes, sir. I have other selections if you prefer . . ."

"No. Sinatra is totally awesome. Thanks." There had to be a dozen hidden speakers. You could hear Sinatra crooning from every corner about checking that list twice. He reached for the champagne. Dom Pérignon. If this was work, he might become a workaholic.

"Is your seat belt securely fastened, sir?" the driver asked.

"Yeah. We're good to go."

The divider slid back up. Scott heard the doors lock. The limo started moving, felt like it was floating.

"This is so fucking awesome!"

Scott took a sip then leaned back and propped his feet up on the seat. He knew the driver couldn't see him through the blacked-out partition, so he stretched out, the better to savor Sinatra. He raised his head just enough to chug the last drops of champagne. He thought about pouring himself another but that would require too much effort.

He had to call Missy, tell her how he was riding home in style. *This* was worth sitting up for, so he opened his briefcase and pulled out his phone.

Maybe we'll take a ride around the block and finish off the champagne together . . .

Weird. There was no signal. The battery was fully charged, he was sure, but he had no bars. He decided he'd go ahead and use the car phone, letting the driver add the exorbitant cost of the call to his bill. There had to be one stowed someplace—in the bar or one of the cabinets or hidden in a seat.

"Oh, driver?"

No answer.

Scott glanced at the control panel lodged in the armrest. He pressed the button for "divider." Nothing happened.

"Driver?"

Still no response.

Fine. I can find it. I mean the car is big, but there can't be that many places to put a . . .

Scott couldn't remember what it was he was looking for.

Man—one glass of champagne and I'm totally trashed.

He heard a whirring sound that reminded him of the hydraulics on an airplane when it begins its final descent prior to landing, when you have to put away electronic devices and your cell . . .

The phone!

That's what he was looking for. He tried to unsnap his seat belt but it wouldn't come undone. He looked down at the buckle and the Lincoln logo looked blurry, crisscrossing crosshairs.

"Driver . . ." he mumbled and wondered if he was going to be sick. Maybe he should take a nap.

Yes, just go ahead and shut your eyes. It'll take about an hour to get home. Sleep it off.

But he wanted to call Missy.

He fumbled for a knob on the cabinet, still hoping to find a phone.

He slapped his palm flat against the door. It flopped open. A piece of paper drifted out. Scott bent forward, straining against the shoulder harness, which didn't budge or give like shoulder straps were supposed to unless they were locked down because you were slamming on the brakes.

He grunted forward, snared the paper scrap off the floor. It was a photograph. A thermal printout.

He smelled something.

Cough syrup. Cherry cough syrup.

He looked up.

The driver had lowered the divider and was bending his arm so he could reach into the seating area.

"Want candy?" the driver asked. "Is Russian. Is good."

Scott felt like a dashboard dachsund, his head bobbling up and down on his neck. His eyes drooped. He forced them open, focused on the fuzzy photo—a fish-eyed image of him sitting in the back seat of a car.

Not a stretch limo.

A Lincoln Town Car.

He heard the driver mutter something. "*Zalupa*. Dickhead."

And then Scott Wilkinson passed out.

25

Melissa Wilkinson was starting to wonder when the glass of milk she'd set out for Scott with his Christmas cookies would start to sour.

The plate next to the glass was empty, with just a smattering of crumbs; she had eaten the cookies herself.

It was two A.M. Saturday.

She had already called his cell phone and office forty different times but had gotten only his voicemail, an outgoing message telling everybody he was in Chicago on business but returning Friday night.

When Scott hadn't arrived home by midnight, she'd gone upstairs and put on a terry-cloth bathrobe. Underneath it was still the Santa's Naughty Little Helper nightie, bought at Victoria's Secret as a surprise. She'd thought he deserved it after such an important business trip, but sexy as it undeniably was, it wasn't very warm.

Suddenly, Tyler had started screaming. She went in and nursed him, then switched on the Fisher Price Sound 'n Lights baby monitor, came downstairs, and waited on the couch with its walkie-talkie receiver snuggled in her lap. She watched Leno and then an infomercial about the Little Giant Ladder, a multifunc-tion product you could use for all sorts of stuff around the house. She fell asleep the second or third time the jolly voice asked her to think about the space she'd save with only one versatile ladder to use and store instead of three or four ordinary ones.

She reawakened at one A.M. and started eating the cookies, one by one, until a half dozen had disappeared. Thirty minutes later, she was scared sick and felt queasy from all the flour, butter, and sugar tumbling around in the acid bath that was her stomach.

Scott had called from the airport five hours ago.

He had said he was on his way, said a car service would be picking him up. He should've been home by ten, eleven at the latest.

She went to the drawer by the phone and found the Yellow Pages.

"Lucky Seven Limousines," she mumbled. She remembered the car company's name because Scott often joked, "They're lucky we don't fire them, they're late so often."

Maybe that's what happened. Maybe they'd been late picking him up at the airport. Maybe there were traffic problems like they always talk about on the radio when they check their jam-cams. Maybe there was conges-tion or a backup at the tunnel or rubbernecking delays or one of those jackknifed tractor-trailers or a multi-vehicle pileup resulting in multiple fatalities.

That's why Scott hadn't come home! He can't! He's dead!

Melissa flipped the pages, raced up the alphabet.

Tea. Taxes. Taxicab Svce.

Lucky Seven Car & Limo Inc. Dial 7-7-7-C-A-R-S. Melissa hated it when she had to spell on the telephone; it took her forever to find the letters.

After fifteen rings, a grumpy woman answered.

"Lucky Seven Limousines."

"Hello. My husband isn't home yet." There was a pause. Like the dispatcher was waiting for Melissa to realize what she had just said. "I mean my husband is one of your customers. A car was supposed to pick him up at LaGuardia Airport."

"Do you have a car number?" Now the woman sounded bored.

"No. No I don't. Scott never tells me those . . ."

Melissa heard a sigh.

"Do you know his arriving flight?"

"He was coming from Chicago."

"I need the airline and the flight number. Do you have it?"

"Yes. It's on the refrigerator. Hold on."

She found Scott's itinerary secured beneath a Cape Cod–shaped magnet—a souvenir from their trip last summer to Hyannis.

"United. United six-five-oh."

"Passenger's name?"

"Scott. Scott Wilkinson. He works for PP&W Advertising."

"Yes, ma'am. I see the reservation in our system."

"Did the car pick him up?"

"No, ma'am."

"What? Why not?"

"His reservation was canceled at four thirty P.M."

"No, it wasn't."

"It's what our computer shows, ma'am."

"Well, your computer's wrong. Scott said he was being picked up."

"Perhaps he arranged an alternative means of transportation. Perhaps he shared a cab with a colleague."

"No. His plane landed at nine-oh-four P.M. at LaGuardia and—"

"The reservation was canceled."

"It couldn't have been."

"Four thirty P.M. The client telephoned, said he wouldn't be needing a car."

"Scott said that?"

"Those are the notes attached to the record. Can I be of any further assistance?"

"No, I . . . wait—are any of your drivers missing?"

"Ma'am?"

"Maybe there was a wreck or something?"

"Not that I'm aware of. Can I be of any further assistance?"

Melissa now heard Tyler begin crying on the baby monitor.

"I . . ."

"Do you need to make future reservations?"

"No . . . I . . ."

Tyler started screaming.

"Thank you for calling Lucky Seven."

"How long has he been missing?"

Melissa looked at her watch. It was 2:30 A.M.

"About five and a half hours."

Another pause from the other end of another telephone call.

"Mrs. Wilkinson," the man said, "technically, we can't consider your husband a missing person until he's been gone for at least twenty-four hours."

"But what if he's hurt right now?"

"Is your husband handicapped, physically or mentally impaired? Is he a depressive, for instance? Suicidal?"

"No. I mean, not that I'm aware of . . ."

Melissa was exhausted. Drained. The middle of the night probably wasn't the best time to talk to the police but she didn't know where else to turn.

"Mrs. Wilkinson, there's not much we can do right now."

"He was at LaGuardia! He said he was coming straight home."

"Maybe he stopped off someplace along the way. Maybe he grabbed a quick beer with some of the guys."

"No. Scott doesn't drink. I mean, he drinks wine with dinner, but he doesn't go out and grab quick beers with the guys! Besides, nobody else from his office was on the plane."

"Maybe he stopped off somewhere else."

"Where?"

"I don't know, exactly. Sometimes, you know, some guys, after a tough day—they like to, you know, unwind a little."

"What do you mean?"

"Look, Mrs. Wilkinson, a lot of times these missing husbands are just out somewhere blowing off a little steam."

"This happens a lot?"

"Some. Especially, you know—this close to the holidays, what with everybody feeling festive and what have you."

Melissa knew the police officer was trying to make her feel better. It wasn't working.

"I see."

"Try not to worry too much, okay? Might be best if you tried to catch a little sleep. I'm sure he'll show."

"We have a baby . . ."

"Let's give your husband twenty-four hours, okay?"

"But what if he still doesn't come home?"

"We'll fill out the forms, okay? We wait the twenty-four, then we fill out the forms. Okay?"

"Okay."

Melissa let the phone drift away from her ear.

She pressed the off button and wished she could do the same thing to her brain. It wouldn't stop racing from bad thoughts to worse.

26

It was 2:30 A.M., and the bachelor party at Johnny C's Carousel Club was still going strong.

A white limousine was parked out front.

Another limousine crunched into the gravel parking lot.

The Carousel Club was a windowless stucco box situated in an industrial zone—right across from a cluster of rusty white oil tanks tucked behind chain-link fencing crowned with barbed wire. A fifty-foot-tall pylon sign let passing motorists on I-80 know what exit to take if they wanted to enjoy the finest adult entertainment in all of New Jersey.

The club's bouncer, dressed in a tuxedo and fur-lined leather gloves, stood in the shadows underneath the canopy shrouding the front entrance. He wondered if there might be trouble when he saw the driver of the black limo walk around his vehicle to open the back door. The guy was wearing black military fatigues with all sorts of flaps and pockets up and down his legs. A knit watch cap was rolled up on top of his head. The driver looked like some kind of cat burglar or military commando.

His passenger looked like some kind of a drunk.

The driver had to drag the bum out of the back seat and haul him across the parking lot.

"He with the private party?" the bouncer asked when the two men finally reached the front door.

"Yes."

"They're in the bar. The groom's shit-faced, too."

"Thank you."

"What the fuck has your guy been drinking?"

"Too fucking much!" the driver joked.

Nicolai Kyznetsoff shifted his weight and adjusted his grip on the body he carried like a sagging sack of bony potatoes.

The bouncer escorted him into the dimly lit bar where a topless girl writhed against a bronze pole as if she were riding her favorite carousel horse.

Men were lined up on stools along the bar. They hooted when the girl dropped to all fours and bounced her bottom up and down like a bucking mule. When they applauded, she slumped down on her belly and slithered across the polished wood stage. Her naked skin squeaked as she crawled. The men tucked more money into her thong.

"We got the hottest bodies in all of Jersey," the bouncer boasted. "See those tits? Those are real. No plastic. Johnny C? He's total class. He don't like no fake tits. He likes they should have a little jiggle, a little bounce. Like I said: total class."

Kyznetsoff nodded.

The club was bathed in the soft glow of red and green beer neons, the pink and blue of gelled lights up in the ceiling.

"The rest of the party got here hours ago. Where the fuck's your guy been?"

"Denver. I picked him up at the airport. I think maybe he had too many martinis on the plane." Kyznetsoff used his free hand to fish a fifty-dollar bill out of his flapped shirt pocket. "I fear he needs private attention."

"I dunno, pal. It's almost closing time . . ."

Kyznetsoff found another fifty inside the pocket of his black commando shirt.

"The VIP lounge is back this way." The bouncer pointed toward a velvet-curtained arch.

"Send in your best girl."

"That'd be Amber. She does this lesbian love thing with Ashley that's pretty damn hot."

Kyznetsoff found a third fifty.

"He'll take them both," he said.

The bouncer stuffed the cash into his pants.

"Let me show you two gentlemens to your private booth."

Kyznetsoff dragged Scott Wilkinson's drugged body into the dark room beyond the curtains.

"You sure he ain't dead?" the blonde girl asked.

"Positive," Kyznetsoff assured her. "Look. See? His eyelid just moved."

Kyznetsoff had propped Wilkinson up on a plush purple couch. The young blonde named Amber, her double-D breasts squeezed into a satin pushup bra, knelt on the sofa, her knees straddling Wilkinson's thighs. She rocked her bottom back and forth a few inches above Wilkinson's crotch.

"You're very good," said Kyznetsoff.

"Thanks." Amber shook her hair in a futile attempt to appear sexy while sweating off her makeup.

"I wish I could be the man sitting beneath you."

A single stained-glass Budweiser lamp dangling from the ceiling lit the room. The air reeked of baby oil and cockroach spray. The scent of spilled beer seeped up from the carpet.

"I would like to be having sex with you, this very minute," Kyznetsoff said as he watched Amber hump and grind.

"At least one of you is enjoying the show!" said the brunette. Her name was Ashley and she was on a bit of a break, having spent ten exhausting minutes performing the calisthenics of the lesbian love scene she and Amber were so famous for. Ashley was a skinny teenager with enormous breasts but no hips. She wore a black bikini with a neon-yellow smiley face centered atop each of her nipples.

While Wilkinson had lain limp beneath the two girls, Kyznetsoff had taken photographs.

Ashley yawned. "He hard yet?"

"Fuck no," said Amber. "I don't think he even has a pulse."

Kyznetsoff let out a fatherly sigh. "I am sorry you girls have had to work so hard tonight."

"Maybe he needs Viagra," said Ashley.

Amber kept grinding. "I can't do this forever, you know." In frustration, she broke the rules. She put her hand directly on Wilkinson's crotch. She made physical contact with her client and started rubbing.

Wilkinson's eyes fluttered open.

"Here we go," Amber said proudly. "I knew he couldn't resist me forever." She ground her hips harder.

Kyznetsoff pulled out his camera. "We take more snapshots."

Amber shook her head. "More pictures costs more money."

"Will this cover it?" Kyznetsoff tucked a hundred-dollar bill in Amber's bra, another into Ashley's thong.

"For a hundred bucks, you can have a free blow job."

"Sorry. I must take a rain check." Kyznetsoff looked through his viewfinder. "Smile, girls. Pretend you're having fun. This one's for the Christmas card!"

27

Scott Wilkinson woke up.

He was sitting in the back seat of a car. The limo. No. A different car, but one that smelled brand-new too.

His head throbbed worse than it had during his legendary New Year's Day hangover, a killer that remained a painful college memory.

He needed to call Missy. Only he didn't know where he was or where his cell phone might be.

He also couldn't move his hands. They were bound tightly behind his back. He looked down at his legs. His knees were strapped together with silver duct tape. So were his ankles.

He looked up and saw the back of the driver's head.

The man turned around and smiled.

"Did you have sweet dreams, Scott?"

"What's going on? Untie me!"

"Answer my question, please. Did you have sweet dreams?"

"I feel sick. I need to stand up."

"Did you dream of naked women? Because it cost me a great deal of money to—"

"What the hell are you talking about? Untie me! Now! Get this goddamn tape off me!"

"You don't remember?"

"Remember what?"

The driver took off his black watch cap and rubbed his stubbly head.

"Scott, Scott, Scott. You must learn to pay attention. To look and listen, to gather intelligence. This way, you can surprise your enemy, no?"

"What do you mean, enemy?" His voice was shrill. His throat felt dry and sticky at the same time. He wanted to be sick, and to wake up from this nightmare. Where was he? He'd do anything for a quick hit of fresh air. And Melissa. He needed to talk to Melissa. "Come on, man. I want to go home."

"Scott. It is fate. What you might call Kismet, though it is a term not much used these days, I think. We meet, you behave badly, things go downhill from there. We are enemies because I have decided it is so. You have no choice in the matter."

"Please. I've got to call my wife."

"Your wife? Not to worry, Scott. We will send her an e-mail. Soon."

"Let me go." It came out as a gasp. It was hard to talk over the waves of nausea.

His captor sighed. Almost as if bored.

"Let me go home and, I swear, I won't tell anybody about any of this." Scott's plea sounded hollow, even to himself.

The driver looked up into the rearview mirror. He stared at his passenger intently.

"Are you pouting?" he suddenly asked, his tone accusatory.

"Huh?"

"You better not pout."

"I told you, I feel sick."

The driver shook his head reproachfully.

"You really do look, to me, like you are pouting, Scott. Boo-hoo-hoo. This is the pouting, no?"

"Please. I have to go home. Now."

"You better not pout, you better not cry. Frank Sinatra tell you this."

"What?"

The driver clicked his tongue and shook his head again.

"Scott, really. Don't you know? I see you when you are sleeping. I know when you are awake. I know if you have been bad or good. And you? You have been very, very bad, Scott."

"Jesus Christ . . ." A tidal wave of queasiness hit and he moaned.

"Do you know—in Russia, we celebrate what you call Christmas on New Year's Day. Santa Claus we call Grandfather Frost. And this Jesus Christ? You may pray to him all you wish because, to me, he does not exist."

The driver started the engine.

"No more talking now, Scott."

"But—"

The driver held up a small black pistol with a slanted muzzle.

"No more talking."

28

On Saturday morning, Kostya Garvonik waddled along the sidewalks of Brighton Beach with Syroslav, whom everybody respectfully called Slava.

"We go to the International Delicatessen," Slava said. "We have some sausage, perhaps a slice of cake."

"Cake would be nice." Kostya weighed close to four hundred pounds. He had eaten a lot of layer cake at the International. He usually took a slice or two with him when he drove his limousine for Lucky Seven. He liked to peel the cake apart and use his finger to knife up the frosting sandwiched between the thin layers. It gave him something to do while he waited for his next fare at the airport.

Kostya finished his cigarette. His friend was still sucking on his. Both men wore leather coats. Slava had his zipped up so the sleek black skin was tight against his chest like a warrior's breastplate. Kostya's coat hung open in front because there was no way to close it on top of his bulging stomach—that enormous beach ball stuffed into his pants.

"You like cherries? Sweet compote?"

"Cherries would be nice."

Slava slapped his hand on Kostya's back. "You eat whatever you like. We call it Vasily's treat today, okay?"

"Okay. Sure."

Kostya was pleased to be seen with Slava. He was an important man because he worked for Vasily and Vasily was the most important man in all of Brooklyn. Kostya knew this. Everyone in Brighton Beach did. That one of Vasily's men wanted to treat a humble limousine driver to sausage and cake and cherry compote was a real honor.

Bright oranges and apples were stacked in crates on the sidewalk out front of the International Deli. Old women, dressed like they were still living in Moscow under Brezhnev, still back in 1972, pushed their grocery carts to block others who might wish to examine the same fruit they did.

"Step aside, *babushka*," Slava said to one old woman. "I need to pass."

She ignored him. "*Kto rano vstayot, tomu bog podayot!*" she said. "God gives to those who wake up early."

Slava sneered at her. "This is America, old woman. Here you may take what you want. There will always be more."

"Who are you to lecture your elders?"

"I am Slava. And you, old hag, are in my way."

The old woman heard the name and put down her potatoes.

"Forgive me, Slava."

He sauntered into the shop. Kostya followed him, basking in his role as companion to such a very important man.

"What will you have, my friend?" Slava asked Kostya.

The two men stood in front of a case filled with mountains of sausages and hams and olive loaves and smoked fish.

"Some ham would be nice."

Slava snapped his fingers. "Galina?" he called to the skinny girl behind the counter. "Give us this ham. A full kilo. And these three sausages. The big ones. Where do you keep the cherries?"

"Behind you, sir," the girl said.

"Ah, yes. *Spasibo*. Thank you."

The pickle jars filled with red cherries swimming in syrup were stacked on a dusty shelf behind the two men.

"No matter how filling the meal, one must leave room for the third course, yes, my friend?"

"Yes." Kostya agreed. "Desserts are what I prefer. They are my favorite part of any meal." He smiled at this always pleasant thought.

"Really?" Slava acted surprised. "Mine, too!"

The girl handed him a thick slab of ham and several sausages wrapped in white butcher's paper.

"And now some cake." He led Kostya into the rear of the store, back to the candy bins and sheet cakes you could slice and pay for by the pound. It appeared to Kostya that Slava had no intention of forking over cash for anything. But why should he? He was Slava, Vasily's right-hand man. Shopkeepers were expected to pay him tribute.

There were several fresh cakes to choose from, all oozing frosting or whipped cream or gooey red fruit between their soft layers. Kostya chose the chocolate.

Seven thin layers of cake. Plenty of chocolate frosting sandwiched in between.

"Now we go downstairs," said Slava.

"Downstairs?"

"Vasily's private dining room."

The dining room in the basement had stained mattresses bolted to the walls. A thick army blanket was draped over the steel door. Mattress pads were bolted to the ceiling as well.

Kostya sat in an antique barber chair set up in the middle of the room. There was a tall wooden table in front of him. All that was left of his luncheon feast was some waxy butcher paper and the sticky dregs of the cherry compote. When he plucked one cherry out of the jar, another fell and rolled toward the drain in the tile floor.

"Did you enjoy your meal?"

"Yes, Slava. Thank you." Kostya reached into his coat and pulled out his pack of cigarettes. "Smoke?"

"Maybe later."

Kostya removed a cigarette and stuck it in his mouth.

"I said, maybe later."

Slava frowned slightly. Kostya slipped the cigarette back into its pack.

"You have enjoyed your lunch. Now we need to talk."

"Of course, Slava. Of course."

"It's warm down here, don't you think? The boiler is in the next room. Take off your coat."

"I am fine."

"Please. Take off your coat. It is too hot in this room."

"Okay." Kostya did as he was told.

"Vasily tells me that your friend has taken some things that do not belong to him."

"My friend?"

"Yes. He took some items that belong to *our* friend and now our friend has asked Vasily to retrieve these things."

"I see. I will do whatever I can to help you and Vasily," Kostya said earnestly.

"So—where is he?"

"Who is it you are looking for?"

"The crazy one. Kyznetsoff."

"Nicolai?"

"Ah. You do know this Kyznetsoff?"

"Of course. He was a driver with Lucky Seven Limousines, the same as I."

"This we know. So—where is he?"

"Kyznetsoff? How would I know?"

"He is your friend."

"But he was fired. Last winter. I haven't seen him since."

"No?"

"No."

"This is how you treat your friends? You lose touch? You do not talk to them?"

"He was never really my friend. We worked for the same company and he would bum my cigarettes, brag about women, maybe, complain about tips, nothing—" He stopped abruptly.

Slava had pulled a pearl-handled razor out of his coat pocket. He snapped it open and walked to the chair.

There was a weathered leather barber's strop attached to its side. Slava began to stroke his razor up and down its surface to sharpen its blade.

"Are you taking a shave?" Kostya tried to joke. "In the middle of the day?"

Slava didn't laugh.

"Where is your friend?"

"I tell you, I do not know."

"Where is Kyznetsoff?"

"I could ask around if you like."

"Tell me—did Nicolai Kyznetsoff ever show you one of these?"

From a pocket in his coat, Slava pulled out a gaily-painted wooden doll.

"A *matryoshka*?" Kostya laughed nervously. "No, why would he?"

"Clever, aren't they? You lift off her head and look—it's the same figure inside. You twist off the next head, here she is again. Smaller, of course, but still identical."

Kostya said nothing. He knew very well how such dolls worked. Breathing heavily, he sat there watching. And waiting.

"There's still one left," said Slava, twisting open the tiny doll. "What's this? *Nichego*. Nothing. Is empty."

"It should not be empty like that."

"No. But it is. Empty."

"There should be one more tiny doll, the smallest."

"This is what I think as well. But this doll? She is empty." Slava shook it near his ear. "*Nem, kak ryba*. As mute as a fish."

"Did Nicolai steal part of your doll? Is that what this is all about? If so, I will gladly purchase a replacement."

"Do you think I am a pussy, Kostya?"

"No."

"Do you think Vasily is a pussy?"

"No, I—"

"Do you think we play with little dolls?"

"No."

"Fedya! Grisha!" Slava yelled at the door.

Two musclemen trooped into the cellar carrying coils of yellow rope. Slava put the doll back in his pocket.

The newcomers tied Kostya to the barber chair. Slava pumped its handle to raise his prisoner up a few notches.

"What are you doing?" Kostya whimpered.

Slava snorted. "See how much rope we had to bring? This is because you are such a sow." He came closer so he could squeeze Kostya's huge cheeks together and pucker the man's lips. "I tell the boys we will need at least fifty, maybe two hundred feet of rope to secure a suckling such as you! Perhaps we should stick an apple in your mouth, you fat, fucking pig!"

His accomplices laughed as they tied their final knots, then backed away from the chair. Slava flicked open his straight razor.

"Now. I ask again. And this time I ask for Vasily. Where is Nicolai Kyznetsoff?"

"I tell you, I don't—"

Kostya screamed as Slava sliced off a tender slab from his upper arm.

"Where is Kyznetsoff?" Slava coyly tickled Kostya's chin roll with the tip of his razor.

"I don't know," Kostya burbled weakly. "Please . . ."

With a few quick slashes, Slava filleted a marbled steak off the other arm. More screams, all muffled by the mattresses lining the walls and ceiling.

Kostya's eyes rolled back in his head. Spittle foamed from his mouth. The only sounds he made now were barely recognizable as human.

Slava shook his head. "Why do you force me to spoil our little picnic like this?"

Kostya was beyond reply. Barely breathing.

Slava shook his head sadly and swiped a surgical incision across the fat man's bloated belly. Blood seeped from the thin red line.

"I have come to the conclusion that you are not cooperating, Kostya. For that reason, I want my cherries back," Slava said as he sliced open Kostya's stomach. Next, he instructed one of the men standing nearby to take photographs. He would show the pictures to Maksim. Slava assumed the older limousine driver would also be wiser, especially when confronted with such compelling motivation.

Maksim would most certainly tell Slava where Kyznetsoff was hiding.

29

The Wilkinsons' home on Canterbury Lane resembled a French chateau.

Solid, impressive brick walls. Five peaked roofs cascading down at incredibly steep angles. A swooping asphalt driveway—still smoothly sealed, still without blemish or bump—wrapped around the McMansion to the three-car garage hidden in the back.

The house was so huge it seemed all the more empty as Melissa kept her vigil inside, waiting for the mandatory twenty-four hours to pass before the police would officially declare her husband a missing person.

It was three P.M. Saturday. Nine days till Christmas. Still no word. No phone call. Melissa had last heard Scott's voice when he landed at LaGuardia seventeen and a half hours ago.

The baby was upstairs napping, unaware that he was currently fatherless.

She had left messages on his cell, his office phone, even his secretary's line, though PP&W was closed for the weekend. She had also contacted the travel agency that made all the arrangements whenever PP&W Advertising executives flew on business. There, too, she had left a message.

Finally, she had called her parents in Princeton. Her father urged her to "calm down."

"I'm certain there's a reasonable explanation," he said. "It isn't like Scott to fall off the face of the earth."

"I know, Daddy," she said. "That's why I'm so worried."

"Let's not make a big scene, Missy. No need to panic more people at PP&W. Let's do as the police suggest. Let's give Scott his twenty-four hours."

Melissa Baines Wilkinson was twenty-six years old and given to wearing cashmere exercise outfits the color of Easter eggs, hues that were just right for her blonde good looks and baby blue eyes. She went to the gym four days a week and still resembled what she not so long ago had been: a buff, bubbly, prep school cheerleader. Her father, Robert Baines, was an extremely wealthy investment banker. Missy had not only received a pony on her twelfth birthday, her father had purchased a small farm in the horse country of western New Jersey and hired grooms and trainers and riding instructors to help turn his princess into a champion rider. The framed blue ribbons could be seen in what Missy and Scott called the horse room, a large study with a fireplace and cathedral ceiling right off the marble foyer at the front of the first floor.

Melissa turned up the volume on the baby monitor. Tyler was sleeping soundly, his breath coming in a steady, untroubled rhythm. Unlike her son, Melissa hadn't been able to sleep at all during the night. She caught her reflection in one of the circular mirrors hanging above the off-white sofa in the living room.

She looked terrible.

She kept some soothing tea eye pads in the refrigerator for just such emergencies. She moved softly across the plush cream carpet, passing through the dining room with its glass-topped table and high-back padded chairs, as she headed into the designer kitchen.

The whole house was done in whites, eggshells, and alabasters, with blonde wood floors and cabinetry. In the kitchen this was accented by pink marble countertops the color of gently steamed shrimp. The room was massive with sparkling, top-of-the-line appliances. Melissa seldom cooked there. She and Scott usually used the enormous center island for unpacking take-out bags and pizza boxes. The refrigerator was stocked with carefully chosen white wines (one of Scott's many passions), Diet Pepsi for her, and jars of gourmet mustard.

She sat down at her desk. Before she took the eye pads out of the fridge, she thought she'd look at her e-mails. Maybe it would provide a distraction.

She had just one new message.

She moved the mouse over the postage stamp icon and clicked. The program opened and displayed the contents of her in-box.

It was from Scott!

No text at the top, just attachments. Photographs. Six of them. Melissa scrolled down the screen and gasped.

He was sending her pornography.

The first picture showed two half-naked girls. They were mouth-kissing each other while straddling someone else's lap. Since one of the girls had her thonged fanny shoved in the third person's face, it was impossible to tell much about him or her.

Melissa scrolled down, saw the second picture. Now she could see the person. It was a man. The room spun around her and she gasped. Closing her eyes, she prayed that when she opened them again the picture would have vanished. That she would realize she'd made a mistake. She opened her eyes.

It was Scott.

He looked drunk.

The girls were on either side of him, sticking their boobs in his face. One of them wore a string bikini top with smiley faces on the tiny bra cups that covered the nipples and nothing more.

Melissa finished looking at all the pictures.

More of the same.

Scott's tongue drooping out of his mouth while they straddled him. His head buried first in one girl's crotch, then the other's.

In the final frame, the two girls were fully naked, leering as they pointed their nipples straight at the camera. Scott, despite the fact that he was wearing their panties on his head, had his eyes closed like he was in heaven.

A bit of text was thoughtfully typed under the last photo: "Having a wonderful time. Wish you were here."

30

The waiting area at the suburban police station reminded Melissa of a doctor's office.

She didn't know why she found this surprising. Two rows of cushioned chairs lined up to face each other across a coffee table bearing ancient magazines. She and her baby were the only ones waiting.

Tyler started crying.

"Hush, honey."

He cried louder. Melissa rocked him, dug a bottle out of his baby bag, gave it to him. It was four P.M.

As far as she was concerned, all bets were off. No more official waiting period. She wanted to know what the hell was going on and she wanted to know now. She didn't call her father because he'd just tell her to calm down, again. Besides, she couldn't show him the pictures. They were too embarrassing. Humiliating, really. What kind of wife drives her husband off to share Kodak moments with prostitutes?

"Mrs. Wilkinson?"

"Yes?"

"I'm Tom Harper."

"Are you a detective?"

"Why don't we step back into the office, okay?"

"Oh. Yes. Certainly. Thank you.

Harper offered a welcoming smile but Melissa caught him twitching his nose. Then she smelled it, too: dirty diaper.

They went through a door into a room filled with several cluttered steel desks. Stacks of papers and file folders were everywhere. Tom Harper appeared to be the only officer on duty.

"How can I help you?" he asked with polite disinterest.

"My husband. He didn't come home last night and then this afternoon . . . I . . ."

She didn't know what to say. She hugged Tyler with one arm and used her free hand to find the folded papers she had stuffed into his diaper bag before leaving the house.

"Today I received an e-mail."

"From your husband?"

"Yes. From Scott."

"So he's not missing anymore?"

Melissa slipped the papers across the desk. The computer printout was five pages long but Melissa had folded them all up in a tight little square to make sure no one could accidentally see her husband's filthy secret.

Harper began unfolding her origami project.

"What did he send you?"

"Pictures." Melissa choked on the words. Then, instinctively, she tried to smile like a beauty-queen contestant does when the judges ask her the wrong question but she still wants to win.

"This your husband?"

"Yes. As I said, he has been missing since last night."

"Uhm-hmmm."

"This isn't like him."

"Uhm-hmmm."

"He usually comes home right away. Takes about an hour from LaGuardia."

Harper folded the papers back up, carefully following the creases Melissa had created earlier. "Mrs. Wilkinson?"

"Yes?"

"You want my professional opinion?"

"Of course."

"You don't need the police."

"I don't?"

"No, ma'am. You need a lawyer. A good divorce attorney. Somebody to make sure this bum doesn't skip out on his child support."

31

First thing Monday, December eighteenth, Special Agent Christopher Miller came out to greet the two Brooklyn detectives he'd been told were waiting for him in the lobby.

Detective Magruder, his tweed cap damp from melting snow, was eyeing the candy canes strung on the building's artificial Christmas tree. His partner, Detective Norbert, didn't appear full of holiday cheer. Miller hadn't spoken to either detective since the day before Thanksgiving, almost four weeks earlier.

"I wasn't expecting to see you guys out here," Miller said. "I was going to call you."

Magruder raised an eyebrow. "Really? Whatever for?"

"I talked to this guy I know, a buddy down in D.C. He did some digging. Took him a month, but he came up with the goods."

"Really?" Magruder nodded. Norbert just glared. "We've been doing some of that ourselves. Digging around, asking a few questions. Only it seems that one of the guys we want to talk to, can't nobody find him anymore."

"Why not?"

"Seems he dropped off the face of the earth after doing lunch with this highly-placed stooge named Slava. Our possible vic, his name is Kostya."

"Fat fuck," Norbert added.

"Fat or skinny," Magruder went on, "we haven't found his body or anyone else's. Sometimes, these Russians like to slice their victims up into teeny-tiny pieces. Pieces so small, you don't ever turn up a body."

Miller listened politely, then said, "What do you guys say we go upstairs and talk in my office?"

Norbert shrugged. "Whatever."

"Lead the way." Magruder stopped to grab a candy cane off the tree, peeled off its cellophane wrapper, started sucking. The two detectives followed Miller into an elevator for the ride up to the FBI offices.

Miller borrowed a couple of chairs from the cubicle next to his.

"This your office?" Magruder asked after the three men were squeezed into the cramped box.

"Yeah," Miller said, scooching his own chair in under the desk so his back didn't bang against the carpeted wall.

"Who the hell did you piss off?" asked Magruder.

"A big shot down in Washington."

Magruder looked at a crayon drawing of an angel pinned to one of Miller's three walls.

"You got kids?"

"Just one," Miller said. "But we ran out of room on the refrigerator door. Look guys, I would've reached out to you sooner, but I just heard back from my guy yesterday. He's doing me a favor. Still some back-and-forth going on between the CIA and the FBI. Turf wars. Who does what, who reports to who."

Magruder moved his head as if to say, *Keep talking—I'm willing to listen.*

Norbert found a paper clip and started twisting it.

Miller had the floor.

"My guy used to be with the Bureau. Sharpshooter. He and I did this thing together a while back."

"He the sniper who took down those kidnappers in West Virginia?" Magruder asked.

"Yeah, but like I said before, that's ancient history."

Magruder shrugged. "Don't matter. I read up on it. And you. I like to know who the man is on the other side of the desk, you know what I'm saying?"

"Yeah."

"Even if it is the dinkiest little desk I ever saw."

Miller couldn't help grinning at this. Neither could Magruder. Then they both started laughing.

"Okay," said Miller, "I know why I'm laughing. What about you?"

"Six-two. Two hundred pounds. Former All-American fullback at Notre Dame and they got you cramped inside a cube the size of my old Yugo. Who'd you piss off?"

"Wait a minute—you drove a Yugo? Who'd *you* piss off?"

"Don't get me started. The list is too long."

Norbert put down his twisted paper clip. He hadn't joined the laugh fest. "So how about you go ahead and tell us what your friend told you?"

Miller picked up the yellow legal pad where he'd jotted his notes. "Like I said, my buddy's with the CIA now. Domestic division. Left the Bureau not too long after West Virginia. Anyhow, I asked him to look into this Russian we're getting jerked around about. Mr. Minister of the Interior. Alexei Bizanko. The old lady's nephew."

"And?"

"You guys already know he runs their oil business."

"Yeah."

"Well, the CIA thinks Bizanko's got a major pay-to-play scam working over there. You want to tap into the black gold, you better show Alexei your green first. Anyway, the CIA thinks he's laundering some of his cash, shipping it out of the country."

"In the form of diamonds," said Magruder.

"No. My guy didn't say anything about diamonds."

"It's diamonds." Magruder pulled a Russian nesting doll out of his pocket. "Small. Portable. Easy to liquidate. Fit nice and snug inside a hollow wooden dolly."

Miller understood. "The *matryoshkas?*"

"Yeah. When the two punks got offed in that alley, we recovered the old lady's entire collection. Or so we thought. We think a little harder, we realize that every one of the dolls is missing a piece. The tiniest one, the last one hidden inside all the others. The solid piece you can't pry open."

Miller nodded. "So, Bizanko used the dolls to mule out his diamonds."

"Bingo. Then he shipped them stateside in like your diplomatic pouch or whatever. Told our customs people they were cultural artifacts under government seal and then had his Russian posse shuttle the goods over to his auntie's apartment."

"What about security?" asked Miller. "The old lady didn't even have a doorman."

Magruder shrugged. "Who was going to look there? Also, we figure he might've made alternative 'security' arrangements."

"With the Russian mob?"

"Maybe. Maybe somebody else."

"So, whoever took out the two boys in the alley, he knew about the diamonds?" Miller asked.

"That's what we're thinking," said Norbert. "The boys probably didn't."

Miller was fascinated. "So how come the Russian mob is just now stepping into all this? Slava? Kostya? Who are they?"

"We're not one hundred percent sure," said Magruder. "But we figure whoever did the alley hit was a pro. Ex-KGB, more than likely. Talented fellows. Could kill you six different ways before you even knew you were dead."

Norbert took over. "It's pretty certain Bizanko had a secret code or serial numbers etched inside his ice. Insurance. Like tattooing your dachshund."

"Anyhow," said Magruder, "we figure our doer got sloppy. Probably pawned a diamond or two someplace where maybe he shouldn't—someplace where they're on the lookout for Bizanko's missing rocks. Maybe the jeweler buys a couple off our back-alley slayer, checks it out under the eyepiece, makes a few phone calls. Maybe he even springs for long distance—calls Bizanko over in Moscow. Bizanko calls Vasily."

"He the boss out in Brooklyn?"

"You got it."

"Did the old lady know what she had?"

"Nope. She was just the storage unit."

"But now that the diamonds are being fenced," Miller said, picking up on the detectives' narrative, "the shit is hitting the fan."

Magruder nodded. "The clock is ticking. Bizanko probably wants to stop this guy from selling off his entire retirement account."

"Maybe my friend at Langley can find out more," Miller offered. "I can give him what you guys just gave me, if that's kosher."

Norbert leaned forward. "Maybe you can give him this, too." He pulled a slip of paper out of his shirt pocket. "Phone number. I copied it off a list we found in the old lady's apartment."

Miller studied the number, then waited to hear what was coming.

"The old lady had it on a list with all her other emergency numbers," said Magruder. "You know: Police, Fire, Ambulance. You recognize it?"

"Sure," said Miller. "It's one of ours. FBI. That's our Washington exchange."

"Yeah," said Norbert.

"I see. Okay. You think somebody in the Bureau is playing you guys?"

"Could be."

"Anyways. So I called the number," Norbert said.

"Of course we put the blocker on," Magruder added. "In case they had Caller ID, which, being the Feebs, you gotta think they do."

"Anyways," Norbert repeated, "some guy answered."

He leaned back in his chair, tilting the cubicle wall back with him. He was letting the suspense kill Miller.

"What'd he say?" Miller asked.

"Who? Oh, the guy who answered?"

"Yeah."

"Well, he told me what I needed to know."

"That being?"

"What he says: 'Executive Assistant Director Owens's Office.' You know this dude? This Owens?"

"Yeah," said Miller. "I do."

"And?"

"He's the guy I pissed off. Leon Owens. He's the one who put me in this damn cubicle."

32

He had been held hostage inside the hunting cabin for two full days.

He felt like a character in a Stephen King book. Only in that one, the guy strapped to a bed, like he was now, had a mattress.

Scott didn't know where he was. He had been drugged for most of the ride out. He was flat on his back, sharp bed slats pinching his skin. He was staring up at a knotty-pine cathedral ceiling. Although it was winter, there was a fan spinning slowly overhead, its light fixture filled with the shadows of dead bugs. Scott knew you couldn't reach the fan without a thirty-foot A-frame ladder.

His captor had gone outside to empty Scott's bedpan—a stockpot he slid underneath the bed frame whenever he gave Scott permission to urinate or move his bowels. The driver would slip on rubber gloves, yank down Scott's pants, strip off his underwear and yell for him to hurry up and finish his business.

Scott was still wearing the same clothes he'd had on when he landed at LaGuardia Friday night. Now his suit, the gray one he'd bought at Brooks Brothers for eight hundred dollars, smelled worse than his son's diapers. Scott had lost his tie somewhere. His hundred-and-thirty-dollar silk knit tie. His red Hermès with the prancing-horse print.

The horse room.

He thought about home, about Missy. Surely she'd gone to the police by now and they were out looking for him. If only he could get his hands on a phone, maybe he could call her. If only he could run outside, find some kind of road, maybe he could even figure out where he was.

Scott only knew he was in the woods because he could see naked tree limbs encased in ice outside the window. And it was quiet. No traffic. No distant buzz of tires on pavement. No noise at all except a dripping sink.

He rolled sideways and saw stools set up in front of a kitchen island. There were more food bags piled on the counter than there had been yesterday. McDonald's. Pizza Hut. This didn't help. McDonald's and Pizza Hut were everywhere.

He raised his head, looked forward, saw a wood-burning stove with a pile of split logs stacked next to it. There were two rifles in a rack mounted on the wall. Both guns looked to be high-powered weapons. Both had telescopic sights. One had a stubby flashlight up front, like the SWAT teams used when they raided a dark crack den on that TV show *Cops*. That rifle was probably equipped with a night-vision scope.

Great.

Scott heard the front door open, then slam shut. Footsteps sounded across the bare plywood floor.

"Who are you?" Scott said to the room. He focused

on the fan. "What do you want? Money? Okay. I can get you money. You should let me make a few phone calls. I could raise whatever it is you're looking for. I have stock options I can cash in . . . and my father-in-law? He's extremely wealthy . . . and . . . my company . . . I'm sure they'll pay whatever you ask . . . so, if we're reasonable . . . if we work out a plan . . ."

Suddenly, his snarling captor showed himself.

"You still do not remember me, do you, you fucking *zalupa*?"

Scott could see the black hairs up inside the man's nostrils. He could smell cherry candy on his breath. The driver tilted his head like he was posing for a close up, giving Scott another chance to recognize his face.

"Dickhead!"

He disappeared from view.

Scott heard wood slide against wood as the driver dragged one of the bar stools closer to the bed. He craned his neck sideways.

The driver was putting on that stupid Santa Claus hat again.

"Okay, Scott. I tell you now who I am, okay?"

"Please. Whatever it takes to get me out of here."

"You want to leave?"

"Yes!"

The driver took a little spiral notebook and pencil out of the knee pocket in his black fatigues. He licked the lead tip of the pencil like Scott sometimes did on the golf course before he entered his score.

"So, you are also ungrateful," the driver said. "I must make a note of this. I offer you the hospitality of my *dacha*, my beautiful country home, and you do not appreciate it? I empty your bedpan, your stinking *govno*, and still you treat me with such disrespect?"

"I'm sorry . . . I—"

"You are so fucking important I am invisible to you? I pick you up, I drive you to the airport, I offer you my cherry candies. You sit in the back seat and play with your papers. You make the important business calls and do not give two shits who I might be. And yet, I know everything about you, Mr. Scott Wilkinson, Forty-four Canterbury Lane, Northridge, New Jersey. Head of Strategic Planning, PP&W Advertising."

Though the mad man seemingly had all this written in his little book, he never looked down at any notes.

Scott racked his brain. He'd met this man before. Where? When?

"Your wife? She is Melissa. Missy. A cute one. Like you, I enjoy the blondes with the big tits. And your son? Tyler? Are you afraid you might miss his birthday next month? It will be his first, yes?"

The driver stopped talking for an instant and held out a pack of cigarettes. "You want one? No. Wait. I forget. You don't like the smoke. You are a pussy."

"What did I ever do to you?"

The driver smiled. Stuck the Marlboro in his mouth, lit it, then waved the match grandly in the air to extinguish it.

"Ah! So now you admit you did something to me?"

"I don't know . . ."

"This is what I am telling you, Scott. First, you ignored me. You sat in the backseat of my Town Car . . ."

"You were driving a limousine . . . at LaGuardia . . ."

"Not the first time, you stupid dumb-ass! The first time was my Lincoln Town Car. With the pine air freshener? You remember the pine?"

"No." Scott's head was throbbing. "When was the first time?"

"I come to your home. Last year. Before Christmas. I pick you up. I am a little late? You are kissing Missy, she is in a bathrobe, you have plastic snowmen singing in your front lawn . . ."

"You . . . you were late . . . then you drove like a maniac."

"Ah. The light bulb in your brain. It glows. You remember. Do you also remember how you complained to my supervisors? How your big important travel department instructed my employers to fire me?"

"You're . . . that driver . . . the crazy—"

"I am Nicolai Kyznetsoff. I come from Russia. When I was seven years old, I joined the Octoberists. At age ten, they promote me to Pioneers. While lazy little American boys were playing Little League I was learning how to defend the motherland."

He paused, letting out some smoke with a pleased snort.

"When I was fifteen, the special committee of the KGB studied my file. They were impressed, so they select me for the Young Soldiers course and then the Special Forces training. Spetsnaz. I do not need to pay for the parachute jump at Coney Island. Me, I have made more jumps out of real airplanes than you have taken cab rides! I can hike thirty miles in one day carrying a rucksack filled with cinder blocks. I can swim one hundred meters with sixty pounds of steel strapped to my back. I practice how to kill with my field shovel. I am good. *Very* good."

Scott swallowed hard.

"Hey, listen. I'm sorry," he said. "I'm sorry I complained about your driving that time. I really am."

"Oh? *Now* you are sorry? Now that you know I am Nicolai Kyznetsoff of the Spetsgruppa Vympel, the most feared Special Forces unit of the KGB?"

"Come on. Just tell me what you want!"

"Do not be in such a hurry. We have plenty of time."

"No. Please. Really. The sooner we can reach some sort of settlement—"

"I am Grandfather Frost. Santa Claus. I see you when you are sleeping, I know when you are awake, I know if you have been bad or good." His tormentor took a long, deep drag on his cigarette. "You? You have been very, very bad. The worst. You, Scott Wilkinson, you are on Santa's shitlist this year. All the way at the very top."

"Look, I'm willing to make good on whatever income you lost. You know, after you left Lucky Seven. I accept full responsibility, okay? Just give me a figure to work with. For your back wages, for what you think I owe you."

"No, Scott. That is not what is on the agenda today. We will not work with the figures. Instead, I think I will call your office. How about I call Mr. Kent Stafford, CEO of PP&W Advertising. He is still your boss, yes? Remember? You called him from my car? Talked about Taco John?" Kyznetsoff gave another snort of pleasure.

"You see how well I am trained? How carefully I listen? How cleverly I gather my intelligence?"

"I'm sure the company will pay whatever ransom—"

"You think you are here because of money?"

Scott had no answer to this. What other possibility was there?

"Listen to me. Listen well. I am already rich. I have become an international jewel merchant." Kyznetsoff gave a low chuckle. "No, Scott—idea here is payback. I lost a great deal because of you. Pride. Respect. And now, you must lose more. Much more. When that is accomplished, then we will see. Perhaps when I feel the wrong has been righted I may show you some mercy."

"Thank you," Scott said softly.

Kyznetsoff leaned over the bed. Smiled.

"I am sorry. Forgive me. My English—it is not so good. I mean to say, if you are lucky, I will kill you."

Kyznetsoff sucked hard on his cigarette, gave it a wet smack.

"Never fuck with drivers, Scott. We know where you live."

33

On Monday morning, Melissa Wilkinson was back at the police station.

It wasn't the second time, or even the third. She was becoming a familiar figure. Tyler, too.

"This *isn't* Scott!" she insisted.

Officer Harper raised an eyebrow. "In the pictures? Now you're telling me that's *not* your husband?"

"No. It's him. But, I mean, it's not *him*."

The police officer smiled a "there, there, honey" smile, one Melissa saw a lot because she was blonde. When it was convenient, when it helped her get her way, she sometimes acted blonde, too.

But not about this.

This was her husband. Her family. Her life.

"Perhaps there's someone else I should talk to?" she said. It was not the first time she had made this suggestion.

"Yeah," Harper said. "Captain Cullen. But he gets a big chunk of Christmas vacation. On account of he's the captain."

"Maybe I should call him at home? Of have my father call the mayor and have *him* call Captain Cullen at home?"

Harper sighed. He squeaked open his file cabinet and found a thick Missing Persons form.

"Fill it out," he said. "If you don't know the answer, just leave it blank and move on. Sort of like taking the SATs. You ever do those?"

"Of course. I got a twelve forty. Six forty Verbal, six hundred Math."

"Great. And, if you don't mind, why don't you bring in some new photographs? Ones with just Scott in them."

Melissa knew the police officer was being a smart aleck but decided to ignore his petty little gibe.

"Like a family portrait," he continued. "Maybe one of those Sears Studio jobs, bring that in."

Melissa moved Tyler to her other shoulder and opened her purse. She had brought along Scott's official PP&W portrait—the one the company had used when Scott's last promotion was announced. "Here's one that should work."

"Thank you, Mrs. Wilkinson. I'll put it in the file."

Harper took the photo, got up from his desk, wandered over to the coffee pot to pour a fresh cup.

Melissa started filling in the State of New Jersey's official Missing Persons form. It looked like the police were supposed to ask you questions, listen to your answers, and make notes. In addition to being annoying, Harper was also lazy.

Once past hair and eye color, height and weight, glasses or no glasses, the questions got more personal.

Did he have scars or tattoos? Deformities? An extra breast, a harelip, a humpback, a protruding lower jaw?

No and no.

Moles? Yes. A cute one on his left cheek. She checked the box: "Buttocks, Left."

When it got to dental records and other resources for DNA samples, such as combs and toothbrushes, Melissa decided it was time to take the paperwork and her baby home.

Later, in the kitchen, she could fill it in in private. Afterward, she'd bring it back to the police station with more photographs. Snapshots of the two of them on their honeymoon three years ago down in Cancún. Maybe she'd even bring in that one of her and Scott by the pool—the one where she had on her string bikini. If Harper saw that picture, saw the happy grin on Scott's face, then he'd understand: this was one husband who had no need for scrawny hookers with silicone boob jobs.

34

When the Brooklyn detectives left, Christopher Miller called his Washington contact.

He was as curious as Magruder and Norbert: why did Elena Bizanko have a number that rang in Owens's office? What was the connection between Owens and her nephew? Was it a special hotline of some sort? And if it was, the question remained: why did an old lady out in Brooklyn have access to it?

Miller's call went into his friend's voice mail.

"P. J.? This is Chris. Look, I think we might need to touch base again. Give me a call. We can talk about that, you know, that fishing trip. Okay. Thanks, man. Catch you later."

Fishing trip?

Miller shook his head. Why, halfway through his message, did he suddenly decide to start speaking in secret code? Maybe because P. J. *was* a spy—just like everybody else down in Langley.

His phone rang.

"This is Miller."

"Please hold." It was the operator. "I'm transferring a call."

"Shirley?"

"What?"

"Who is it?"

"Some woman. Needs to talk to somebody. She sounds pretty worked up."

"Okay." Miller checked his watch. It was still early: eleven A.M. "Put her through."

"Please hold."

Miller sighed. After eleven months on probation, it seemed Shirley, the receptionist, had demoted him further—to handling cold calls from concerned citizens. Usually, this kind of public interface involved suspicious-looking packages that typically turned out to be somebody's bologna sandwich left behind on a bus or park bench.

"Go ahead, ma'am," said Shirley, passing off the call.

"Hello?" The woman's voice was soft but strong.

"Yes, hello. This is Special Agent Miller. How may I be of assistance?"

"Are you in charge of kidnapping?"

"No . . . I'm—"

"I specifically asked to be connected with the person in charge of kidnapping."

"Well, technically, I don't think that's anybody's job description. However, I've done extensive work on kidnap cases in the past and perhaps—"

"Thank God. I need your help. Please."

Miller heard the strength evaporate from her voice. She sounded exhausted. He found a clean legal pad. Picked up a pen.

"What seems to be the problem?"

"My husband's missing."

"Have you contacted the police?"

"Yes, but they don't believe me. They think he ran off with some hooker or something."

Miller cleared his throat. "You mean, your husband?"

"Yes. Scott Wilkinson."

"And you are?"

"Melissa Wilkinson."

"Okay." He wrote it all down. Habit made him write "Wilkinson Case" and "12-18" at the top of the pad and underline it, just like on his homework for the Jesuits back in high school.

"And you think it's a kidnapping because . . . ?"

"Because he hasn't come home!"

"Uhm-hmm. So, how long has Scott been missing?"

"Two . . . almost three days."

"And your last contact was?"

"When he landed at LaGuardia last Friday. He was on United Flight Six Fifty from Chicago. The plane landed at nine-oh-two P.M. He called me as soon as he was in the airport. He always does."

Miller made notes. "We do the same thing," he said.

"You and your wife?"

"Yes, ma'am. She likes to know when I'm safe and sound on the ground."

"He was on his way to baggage claim. He didn't have any suitcases but that's where his driver was supposed to meet him."

"Did you call the car company?"

"Yes. They told me Scott had canceled the reservation Friday afternoon."

"Interesting."

"It's not right."

"Have you received any ransom demands?"

"Ransom?"

"Well, in most abductions, the kidnapper wants something. Usually money."

"No. No, I haven't heard from anyone."

"Has somebody made contact? Offered proof of life?"

"Proof of life?"

"Some evidence that your husband is alive. Maybe a video or a photograph?"

"Somebody sent me pictures of Scott." She paused. "Dirty ones."

"Dirty?"

"Pornographic." She suddenly sounded even wearier.

Miller leaned back in his chair.

"Pornographic?"

"In the pictures, he's with . . . these girls. They don't have much on, and Scott, he looks weird. Maybe drunk. Or drugged."

"These photographs, they came in the mail? FedEx?"

"E-mail."

More notes.

"Okay. E-mail. What was the sender's address?"

"It was Scott's. Someone used his e-mail account."

"Was there any message? With the pictures?"

"Yes, but I know Scott didn't type it."

"What did the message say?"

"'Having a wonderful time. Wish you were here.'"

Another pause.

"Okay."

"Scott didn't write that."

"Okay."

"He has an MBA from Harvard, Special Agent . . ."

"Miller."

"Mr. Miller, that's such a hokey cliché. Scott hates clichés. I was too upset at first to realize it, but now I see it's more like a taunt. Scott's not like that at all. We have a baby."

"Boy or girl?"

"Boy. Tyler. Eleven months. Are you going to tell me I need to see a divorce lawyer?"

"No, I was going to suggest—"

"That's what everybody says. That my husband has run away from home, that he's tired of me. But no one at PP&W has heard from either."

"What's PP&W?"

"That's where Scott works. It's one of the biggest ad agencies in the whole world and they can't tell me where Scott is. They've been calling here. Wondering why he didn't show up for work today."

"Mrs. Wilkinson, I'd like to help you out. Honest. But I'm more or less confined to base here."

"What?"

"I'm on what you might call limited desk duty."

"Why?"

"Long story."

"Then why did the woman who answered the phone send me to you? I specifically asked for the agent in charge of kidnapping."

"Yes, ma'am. And like I said, I used to do a whole lot of work pertaining to kidnappings and—"

"I don't need a 'used to' person. I need a 'right now' person."

"Tell you what—I'm going to take down your phone number and we'll get back to you."

"I don't want you calling me just to tell me you can't help me because you're on desk duty or retired or whatever."

"I'll have the right person contact you, okay?"

"Soon?"

"Soon as I can. You have the police out looking for him?"

"I filled out their form. Yes."

"Okay. Good. That's a start."

Miller walked down the hall to the vending machines. He needed to stretch his legs, needed to think.

Christmas was coming fast. He had to go to Toys "R" Us. Angela wanted an Elmo. The one who sang or roller-skated or danced the Hokey Pokey or something. She had also asked Santa to bring her a "big-girl" bicycle with training wheels. So, one of the things Miller knew he'd be doing on Christmas Eve was wrenching together a bike, and that could take all night.

But that was okay. The holidays were for family.

Miller remembered what somebody had once told him: family are the people who, if you don't come home, will go out looking for you.

People like Melissa Wilkinson looking for her husband, Scott.

Miller sipped the watery coffee he'd just bought from the vending machine and decided it tasted so bad it wasn't worth any extra trips to the men's room. He chucked the cup into the trash.

He marched back to his cubicle and made another phone call to another friend. This one worked for the Port Authority Police out at the airport.

They shot the breeze for a minute or two, commiserated about fighting the crowds in the malls and putting together Chinese-manufactured bicycles on Christmas Eve with instructions written in badly translated English.

Then Miller popped the question:

"Jimmy—do you guys have security cameras out at LaGuardia? Down near baggage claim?"

35

The big car crawled out of the shadow cast by the rusting subway trestle.

In the sunshine on Brighton Boulevard, Maksim Demichev's Town Car looked filthy, more gray than black because of the road salt cloaking its body and windshield.

Maksim parked in front of the Lucky Seven office. He wanted to drop off a small holiday gift for the dispatchers: a box of Russell Stover chocolates he'd purchased at a gas station food shop when he filled up after his last run out to JFK.

Three men were waiting for him on the sidewalk.

"Maksim Petrovich Demichev!"

Maksim squinted. It was Slava and two other men who also worked for Vasily. Large men. Thick necks.

"How are you this lovely day?" Slava smiled. The other two, the muscle, didn't smile. Their type seldom did.

"I am fine," Maksim said cautiously. "How are you, Slava?"

"*Pizdato*," Slava said. "Fantastic! Are you hungry for lunch, Maksim? I thought perhaps we could eat together at the delicatessen."

Maksim was sixty-four years old. He had lived in Brighton Beach for nearly two decades. He knew who Slava was, what he did, and whom he did it for. He had also heard rumors of what went on at the International Delicatessen. A couple of people he knew worked there. The meat butcher. The old lady who stocked the cheese. They both said some people who went downstairs never came back up.

"I had a big breakfast," Maksim said, patting his belly.

"Me, too." Slava dropped his cigarette to the sidewalk and ground it into the concrete with the toe of his shoe. "Perhaps we should take a stroll along the beach?"

Maksim held out the Russell Stover box. "I brought chocolates. For the girls."

"They can wait."

Maksim nodded and placed the slender white box on the roof of his car. Slava gestured for Maksim to join him on the sidewalk.

"Come. We go down to the boardwalk. We smell the ocean. We soak in the sun."

"Okay."

The boardwalk was a public place, Maksim thought. If Slava meant to kill him, he would not choose such a spot.

"Come," Slava said, wiggling his fingers to summon Maksim closer. "We go together. You and me and my two friends."

"Okay."

Maksim stuffed his car keys into his pocket and wondered if he would ever see his dirty Lincoln again. He had hoped to visit the car wash this afternoon. He had hoped to have it washed and waxed. He left the box of chocolates on the roof to melt in the bright December sun.

"Sit," said Slava when they reached an empty bench facing the ocean. "We talk."

Maksim's knees felt rubbery. He ran his hand through his thick hair. It was as grimy as the road grit slathered across his car's hood.

"So, Maksim, do you know Nicolai Kyznetsoff?"

"Yes."

"He is your friend?"

"Nicolai has no friends."

"Really? This is so sad for me to hear. So close to the holidays and he has no friends, no family?"

"He is a lone wolf."

"Ah, but even the lone wolf roams with the pack from time to time, no?"

"Yes. From time to time."

Slava pulled down the zipper on his taut leather jacket and reached inside.

"Do you need a cigarette?" Maksim asked. "I have a fresh pack."

"No, thank you, Maksim." Slava found what he was looking for. "I have some snapshots which I thought you might enjoy."

He showed Maksim what he had done to Kostya.

Maksim felt his breakfast rise up into his throat.

"Did you know the fat boy?" Slava asked.

"Yes."

"He was your friend?"

Maksim didn't know what answer Slava wanted.

"He was another driver for the company," he said. "For Lucky Seven."

"I guess he was not so lucky, eh?" Slava smiled and Maksim could see the gold capping two of his bottom teeth. "Tell me, Maksim, was not Nicolai Kyznetsoff also a driver for this same company?"

"Yes. Please. Can you put those away? I do not wish to look at Kostya this way."

"No?" Slava had arranged the photographs in chronological order, from grisly to gruesome to worse. He flipped them one at a time into Maksim's lap. "You don't wish to see what happens to those who do not tell me what I need to know?" He laid down the final picture: Kostya's slimy intestines coiling out of his enormous belly.

Maksim turned his head and retched.

Two old ladies looked over to see the man who had taken ill. They turned away quickly when Slava smiled in their direction.

"Okay." Slava draped his arm around Maksim's shoulders, helped him sit up straight. "Now, we talk. Okay, Maksim?"

"Yes. We talk."

Slava patted Maksim's knee.

"Good boy. *Berezhyonogo bog berezhyot*—no? God keeps safe those who keep themselves safe, *da?*"

"Yes."

"We have friends who tell us Nicolai came into their shop and sold them diamonds which he did not really own."

"Did he steal them?"

"Yes."

"Did he kill someone when doing this robbery?"

"Yes. Two *chernye*. So we do not care that he kills these two boys."

Maksim looked up. Pointed down the boardwalk at the parachute jump off in the distance. Coney Island might as well have been Paris, the parachute jump the Eiffel tower, Maksim felt so cut off from the ordinary world after seeing those photographs.

"Nicolai is Spetsgruppa Vympel. KGB. He showed me the arm patch. With the parachute."

"We know this. We know what he did in the old country."

"So what do you want from me?"

"The one thing we do not know. Where is he?"

"I do not know . . ."

Slava reached back into the jacket, ready to show Maksim the photographs again.

"I mean," Maksim stammered, "I don't know for sure."

Slava pulled out his pack of cigarettes, offered one to Maksim.

"Thank you."

Maksim jabbed the cigarette into his lips. Slava took his time. Slipped a smoke into his mouth. Dug in his side pockets. Found the lighter. Lit Maksim's first. Then his own.

"What do you *think* you know?"

"Well . . ." Maksim took a long drag, tried to think.

"If he had money, where would Kyznetsoff go?"

"Okay. Okay." Maksim sucked so hard on his cigarette he could feel the filter searing his lips. "Okay. This one time, over a year ago, we went hunting."

"Hunting?"

"Yes. Nicolai had a *dacha*."

"He did?"

"So maybe if he needs to be away from Brighton Beach, maybe he has returned there?"

"Where is it?"

"Pennsylvania."

Slava gave Maksim a look. He needed more.

"Browndale! Yes, I remember. There was a firehouse nearby. The Browndale Volunteer Fire Department. This I remember because they are all Polish and Lithuanian and have a festival that weekend we are there. They sell pierogies and kielbasi."

"Do you know how to find this Browndale?"

"Is easy. It is near to Scranton, but not so far. It is in the mountains. I can draw for you a map."

Slava was impressed. "*Horoshow*. Very good."

"Nicolai made me drive. His own car, it was in the shop. So I drive him to his cabin."

"So his *dacha* is a cabin?"

"Yes. A shitty little shack. Nicolai tells me he owns one hundred acres, all the forest, as far as my eye can see. But his *dacha*? It is shitty shack."

"What does it look like, exactly?"

"I can show you photograph."

"Really?"

"Yes! When Nicolai kills turkey early in the morning, he makes me take the photograph of him holding his trophy. I still have the film. The negatives."

"His cabin? It is in this picture?"

"*Da*. It is directly behind Nicolai and his turkey."

Slava took one final drag on his cigarette and patted Maksim on the knee again.

"Good. We go to camera shop, have them make photographs from your film. And you? You will draw me this map."

"Okay."

"You are a good friend, Maksim. This I will tell Vasily. You are a very good friend indeed."

36

Kyznetsoff dumped the contents of Scott Wilkinson's briefcase on the floor.

He pushed the pile around with his combat boot and kicked over a paperback novel. A thriller. The kind with a shiny, embossed cover.

"You are reading this? On the airplane?"

"Yes."

Kyznetsoff squatted, picked up the book. "This says 'a real page turner.'" He found where Scott had bent down a corner to mark his place. "I suppose you are curious as to how it will end, no?"

"Not really. It doesn't seem very important now."

"That is not the proper answer. Do you understand?"

"Sure. Fine. Whatever you say."

"Hey, no problem, Scott. Here. Read it now." Kyznetsoff slammed the book down hard on Scott's chest.

Now Kyznetsoff unsnapped a button on his chest pocket and pulled out one of Scott's business cards. "You are the Head of Strategic Planning."

"Yes."

"But you didn't plan for this, did you?"

"No."

"Tsk, tsk, tsk. They might demote you." Kyznetsoff took a black jacket off a hook, found his rolled-up watch cap in the pocket, and moved toward the door. "Tell me—this Brand Asset Builder you designed for PP&W Advertising—"

"How do you know about that?"

"I check the Internet. Once I decide you must be punished, I do my research."

"I see."

"Yes. Maybe you are starting to. Another thing I know is that your boss will consider this Brand Asset Builder to be proprietary information and he will not like hearing that you are talking about it to Omnicom and Interpublic, your two major competitors. In fact, you might lose your job when I phone Mr. Stafford— just as I once lost mine because of a call *you* made. Oh, well: rooster today, feather-duster tomorrow."

Kyznetsoff drove twenty miles to the truck stop located at the Route 191 exit off I-84. The signs indicated he could take 84 west to Scranton or east to the Delaware Water Gap National Recreation Area. He wasn't inter-ested in either destination. He pulled into the asphalt parking lot.

The truck stop had a bright red canopy sheltering a dozen or more pumps. A long, vinyl-sided building topped by a brown shingle roof and twin satellite dishes served as a convenience store. The building backed up against an eroded hill of scraggly pines and rocky clay.

Kyznetsoff parked near the phone booth at the side of the building, back near the corroded ice machine. He unwrapped a cherry candy and popped it into his mouth. He went to the pay phone and punched in the number he wanted to call, as well as his prepaid calling card number. The card would make his call untraceable.

He talked first to the woman who was the head of the research department at Omnicom. Kyznetsoff had found her name online, using Scott's laptop. Next, he called Interpublic.

In both instances, he identified himself as Scott Wilkinson. The other advertising executives had heard of Scott, admired his work, but had never met him. So, when Kyznetsoff said his name, they had no reason not to believe him—especially since he spoke slowly and chose his words very carefully in a concentrated effort to mask his accent.

When he told them of his—Scott's—dissatisfaction with PP&W, both rival agencies were excited about setting up a meeting. Interviews were arranged for the week after Christmas.

Next he called Kent Stafford, Scott's boss. His number was listed in Scott's BlackBerry. An administrative assistant answered on the second ring.

"Mr. Stafford's office."

"Hello. I need to speak with Mr. Stafford," Kyznetsoff said.

"I'm sorry, Mr. Stafford is in a meeting."

"This is a matter of extreme urgency."

"I can take a message . . ."

"I know why Scott Wilkinson has not come in to work today."

"Excuse me?"

"I know why he is not currently at the meeting with . . ." He glanced at Scott's daybook. "Fifer Pharmaceutical."

"Who is this? Because Mrs. Wilkinson has been leaving messages all over the building—"

"I could call back in ten minutes if that's more convenient. It is, as I say, a matter of some urgency. It is about what Scott Wilkinson is planning to do, now that he's set up meetings with Omnicom and Interpublic."

"What?"

"Should I call back tomorrow?"

"Make that five minutes."

Kyznetsoff strolled into the convenience store.

He was hungry for something sweet and saw the racks of brightly colored Christmas candies fronting the cash register. He grabbed a fistful of marshmallow snowmen. He liked to squish them into a gooey wad, then peel off the foil and jam the mashed ball into his mouth.

There was a young girl at the magazine rack watching him mangle the candy. She licked her lips when Kyznetsoff squashed another sugary mess in his fist.

"You gotta pay for those," the guy behind the counter said. "You can't do that and put 'em back."

Kyznetsoff, his eyes riveted on the girl, reached into his pants and pulled out a ten-dollar bill. He tossed it on the counter and moved toward the girl. He noticed she was reading *Penthouse*.

"Hey, mister," called the cashier. "You forgot your change. Marshmallow snowmen are two for a dollar."

"Give it to the dogs." There was a charity coin canister on the counter. It showed the pathetic picture of an abused dog. "I like dogs. Especially the skinny ones with all their ribs showing."

As he drew closer, Kyznetsoff saw that the girl was really a child. Fifteen. Maybe sixteen. But the pink lip-gloss and white eye shadow made her look much older. So did the midriff-baring top she was wearing even though it was 28 degrees outside. Most likely she was working here as a prostitute—a "lot lizard" turning tricks with truckers.

"Aren't you chilly?" Kyznetsoff asked with a sly smile.

"No," the girl said. "I'm actually kind of hot."

"I would agree. Do you like the dirty letters in *Penthouse* magazine?"

"Do you?" she asked coyly, moving close enough for Kyznetsoff to smell her cheap scent. "'Cause anything they write about, I can do better, baby."

Kyznetsoff nodded. Leered admiringly. "Of this I am quite certain."

"You want to go out to your rig? You gotta rack in back?"

"No." Kyznetsoff reached into his pocket and pulled out a thick roll of hundred-dollar bills. "I would like to invite you to my secret chalet." He peeled off a bill. "Once there, I will feed you caviar and champagne." Another bill crinkled off the roll. "Afterward, we shall soak in my hot tub. After that? Who knows?" He put three hundred dollars in her sweaty fist.

The girl's eyes went wide. Her breath became quick and shallow. Kyznetsoff checked his watch.

"Would you do me a favor?"

"Maybe." The teenager attempted to regain her sexy swagger.

Kyznetsoff handed her a fourth hundred-dollar bill.

"Will you kindly purchase this magazine plus anything else you think the two of us might enjoy as we spend our afternoon together?" He leaned in closer and she could smell his cherry breath. "Perhaps some chocolate sauce? Whipped cream? Have you read of such things in *Penthouse*?"

"Yeah," her voice trembled. "I read about, you know, about licking it off and stuff . . . putting it on a guy . . . you know . . . down there."

"But I want to pour it on *you*," Kyznetsoff whispered. "Down there." He took her hand, bowed, and kissed it softly. "I will see you outside in five minutes, yes?"

"Okay," the girl said, finding it hard to breathe.

"Do you like the maraschino cherries?"

"For the whipped cream?"

"One for each breast."

Kyznetsoff smiled. Money tossed around in such a fashion was bound to prove irresistible to the young girl.

Besides, he knew he would soon retrieve all the hundred-dollar bills he had just handed her.

37

"Who the hell are you?"

"I would rather not give my name."

Kent Stafford was furious.

"Where are you calling from? I don't recognize this area code."

"I am using a phone card. I prefer to remain anonymous."

"Where's Scott?"

"Here at Omnicom."

"What?"

"He is offering to sell us your Brand Asset Builder. They have agreed to double his salary."

"Jesus. You work at Omnicom?"

"In the research department. Mr. Wilkinson is also talking to Interpublic. He told us he will auction off your research tools to the highest bidder."

"The bastard."

"Mr. Stafford, I have always dreamed of working for PP&W. I have the PhD from Warsaw University, but here I am only a junior assistant."

"Call me after the holidays," Stafford barked. "If this information pans out, we'll talk."

"Thank you, sir!"

The line went dead.

Kyznetsoff wasn't certain whether Scott would be fired today, tomorrow, or next week. But he knew people at PP&W would soon start asking questions. They would call their friends working for Omnicom or Interpublic and, eventually, at least one of those friends would say, "Now that you mention it, I heard Scott Wilkinson has set up a lunch meeting with our personnel department for right after the holidays."

Kyznetsoff had also confirmed, through Mr. Stafford's secretary, what he suspected: Missy Wilkinson had been calling PP&W, searching for her husband. Now, however, the people at PP&W would avoid her. They would assume Scott was stealing from his employer *and* cheating on his wife. Perhaps, they would conjecture, he was selling out PP&W's secrets to finance his latest fling and impending divorce.

The girl came around the corner carrying a bulging grocery bag. "They didn't have whipped cream so I bought Cool Whip instead."

"*Horoshow.* Marvelous."

The girl giggled. "You talk funny. What's your name?"

"Vladimir."

"Are you like a foreigner or something?"

"*Da.*"

"Does that mean yes?"

"Yes."

"Cool. Look, I gotta be back here by six. One of my regulars is coming in from Ohio."

"Of course. No problem."

Kyznetsoff held open the door and the girl hopped into the Expedition. He wasn't sure how many times he would have sex with her. He wasn't certain whether he would make Scott watch or whether he would use the naked teenager to photograph a whole new sex show to e-mail Missy.

He only knew one thing: when he was finished doing whatever he wished to do with this comely young whore, he would most certainly kill her.

38

At 5:15 P.M., Christopher Miller sat in the front seat of his car with his daughter.

Angela had never heard the Supremes do "Santa Claus Is Coming to Town," the tune currently spinning in the CD player.

"Now, let me show you how to make the moves," Miller said, shoulder-shooping to one side, then the other. "The moves are the whole show if you want to be Diana or one of the Supremes."

Angela giggled. Miller loved the way his daughter thought he was funny.

"Pay attention, sugar. Twirl your hands in front of you. That's right. Roll 'em on top of each other like you're wrapping up a rope, or making taffy."

"Taffy? That's silly, daddy!"

"Roll one on top of the other . . . like this . . . like a referee does when, you know, there's illegal procedure on the field."

"What?"

"Encroachment. Like in football."

"Football? I thought this was dancing."

"It is, sugar. We're car-dancing. Roll your arms. One on top of the other and around."

"Like this?"

"You got it, girl. Now snap your fingers and point and snap again and point and sweep your arm slowly to the right and shake your finger at all the naughty little boys and girls who better not pout."

She dropped her arms and held her stomach and giggled so hard she had water pouring out of her eyes. "You're the silliest daddy in the world! Stop!"

"Stop? Can't stop now, sweetie. No, sir. This is the best part. . . comin' on up."

Miller's wife, Natalie, had dropped by his office with Angela and was currently inside delivering holiday goodies to the gang down in Investigative Technologies—the department where she used to work running finger-print searches while she night-schooled on her PhD.

It was his job, in the meantime, to baby-sit Angela out in the parking garage.

"Sing along, honey . . ."

"Oh, you better wash out, you better not cry, you better not pop, I'm tellin' you why . . ."

Miller knew "pout" was one of those words you learned when you were eight, maybe nine. Not six. Besides, Angela never pouted, she always smiled. Always. Her face was a radiant ball of perpetual sunshine.

They did a daddy-daughter duet on the chorus.

"Santa Claus is comin' to town, Santa Claus . . ."

Someone tapped lightly against Miller's window. He turned and saw a pretty young blonde woman with sad eyes.

"I'm sorry," she said. "I didn't mean to . . . Mr. Miller?"

Miller punched off the CD player. Angela crawled across the bench seat and into his lap.

"Daddy? Who's she?"

"I don't know, angel." Miller scrolled down his window. "Can I help you, miss?"

"Are you Special Agent Christopher Miller?"

"That's right."

"I'm Melissa Wilkinson. We talked on the phone? Earlier today? I called you because my husband—"

"I remember," Miller said, holding up his hand to stop the blonde woman before she used any words like "kidnapped" in front of his baby girl.

"I found your photograph. On line. Lots of articles, too. You really *are* a kidnapping expert." She started digging inside her purse, pulling out folded inkjet printouts. "I Googled you," she said. "I know you rescued a small child in West Virginia . . . you ran out of a barn and had her cradled in your arms and they shot at you and—"

Miller nodded toward his daughter. "Mrs. Wilkinson, I wonder if maybe we could talk about this a little later? Maybe tomorrow during normal business hours?"

"Scott's office called this afternoon. They wanted to know if I've heard from him because they said they had some questions they needed to ask him."

"Well, that seems like—"

"It was one of their lawyers! From the PP&W legal department. He said something about ethical violations and noncompete clauses and how Scott could be putting himself and his whole family in serious jeopardy if he continued doing whatever it is they think he's doing. He said the company wasn't afraid of going to court and so I lied and told them I'd tell Scott to give them a call when he came home, that he was out Christmas shopping and—"

"Who are you?" Natalie Miller now came up behind Melissa Wilkinson.

"I'm sorry."

"Why are you badgering my husband?"

"Because *my* husband is missing!"

Miller stepped out of the car. "Ladies?" He looked at his wife, nodded toward the car. Angela. "Mrs. Wilkinson, like I said, we need to continue this discussion inside. Tomorrow." He leaned down and whispered at her. "My daughter is six. A couple of seconds ago, we were singing Santa Claus songs, which is what a six-year-old girl should be doing this close to Christmas."

"I'm sorry. I—"

"I understand your husband's missing and you're upset but you need to understand I have to protect my family."

"I am so sorry . . . I didn't mean to . . ." Melissa bit her lip. Miller could see her contort her cheeks, try to stop any tears before they started down her cheeks, before they frightened the little girl.

"Look," Miller said, "I was going to call you first thing tomorrow."

Melissa took a deep breath, found her composure. "Tomorrow might be too late," she said.

"Has there been a ransom demand?"

"No. No ransom note."

"What's going on here?" Natalie moved closer, turned her back to the car. She, like her husband, wanted to shield Angela from whatever had brought this terrified woman into the parking lot of an FBI field office. "Chris?"

"Mrs. Wilkinson's husband is missing. Has been for three days. She suspects foul play."

Natalie nodded, shifted into her Betty Bureau fact-gatherer mode. "Kidnapping?"

"One theory. The police don't buy it."

"And you? Have you seen or heard anything that might substantiate her claim?"

"Well . . ."

Miller knew if he answered truthfully he was stepping into this thing big time. There would be no turning back; he'd be up to his eyeballs in it and somebody else might have to figure out the Chinese bicycle instructions on Christmas Eve because he would probably be at the office or out in the field, logging another eighteen-hour day, running down leads, strapping on his Glock M22, chasing after a bunch of bad guys while simultaneously trying to keep it quiet so Leon Owens, who still had Miller on some kind of permanent temporary suspension, didn't bust him before he had the chance to find out why Owens was handing out a private FBI phone number to an elderly Russian auntie in Brighton Beach who just happened to collect nesting dolls with illegally smuggled diamonds hidden inside them.

Man. Sometimes the truth could be a mother.

"Yeah," he said. "I might have something."

Melissa's eyes shifted back and forth between the two

Millers. "What? Can you help me? Can your husband help me?"

Natalie sighed. "Can you, Chris?"

"It might be nothing."

Natalie knew her husband better than that. "Or it could be something, right? Something huge?"

"Yeah. Could be. Maybe."

"What? What is it? Mr. Miller? Please?"

Natalie turned to Melissa. "Tell me, ma'am—do you bake banana bread?"

"Banana? No, I—"

"Good." Natalie held out her hand for Christopher to turn over the car keys. "He gets enough of that already from the neighbors. All that banana bread is making him soft, giving him a cute little banana bread belly."

"Hey!"

"Go back inside, Christopher. Help this woman."

"What about—?"

"Toys 'R' Us? I'll handle it."

Angela heard that.

"Are we going to Toys 'R' Us, Mommy?"

"No, honey." She turned back to Mrs. Wilkinson. "You're in good hands, Mrs. . . . ?"

"Wilkinson. Mrs. Scott Wilkinson. I mean I'm Melissa . . . Missy . . . my husband is Scott."

"Okay. My husband? He'll find yours. He's actually quite good at it. In fact, I'd say he's the best. I think that's why I married him."

39

Miller escorted Melissa past lobby security and up to the floor where he worked.

The place was nearly empty—the cleaning crew was rolling their carts down the halls. Here and there, agents tapped computer keys or made one last phone call. They all waved to Miller; he waved back. He led his visitor into his cubicle and picked up a small digital cassette case sitting on his desk.

"After you called," he said, "I talked to one of my buddies who works with the Port Authority cops out at LaGuardia. Played a hunch. He sent this over about an hour ago."

"What is it?"

"Security camera footage from baggage claim, near one of the escalators everybody has to use on their way out, whether they're picking up luggage or not. There's also a camera mounted above one of the carousels looking out toward the doors and the curb. Since you told me Scott's plane landed Friday night at nine-oh-four, I asked my guy to pull and send over everything they had from nine P.M. on. I was able to scan through it quickly."

"Is he on the tape? Did you see Scott?"

"I'm not sure. I saw something that got my curiosity up, but since I don't know what your husband looks like . . ."

"This is him," Melissa laid a wallet-sized print of the official PP&W portrait on Miller's desk.

"Okay, but—"

"This is him, too." She pulled out one of the photos she'd received via e-mail.

"Okay," Miller said. "We'll talk about that one a little later."

"We can talk about it now if you like," Melissa said bravely.

"Later will be fine. Come on."

He led Melissa down a hall and into an empty con-ference room equipped with video decks and a flat-screen monitor. He slipped the small cassette into the mouth of the digital player. The screen filled with a familiar scene: a crowded airport after several planes have just landed. Business people, college kids, families. All shuttling down the escalator, jostling over to the carousel, heading to the exits with their carry-ons.

The perspective changed.

"Okay. This is the other camera. The one looking toward the doors. What I noticed was in this cluster of drivers . . . here . . ."

"From the car services?"

"Right. That's where the limo drivers all congregate, hold up their signs, and meet their passengers."

"The company said Scott canceled his reservation," Melissa reminded Miller.

"I know. But I saw something. Here it is." He pushed pause. He pushed another button and zoomed in on the still frame until he was focused on one driver holding up a sign. "I think that sign says Lucky Seven. See? And underneath, the name of the passenger."

"Wilkinson. It says Wilkinson!"

"Right. Now, it could be another Wilkinson coming in at approximately the same time."

"Impossible! It has to be Scott. Did you see Scott?"

"You tell me."

Miller pushed the play button twice. The scene rolled forward in super-slow motion. A tall man with sandy hair, his back to the camera, approached the driver holding up the Wilkinson sign.

"That's Scott! That's my husband!"

"You're sure?"

"Positive. That's his coat."

"Okay."

"That driver. Does he work for Lucky Seven? I want to see his face," Melissa said, suddenly furious.

"So do I," said Miller. "Unfortunately he never drops his sign while he's facing the camera. See how he holds it up high like that? Blocks his face the whole time. He only lowers the sign after he's turned around and is standing next to your husband to help him with the rolling bag."

"Because he knew about the security cameras?"

"Maybe." Miller rewound the tape to the spot where the driver was holding up the sign and hiding his face. He froze the image. "But here's something. Could be a clue. Might help us ID the driver." He tapped the screen with his pen.

"What? The sign?"

"No. Right above it." Miller twisted a few dials, forcing the pixels on the screen to become sharper. "I'm not a hundred percent certain, but that sure looks like a Santa Claus hat."

40

The morning sun streaming through the window blinded Scott Wilkinson.

He couldn't move because he was still strapped to the metal bed frame. He raised his head about an inch and saw the silhouette of his captor, Nicolai Kyznetsoff, dragging the dead girl's naked body across the rough floor.

"You killed her."

"*Da.*"

Scott's whole body shuddered. He had never been this close to violent death. He could smell the gas exiting her entrails, the sharp metallic stench of her blood.

Kyznetsoff shrugged. "It is of no consequence. Her life was small and she was bored with it. So she is dead. We all die, Scott. And this slut? She was dead long ago with nothing to live for but her next fuck session. At least she went out with a bang!" Kyznetsoff laughed. "I make a joke, Scott. She went out with a bang? I banged her a dozen times! Was it a dozen?"

"I don't know," Scott swallowed.

"What? I told you to keep count!"

Scott turned his head away from Kyznetsoff, away from the sun burning through the filthy glass.

"She stinks, no? First your *govno*. Now hers. My *dacha* stinks like a latrine." He tugged on the teenager's limp arms. "Tell me, Scott—when you called the car company, when you complained about me, what did they say?"

"I don't remember."

"What? You lie there strapped down for days and days and you do not remember every word, every detail of what transpired? You would never make Spetsgruppa Vympel, even with your fancy Harvard MBA. You are too stupid. You are a soft, worthless . . ."

"They told me," Scott snapped, "that you would be dealt with."

"I would be 'dealt with?'"

"Yes."

"I see. Okay. Thank you. Now I deal with you."

Scott heard metal slide against metal.

"I am tired of emptying your bed pan. Tired of you not doing what I ask you to do. I tell you to watch me with this whore and you turn your head? You *petuh!* Sissy boy."

Scott felt cold steel press against his temple.

"So maybe I kill you, now. Maybe I splatter your brains on the floor. I have to clean up her mess, I might as well clean up yours, too."

Scott heard another click.

"But, then again, I do not wish to become bored like this dead whore. So, maybe we wait. Just a little longer. It will thrill me to see you lose your wife, your job, your home. Yes. This would be good. To see you crawl along the gutter begging for nickels and dimes. I must make you lose your house as well as your wife and your job."

Now the sound of Velcro.

Scott dared look.

Kyznetsoff was putting his pistol back into its holster. In his right hand he carried a military shovel that looked like a gardening trowel, only three times bigger, its black metal edge sharper.

"I am going outside to bury this pig in the forest."

"What about her family?"

Kyznetsoff shrugged again. "Their daughter was *shalava*, a slut. She turns tricks at a truck stop. What do the parents care if she is dead?"

Scott heard Kyznetsoff drag the body toward what must be the cabin's front door. The door creaked open and, after a minute, there was a series of thumps. Like a heavy leather medicine ball bouncing on the porch planks.

The girl's head working its way down a flight of wooden steps.

41

Kyznetsoff dug a shallow pit and pushed the girl's naked body into it.

He used his entrenching tool to rake in some dirt and leaves, to blanket the corpse with an inch or two of earth. He was about one hundred meters from the front of the cabin, deep in a stand of spindly trees and jagged stumps. He didn't care if wild animals dug up the body and feasted on her. He just wanted her putrid stink out of his cabin. He thought about going into town, to the hardware store, to pick up a bag or two of lime to cut the stench of death. But the hardware store was currently stocking snow shovels, not lawn fertilizers.

He heard car tires crunch gravel. He collapsed to his stomach, stretched into a prone combat stance. Someone was coming. Reflexively, he rolled down his ski mask. He peered out its two small eyeholes, breathed through the opening for his mouth.

A white Suburban wound its way down the cabin's rutted driveway.

Kyznetsoff wasn't expecting visitors.

His fingers found the small pair of high-powered

binoculars in his left hip pocket, and he focused on the action at the bottom of the hill.

He saw Vasily's main man, Slava, and two goons.

Kyznetsoff could only smile.

Vasily must have figured out who currently had possession of Comrade Bizanko's diamonds. Kyznetsoff realized he had probably pawned a stone to the wrong jeweler, someone with connections back to the thieves-in-law in Brooklyn.

Perhaps an unwise move.

But he had needed the money to finance the Wilkinson operation. The stretch limousine. The special electronics to block cellular communication and control the locks and seatbelts. The drugged champagne. The Ford Expedition. The new weaponry and uniforms. All of it. He had paid cash for everything.

The three Russians climbed out of the SUV.

Kyznetsoff levered the zoom lens on his binoculars and noted that each man carried a high-powered hunting rifle, as well as an automatic pistol strapped to his side.

Someone had talked to Vasily. But who? Who knew of this secret place? Who had ever been to this cabin deep in the Pennsylvania woods?

Of course.

Maksim.

He was the only man who had ever seen this hideaway.

Obviously, it had been a mistake for Kyznetsoff to maneuver the old fool into driving him up here that one weekend when his own car was in the shop.

No matter. Maksim would be "dealt with."

They would all be dealt with.

Kyznetsoff gripped his entrenching tool and crawled across the wet leaves until he came to a patch of melting snow near a stump—an excellent vantage point for spying on his three most immediate enemies.

He watched Slava stride toward the cabin. He saw him stop and point to the Ford Expedition at the far end of the driveway. He pointed again, this time up into the forest—almost directly to the stump where Kyznetsoff lay hidden in the shadows.

Slava was splitting up his troops. Sending one man to check the car, another up the hill. Slava, himself, it appeared, would search inside the cabin.

He, of course, would discover Scott Wilkinson.

No matter. Most likely, he'd pump Nicolai's house-guest for information and, when he'd learned what he could, make an end of him. Not the end Nicolai had envisioned for Scott but, sometimes, that happened.

Slava would not care that he had ruined Nicolai's revenge. Slava was a kindred spirit. A fellow predator. He took care of no one except himself.

The three new arrivals set out on their appointed missions.

One of the big men trudged across the small stream at the base of the hill and started climbing up the mucky slope, unknowingly heading straight for Kyznetsoff.

He would become target number one.

42

"Who are you?" Scott asked when he saw the man in the black leather jacket.

The man moved closer to the bed.

"I need help! My name is Scott Wilkinson."

The newcomer had a rifle.

"A man named Nicolai Kyznetsoff kidnapped me. Brought me here. Tied me up like this. Please—I need your help. I don't know where he keeps the keys to these handcuffs but . . ."

The man looked around the room.

"He's up in the woods somewhere. He went outside to bury this girl he raped and tortured and . . . it was horrible. He cut her. Hacked at her with a kitchen knife. I couldn't watch."

The man with the rifle walked to the door.

"Please," Scott pleaded. "I need your help!"

He heard the cabin's front door open, then close.

43

Kyznetsoff threw a shovelful of dirt into the first man's face.

While the flying debris blinded him, Kyznetsoff rotated the shovel handle in his fist and punched the tool up under the man's chin. Its sharpened steel tip dug into the carotid artery and, when Kyznetsoff thrust it forward, nearly yanked the man's head off his neck.

From his training and experience in Chechnya, Kyznetsoff knew this simple tool could prove a valuable weapon. It was mobile and maneuverable, like his knife, but it carried more striking power, could deliver more force.

He looked at the man's fallen body, his head wrenched backwards like one of those plastic dispensers where the candy tablets slide out of the neck of a cartoon character.

The shovel had done its job.

Kyznetsoff tumbled sideways onto a soft bed of pine needles, assuming a ready combat crouch, and making no sound.

He would work his way down the hill, heading west by northwest. He would sneak up behind the man currently attempting to jimmy open the locked doors on the Expedition.

He would take out target number two.

"Fedya?" Kyznetsoff heard Slava call to the man working on the car doors. "Has Grisha returned?"

"No. He is still up the hill."

"What the fuck are you doing?"

"Trying to open this goddamn door."

"You think Kyznetsoff is hiding inside his car? What? Is he underneath the seats?"

"The windows are all black. I cannot see inside."

"There is a man inside the cabin."

"A man?"

"He is in there pissing in his panties he is so scared."

"Maybe he is Kyznetsoff's *petuh*. Maybe he screws this man because he has no girl."

"He had a girl. He is somewhere in the woods now burying the bitch's body."

"Where?"

"I will go ask the man more questions. You? Forget the car. Go up into those trees. See if you can find our gravedigger."

Kyznetsoff hunkered behind a mammoth outcropping of rock.

Good, he thought. Slava is sending another lamb up the hill to be slaughtered. Kyznetsoff was skilled and proficient in all manner of weaponry. The cold steel of the combat knife was one of his favorites.

He pulled it out of his boot.

The second man moved closer. Slava returned to the cabin.

Kyznetsoff heard the cabin's screen door slam shut and used the noise to cover his grunt as he flung the knife ten meters at his next victim.

The man called Fedya sank to his knees, both hands clutching the knife sticking out of his forehead. Blood cascaded down his face, covered his eyes. He was too stunned to scream before he died. Besides, the knife's tip had pierced the soft tissue of his brain and rendered him speechless, just as Kyznetsoff knew it would.

Kyznetsoff scurried down the hill, using the trees to cover his movement.

He crept up onto the cabin's porch.

Now it was time for target number three. Slava.

44

"Thank God, you came back," Scott said when he heard the man walking around the cabin, opening drawers, emptying shelves, knocking over furniture. "We need to call the police! Call the FBI! I was kidnapped!"

"The FBI?" the man said.

He had a thick Russian accent.

"What do you know of the FBI?" The Russian approached the bed. "Do you work for Miller?"

"Miller?"

"Christopher Miller. Do you work with Bizanko's friend at the FBI? Is this why you are here in the woods hunting Kyznetsoff?"

"No. I don't know any . . ."

The man hovered over the bed. "You are attempting to retrieve the diamonds yourself and Kyznetsoff, he catches you?"

"No, I swear . . ."

Scott saw the man reach into his black leather coat and pull out what looked like a pearl-handled barber's razor.

"Are you with the FBI?"

"No. I swear. I was kidnapped . . ."

The man snapped open the blade.

"Did Comrade Bizanko fail to inform you that Vasily has taken over this assignment? Or maybe you greedy pigs have decided you will steal our cut?"

Scott could feel the edge of the razor as it scraped down his stubbly neck and came to rest over his Adam's apple.

"Did you come here to steal our slice of the pie? Are you FBI? Perhaps *you* are Christopher Miller."

"No . . . I swear . . . I am not with the FBI . . . I don't know anybody named Miller . . . I don't know Bizanko . . . I don't know . . ."

Scott heard a soft thwick-pop. The man above him winced. Blood sprang from his head. Another thwick-pop. The man dropped the razor. Another thwick-pop and the man fell forward, his dead weight sprawled across Scott's chest.

"Jesus!" Scott screamed. "Jesus!"

Kyznetsoff leaned over the bed, smiling.

"Did you piss your pants, Scotty?" He pulled off his ski mask, used it to wipe the sweat dripping down his brow. "I see you have met Syroslav Ivanovich Gubina, the one they call Slava."

Kyznetsoff put his boot to Slava's back and rolled him off Scott's chest. The body tumbled to the floor. "They also call him the Brooklyn Butcher. He is quite skilled with his straight razor. What do you know—I just saved your life."

Kyznetsoff holstered his pistol.

"I could have used a razor on him as well, perhaps a paint scraper. Maybe even the sharp lid off the top of an old sardine tin. Something dramatic. But you see, Slava was the last man for me to eliminate. Therefore, I no longer had any need to maintain silence. So, I shoot him. Bang-bang." He raised his shoulders and let them drop. No big deal.

Kyznetsoff walked away, disappearing from Scott's limited field of vision.

"I am hungry," Kyznetsoff said. "Hunting turkeys always makes me hungry. I'm going to fix a sandwich. A turkey sandwich."

"Thank you," Scott said, his voice quavering.

"What?"

"Thank you, Mr. Kyznetsoff. For saving my life. Thank you."

Kyznetsoff laughed.

"You think I give two shits about your life, Scott? Do you? If so, you are a fool. To me, you are the *piz dyulina*— the thing that does not matter. One day, when you no longer amuse me, when I am no longer interested in watching you suffer, I will be the one who slits your throat. I will use the barber's razor or rip off your head with my field shovel. This I promise you I will one day do."

He moved into the kitchen. Yanked open the refrigerator door.

"But, first, I must do more reconnaissance work. You see, Scott, I have no interest in sharing my diamonds. Not with Slava. Not with Vasily. Not with this *petuh* from the FBI he speaks of, this man, Christopher Miller."

"I swear—I don't know him!"

"No matter. As you say, Christopher Miller 'will be dealt with.' He will be next."

45

Six days before Christmas, Christopher Miller was driving out to Brooklyn again.

He had told his boss that he needed to follow up on "that thing with the little old lady" for Leon Owens. He was really heading out to Brooklyn so he could visit the offices of Lucky Seven Limousines.

It was weird. Two different cases, both sending him in the same direction, both taking him to Brighton Beach. Of course, there was no connection, Miller told himself, not between the stolen dolls and Melissa Wilkinson's missing husband. It was just weird.

Miller pulled in behind a row of Town Cars double-parked along the curb. He hadn't called, so nobody was expecting him. Sometimes it worked better that way.

He climbed out of his vehicle and closed up his coat. It was cold this morning. Snow flurries swirled into a whirlwind every time a subway car screeched past on the elevated tracks.

A man with greasy gray hair stood beside one of the Town Cars smoking a cigarette. He stared at Miller. Studied him. Acted like Miller must've taken a wrong turn, didn't belong in Little Odessa. Like he belonged over in Bensonhurst with the rest of his black brothers.

Miller smiled.

Greasy hair didn't smile back. He raised his cigarette to his lips, took in some more smoke.

"You work here?" Miller asked.

The man hunched his head, raised his shoulders. "No English. *Russkovo*."

Miller moved closer.

"Okay. No problem." He put on his friendliest face. "By the way, your zipper is wide open. You're just flapping in the breeze down there, brother."

No reply.

Miller turned away, headed down the sidewalk.

Before he opened the door to the office, he couldn't resist: he snuck a quick peek back over his shoulder.

The guy was checking his fly.

Busted.

A heavyset woman sat behind a gunship-gray desk. Miller figured she weighed close to three hundred pounds. When he walked in, she tried to hide a half-empty box of Entenmann's Christmas cookies that she'd been dipping into.

"May I help you?" she asked.

"I hope so. I'm Special Agent Christopher Miller with the FBI." He flashed her his badge.

"Is there a problem?" the woman asked. "Did one of our drivers smuggle something from the airport or something? Was it drugs? Not again—"

"Whoa. Hold on. I just need to ask you a couple of questions."

The woman now reached for a bowl of red-and-green M&Ms. She popped a handful into her mouth.

"Oh. Okay. Whew. I got all nervous when you said 'FBI' like that."

"I'm okay with waiting until you feel more relaxed."

"It's all right." She fanned the air around her face, which was mottled with red panic patches. "Sometimes I sort of lose it. So—how can I help you?"

"You are?"

"Julie."

"Julie, does your company work with PP&W Advertising?"

"Yes, sir. They're our biggest client. They sent me a tiered popcorn tin this year. It has caramel and cheese and regular popcorn, too."

"Is that so?"

"Yunh-hunh. There're dogs and cats on it. It's super cute. Let me show you . . ."

She twisted around in her swivel chair to retrieve it.

"That's okay."

She swiveled back.

Miller flipped open his notebook. "On Friday, December fifteenth, a PP&W executive named Scott Wilkinson was scheduled to be picked up by one of your drivers at LaGuardia airport."

"Did we miss the pick-up?" She hastily grabbed more M&Ms. "Some of the guys do that sometimes. They screw up, and the customers all call here to yell at me."

Miller pointed to the boxy computer sitting on her desk.

"Would you have Mr. Wilkinson's reservation in your system?"

"Sure."

"He was on United Flight Six Fifty out of O'Hare. Landed at nine-oh-four. LaGuardia."

"Wilkerson?" Julie asked, wiggling her fingertips over the keyboard, her hands becoming chubby Olympic swimmers limbering up before leaping off the starting blocks.

"Wilkinson," Miller said. "With a 'k-i-n.'"

She tapped keys. "Here we go. Wilkinson, Scott. That reservation was canceled."

"You sure?"

"Yes, sir. The passenger called, said he wouldn't need a car."

"Did you take that call?"

"No. I worked the late shift Friday. But I bet we were happy to have the cancellation."

"How come?"

"Of-fice par-ties." She sang the two words with a fluttering trill. "We were running short on cars all night. Kept getting calls from clients who'd had a little too much holiday cheer. 'Where's my effing car, you effing idiot?' Stuff like that. So cancellations are always welcome, especially this time of year."

"I see." Miller handed her an image lifted off the surveillance tape. "Is that one of your signs?"

"Looks like it."

"This man here?"

"With his back to the camera?"

"That's right. That's Scott Wilkinson."

"No!"

"Yep."

"So he didn't cancel?" Confused, Julie dug for a foil-wrapped Reese's cup buried beneath the few remaining M&Ms.

"This driver. Do you know him?"

"Let me look . . ."

Miller felt cold air. Somebody had come in the front door. He turned to see who it was.

The guy from out on the street. He carried a Russian language newspaper and sat down on the ratty sofa.

"He work here?" Miller asked Julie.

"Who? Maksim? You bet. He's been with Lucky Seven for years."

"Maybe I should show him this picture . . ."

"Why?" she asked. "It's a terrible shot. All you can see is the top of the driver's hat. You know, like those ski caps with the fluffy little ball up top."

"Or maybe a Santa Claus hat?"

"You're right! It kind of sort of looks like a Santa Claus hat, doesn't it?"

"Do any of your drivers wear a Santa hat?"

"On the job? No."

"Who's that?" Miller pointed to a row of framed photos on the credenza behind the woman's desk.

"That's Noodles. My cat."

"How about the one next to it?"

"Oh. That's just me horsing around with a guy at last year's Christmas party. We had it at the Odessa. It's this nightclub that serves totally yucky Russian food. That's my old boyfriend. Nick. He said he was Grandfather Frost. That's what they call Santa Claus over in Russia."

"Can I see it, please?"

"Sure." Julie handed him the photo. "My dress is kind of risqué . . . sorry about that . . . of course I can't wear it this year . . . put on fifty pounds . . . I have a glandular problem."

Miller was only half listening. He was comparing the two pictures. The two hats. There was something about them, something similar.

"What's this pom-pom made out of, you think?" he asked. "It looks kind of dark. Gray."

"It's mink. Nick told me. Real mink."

The pom-pom was the same on the hat in the airport surveillance photo.

"Does Nick have a last name?"

"Kyznetsoff. Nicolai Kyznetsoff. He's cute, isn't he? Good kisser, too."

"Is he a driver?"

"Used to be."

"What happened?"

"He got fired. I forget exactly why. Hey, Maksim?"

The driver on the couch looked up from his paper.

"Do you remember why Ramirez fired Nick?"

He shrugged.

"When was the last time you spoke with Mr. Kyznetsoff?" Miller asked.

"Well, we stopped dating a while ago."

"I see."

"Just one of those things. He's real sweet and all but, well—he's *fifty*-something years old!"

Miller tried for what he hoped was an appropriate expression.

"Have you talked to him since you two broke up?"

"No. Wait. Yes. Once. About a month ago. He called to tell me he was starting his own car company."

"Really? And why did he call you?"

"He wanted to know if PP&W was still our client because he didn't want to poach any of our existing customers. I told him they sure as heck were our clients and he better not try to steal them from us. He laughed at that. He's a sweetie. But like I said—"

"He's fifty?"

"Exactly."

"Do you have his employment file? Maybe a copy of his hack license?"

"Sure. It might be in storage or whatever because he hasn't worked here in nearly a year."

Miller handed her his business card. "Please find that file, ASAP. Fax it to me."

"Okay. I'll check with Ms. Ramirez. She's the head of Personnel and Customer Relations and that kind of junk."

"Julie?"

"Yes, sir?"

"I need that file."

"Yes, sir."

"I want to talk to Ramirez."

"She's in Puerto Rico. Visiting family."

"Do you know where Mr. Kyznetsoff is now?"

"No."

"Any idea?"

"Well, I never went to his apartment or anything, if that's what you mean. We used my place that one time we, you know—got busy. Hey, Maksim!" she shouted. "Do you know how to get in touch with Nicolai?"

"*Nyet.*"

"That means 'no,'" Julie explained. "Sorry."

"Okay. Fax me his file. Call me if he contacts you again."

"Did Nicolai do something bad?"

Miller didn't want to see Julie panic again. Her candy bowl was nearly empty.

"No. I don't think so. I just want to find out where he bought that Santa hat. Don't see one like that every day, not with a mink pom-pom. Thank you for your help." Miller headed for the door. He stopped when he reached the couch. "Maksim, if Nicolai calls you, let me know." He handed the man one of his business cards. "Dig?"

"Yes," the old man said, stuffing the card into the pocket of his shirt. "I understand."

Miller pushed open the door and stepped outside.

Detectives Norbert and Magruder were waiting for him on the sidewalk.

Norbert had that look on his face again: he wasn't happy.

"Hello, Agent Miller," Magruder said cheerfully. "Whaddya say we all take a little ride?"

46

Scott Wilkinson was mad.

The sun had been up for hours. His third, no, fourth day strapped to the bed frame. He was losing track of time.

Needing to calm down, he took in a deep breath, pulled in a chest full of air through his nose.

He nearly gagged.

The room stank. The body of the crazy Russian butcher, the maniac with the straight razor, the man Kyznetsoff killed yesterday, lay rotting on the floor.

"Goddamit! Where the hell are you, you goddam bastard?!"

He heard the front door open.

"Mr. Kyznetsoff?" He still couldn't see his captor— he could only hear someone behind him, someone shifting their weight, creaking the floorboards. "Look, this is stupid and I don't think you're a stupid man. You've made your point. Let's move on. I can tell my wife to wire you a million dollars. You can put it into some sort of offshore account. We can set that up for you. My father-in-law deals with . . ."

Another creak of wood.

"Mr. Kyznetsoff?"

Nothing.

Scott sighed. Gave up. Stared at the ceiling. The fan. The knotty-pine paneling.

The same thing I've been staring at for four days!

Kyznetsoff's face popped into view.

"You want to negotiate? Fine. What do you have to offer, Scott?"

The Russian was upside-down. When he grinned, Scott saw yellow clumps of scrambled egg stuck between his teeth.

"I am offering you money. A million dollars."

Kyznetsoff shrugged. "I have money."

"Please," Scott pleaded. "Tell me. What is it you want?"

"I want to punish you. I am Grandfather Frost. You have been a naughty boy."

"What else?"

"Oh, now *you* are Santa?" Kyznetsoff sneered. "Asking me what I want for Christmas? Ho, ho, ho!"

"What the hell do you want?"

"Christopher Miller."

"Who?"

"Bizanko's friend at the FBI."

"I don't know any Christopher Miller."

"Too bad. Apparently, he is an FBI agent who wants my diamonds. This could make it difficult for me to continue liquidating my assets."

"I don't know—"

"Comrade Alexei Bizanko? Have you not heard of him?"

"No, I—"

"A big shot in Russia. With friends in your stinking

American government, friends he can call on to help him locate his lost treasure. But if we listen carefully to Slava, we also hear him say that Vasily wants to take over the treasure hunt, wants to push the FBI out. The FBI, however, does not agree, so they send this Christopher Miller to hunt me down. Fine. I take care of Slava, next I must deal with Miller."

"Fine." Scott looked away. "Everybody's out to get you. The FBI. Vasily, Bizanko—hell, all of Russia."

"You know what, Scott?" Kyznetsoff pulled out his pistol and aimed it down at Wilkinson's mouth. "You begin to bore me."

"Wait! You don't have to do this!" Kyznetsoff forced the gun past Scott's lips, made him taste its tart barrel. "Wait!"

Kyznetsoff sighed.

"What do you want?" Scott begged. "Please. Just tell me. Please." The gun hovered near his face, but, at least, it was no longer jammed inside this mouth.

"You are such a pussy. Pissing into your panties. Please, please, please. Pussy."

Scott decided, for the first time, to try another tack. "What the hell do you want, you goddam asshole?"

Kyznetsoff tightened his lips. Smiled. The outburst impressed him.

"I told you," he said. "I want Christopher Miller. Where do I find him?"

"Did you Google his name?"

"Of course. I find only stupid newspaper stories. Headlines."

"That's the raw data," said Scott. "You need to sift

through it now like a miner panning for gold." Suddenly, for the first time in days, Scott felt empowered. It was, after all, the same stock speech he gave clients—extolling the virtues of data mining as tool in targeting customers. Now they were in *his* area of expertise. Every day, he helped marketers find nuggets of insight hidden under sales data using decision-tree algorithims and other tricks of the trade.

"This is what you do, Scott? With your strategic planning, you help companies find customers?"

"In the simplest terms . . . yes."

"So, in the simplest terms—you will help me find this FBI bastard?"

"You say he's crooked?"

"If he is an ally of Bizanko, he stinks like fish guts in the sun."

Finally. A crack. A way in. Maybe a way out.

"In that case, sure. Fine. I'll help you find this corrupt agent. We can use my laptop. Find a WiFi hot spot."

"Computer is gone. I used it, I dumped it."

"Okay. No problem. We still have my BlackBerry. It can be used as a handheld Web browser."

"I know this, Scott. I do not need you to tell me this."

"But I can help you sift through the data. Analyze patterns. We can find this guy you're looking for."

And maybe send an e-mail to Missy, too.

47

They drove down the mountain in search of a wireless hot spot.

Scott was blindfolded, and gagged with duct tape.

His hands were cuffed behind his back. His waist was belted with a heavy chain, which Kyznetsoff had then anchored underneath the back seat of a vehicle that rode like an SUV. Scott only knew they were driving down a mountain because he felt every curve.

After fifteen minutes, the road settled down. Fewer twists and turns. Scott could hear traffic. Other cars. Passing trucks. Motorcycles. They must be nearing civilization.

He heard Kyznetsoff flick on the radio.

"Grandma Got Run Over By a Reindeer."

For the first time in his life, Scott didn't mind hearing the horribly annoying Christmas song. When it ended, maybe the disc jockey would report the news. Maybe he'd talk about the weather or make an announcement for some local charity. Maybe he'd give Scott some hint as to where the hell he was.

The song ended. A commercial took its place. Scott paid close attention, strained to pick up a clue. This was the data he truly needed to mine. First he learned it was December nineteenth because his "good friends" at Flannigan Furniture wanted to remind everybody there were only five shopping days left if they wanted to put a new Broyhill sofa under their tree. "So hurry into either of our two convenient Scranton locations . . ."

Scranton. Northeast Pennsylvania. That made sense. There were all sorts of cabins scattered in what they called the Endless Mountains near Scranton.

The radio snapped off.

"We are here," Kyznetsoff said.

Scott flinched when the duct tape was torn off his eyes.

The first thing he saw was Kyznetsoff sitting in the front seat of a big car, a Ford Expedition. He was holding the BlackBerry 7730. "We have signal. I Google Christopher Miller." He tapped the tiny keyboard.

"Add 'FBI,'" Scott tried to say.

"What?" Kyznetsoff turned around and tore the duct tape off his mouth.

"Add FBI. Put it all in quotes. Narrow your search."

"Put in quotes? I have to retype everything?"

"No. Move the cursor back . . . insert the quote . . . scroll forward—"

"What?"

"Just hand it to me. I'll do it."

"You will?"

"Yes. It'll be faster."

"How kind of you, Scott. And, perhaps, while I am sitting here being lazy, you can send out some e-mails? Send a little love note to Missy? Forward some jokes to your friends at the office? Text-message the police?"

"No, I just thought it would be quicker if—"

"You are such a dickhead." Kyznetsoff tapped the miniature QWERTY keys. Manipulated the trackwheel.

Scott glanced out his window. They were in a parking lot. A grocery store.

"Not much," Kyznetsoff said. "Very little data."

"Let me see."

Kyznetsoff rotated the screen around so Scott could read it.

"Okay. Good."

"What? Is just the same newspaper story. Over and over. 'The Man in the Moon.'"

"No. It's good. It's gold."

"What is so good about the same stupid story?"

"You really don't see it?"

"Oh, you are so fucking smart, aren't you, Scott Wilkinson? Mister Head of Strategic Planning. Do you think I won't shoot you? That I will not slit your throat? The windows of this vehicle are tinted black for a good reason: no one can see what I do to you in here."

"Jersey City," Scott said quickly, sounding a lot less cocky. "Christopher Miller lives in Jersey City, New Jersey. See how they all call him a 'Local Hero?'"

"No."

"Fourth paragraph in the AP story. Second in the *Post*. So we can deduce that he lives in Jersey City . . . we know he worked undercover . . . posed as a driver for the Jersey City Cab Company . . . says here he went to high school at Saint Peter's Prep . . . also in Jersey City . . . then played football at Notre Dame. We should check out their alumni databases . . . do a simple classmate-finder type search."

"No need. This is plenty." Kyznetsoff flung the BlackBerry into the front passenger seat.

Something outside the SUV had caught his eye.

48

"You see her ass? In the green? Is nice ass, yes?"

"I wouldn't . . ."

Kyznetsoff turned to face Scott.

"You will wait here," he said. He fumbled under the passenger seat. "Where is the fucking duct tape? Shit. She's getting away. You do not see many good asses up here, Scott." He dug frantically under both front seats, searched for the roll of silver tape. "Mostly you see fat Polish women who eat too many pierogies so their butts are dimpled like clotted farmer's cheese. Shit. Wait here."

Kyznetsoff forgot about the tape and practically leapt out of the car.

Scott couldn't believe his luck.

He was alone. No gag. No blindfold.

The car's engine was still running.

He watched Kyznetsoff talking to the girl. She seemed to be giggling. They chatted a little longer then strolled together into the grocery store.

This was his chance.

Scott leaned forward. His hands were still cuffed behind his back, his waist still chained, but if he could bend forward far enough, he might be able to twist sideways and reach the BlackBerry lying in the front seat. He might be able to snare it, somehow, maybe with his teeth.

He could snag it, bring it into the back seat, drop it into his lap and then use his teeth to grab some sort of stylus. A pen. A straw. A screwdriver. There had to be some kind of stick he could use to poke out an e-mail. All he had to do was hit a few keys, tap out H-E-L-P. Maybe SCRANTON. CABIN. A quick, concise, text message to send a search party in the right direction.

He bent forward as far as he could. His shoulders jammed against the two front seats. He pushed hard against the seat backs but they wouldn't budge. He retreated, tried again: he leaned forward, twisted his torso, squeezed in over the armrest dividing the front seats.

Better.

Closer.

He was facing the passenger seat and could see the BlackBerry sitting in the leather chair but he couldn't reach it. He pushed his body, felt muscles spasm in his lower back. He grunted. Stretched. Tried again. Still no luck. If only he were two inches taller. He tried again.

Shit!

He groaned and made a third attempt.

It remained beyond his reach.

Damn!

This wasn't going to work. He rotated his trunk, felt a cramp somewhere near his kidneys, slammed backward into the seat cushion.

Shit, shit, shit.

Now what?

He looked around the back seat. What did he have? What could he use? He would pull an Apollo 13: use what he had on hand to engineer a solution. He took inventory, which was easy because he had nothing. No hacksaws. No screwdrivers. No twisties or pipe cleaners or paper clips.

What about the windows?

Scott couldn't remember. Did Kyznetsoff lock the power windows before he left? Or was he too distracted? Did he forget to lock the windows?

The engine was running. The windows should work.

Scott tipped himself sideways until he felt the armrest rub against his right ear. He rotated his head, positioned his face over the recessed controls. He lowered himself slowly and used his nose to push down on the indented window button. He heard a familiar whirr, felt a sharp blast of cold wind. He nosed the button again. The window opened wider. Now he could hear traffic. Cars on the highway, pulling into the parking lot. One more push. The window moved halfway down.

Scott heard the rattle of a wobbly-wheeled grocery cart.

Someone was coming. Scott kept nudging the button, trying to open the window as far as he could. The more it was open, the more his rescuer would be able to hear him.

"Help!" Scott screamed. He rocked his head, nosed the button. "Help! Hey! Over here!" One more nose push. He heard the window come to a stop. Heard the shopping cart roll closer. Felt cold air blanket his back. The window had to be wide open. "Help!"

"Hey look! Your window's open. You need to take better care."

Scott looked up. It was Kyznetsoff.

"You could catch a fucking cold."

Now what was going to happen?

"You dumb dickhead." The whole truck rocked when Kyznetsoff slammed the shopping cart against it. The window scrolled up. Kyznetsoff had some sort of remote control for it. Trapped again.

"Guess what, Scott," Kyznetsoff said as he climbed into the front seat. "The grocery store? They sell duct tape up front near the cash registers. So, I stole a couple rolls." Scott heard the familiar rip of fabric. "Maybe I should cover your fucking nose, too? Make you fucking suffocate."

Kyznetsoff wrapped the roll around and around Scott's head, pulled it tight into his hair and across his mouth, leaving the nostrils open.

"Oh. I forgot to tell you. Mrs. Green Pants and I will go on a date as soon as I return from New Jersey."

He picked up the BlackBerry off the passenger seat.

"What do you say, Scott? Shall we send Missy that e-mail? Let her know where you are?"

Scott's eyes widened. Kyznetsoff couldn't be serious.

"You are right. Why bother?" He leaned out the window. Tossed the unit out onto the asphalt. "I will personally give Missy your regards. I plan on seeing her as soon as I am done with Christopher Miller. Perhaps I will bring you pictures."

Kyznetsoff put the truck in reverse.

Scott heard the crunch of plastic.

His BlackBerry—crushed under a tire.

49

Miller rode up front in the sedan with Magruder.

Norbert was in the back, glaring into the rearview mirror, trying to burn a hole in the side of Miller's head. They made their way down Brighton Avenue, away from Lucky Seven Limousines, past the knish shops and fruit stands and caviar kiosks.

"So what did I do this time? Why are you giving me the evil eye?"

"Aw, he's not giving you the evil eye," Magruder said. "He's squinting. Robbie has hazel eyes and people with hazel eyes? The sun makes 'em squint. Right, Robbie?"

Norbert said nothing. He stared. Or squinted. Miller figured it was a little bit of both.

"Where we headed?" he asked.

"Elena Bizanko's place."

"Why? You two dig her furniture?"

Magruder took off his tweed cap and rubbed the top of his matted hair. "Your boss told us you were coming out this way to check up on the old lady for Leon Owens."

"You called Charlie Lofgren?"

"Yeah. Right after Mrs. Bizanko called us."

"And why did Mrs. Bizanko call you? Is one of her cats stuck in a tree?"

Norbert finally spoke: "Vasily."

"Vasily?" said Miller.

"Yeah."

"The mob boss?"

"It sure ain't the name of her cat."

The apartment was even uglier than Miller remembered. The butterscotch-and-chocolate checkerboard couch. The pea-green wallpaper. The red rug with paisley squiggles resembling pink bacteria. Miller finally figured it out: Elena Bizanko was color-blind except when it came to black people.

"Mrs. Bizanko," Magruder said, "you remember Christopher Miller from the FBI?"

The old woman grunted. She was hunkered down in a far corner of the couch, trying to keep as far away as she could from Miller.

"*Da*. I remember."

"Why don't you tell him what you told us?"

"Why? Why you not tell him? Why you bring this black man into my home again?"

Magruder smiled politely. "Sometimes it's better for an investigator to hear things firsthand."

"Why?"

"Standard police procedure."

"Is standard horseshit," she muttered.

"Tell him," Norbert snapped. "Now. We don't have all freaking day here."

Mrs. Bizanko hiked up her considerable chest and inhaled her disgust.

"Vasily come here," she said. "He is very important man and he come here to see me. He no send Slava—he come himself."

Miller decided to sit down since nobody was going to ask him if he wanted to. Mrs. Bizanko grimaced when he did.

"Why did Vasily want to see you?" Miller asked.

"Because my nephew, Alexei, is even more important. He is Interior Minister of all Russia!" She puffed out her cheeks as she said this. "Vasily tell me to tell Christopher Miller we no longer require his assistance."

"Excuse me?" Miller wasn't sure he'd heard right.

"Vasily say to me—'call off that FBI guy!' We no longer need you no more. Vasily will find Alexei's dolls. That is the message I am to give."

"I don't understand," Miller said.

"Really?" Norbert said. "It's simple. Someone, who seems to be Alexei Bizanko, her nephew, wants you, Christopher Miller, to back off."

"Maybe there's some other Chris Miller at the Bureau, down in Washington."

"Nope," Norbert said. "We checked."

"I call your number but you no answer." This from their hostess.

"You called my number? In Newark?"

"Newark? No. Why would I call Newark?" She gestured toward the kitchen. "I call special, emergency number. The one I call the first time."

"I don't have any 'special, emergency number.'"

"Do not play at being stupid! When Alexei ship his *matryoshka* dolls, he give me instructions. Very many details. If ever there comes a problem, if ever I lose even a single doll, I am to call FBI and ask for Christopher Miller. You are Christopher Miller?"

"Yeah."

"So why do you act like you not know this is the way it is to be done? You came the first time I called."

Magruder sat down opposite Miller. "You got some sort of explanation here, Chris?"

Miller rubbed around his mouth, focused.

"When did you receive the first doll?" he asked.

She looked at the two cops.

"Tell him," said Magruder.

"When?" Miller asked again. This time, he sounded like he might get upset if she didn't answer.

"Five, maybe six years ago. First, I thought Alexei make me a gift. Then, I read all the instructions."

Miller had a far-off look in his eyes. Something was starting to make sense.

"Diamonds," he said aloud.

"What is this about diamonds?"

"Sit down, Mrs. Bizanko," said Magruder.

Miller stood up. "Where's this special phone number?"

"Side of the fridge," answered Magruder.

"It's the same number we told you about before," said Norbert. "The direct line to Owens's office. I understand you used to work for him. Maybe it's one of those relationships that's hard to quit. You know, breaking up is hard to do and all that."

"What's that supposed to mean?"

"I dunno. Maybe you're still working for him—only you don't want us knowing about it. So you tell us Owens is the one who put you in that crappy cubicle."

"You mean I lied?"

"Something like that."

Miller held Norbert's stare.

"So?" said Magruder. "You gonna tell us what's going on here?"

"Yeah. Just as soon as I find out." He marched into the kitchen and found the list of emergency numbers, yanked it out from underneath a magnet, headed back into the living room.

"Call it," he said, passing the paper to Mrs. Bizanko. "Ask for Christopher Miller."

"What? Why? You are Christopher Miller! I already give you Alexei's message."

"Call it!"

She looked defiant the way only a bad-tempered old lady can.

Magruder picked up the phone, handed it to her.

"Place the call."

"Is long distance!"

"The City of New York will reimburse you."

She took the phone, glanced at the number, pressed the buttons.

The call rang through.

Miller heard the tinny sound of a man's voice leaking out from the earpiece.

"Leon Owens's office. How may I be of assistance?"

"I need to speak to Christopher Miller," Elena Bizanko said grudgingly.

"One moment."

Miller held out his hand.

"Give me the phone."

Bizanko looked to Magruder. He nodded. She slowly passed the phone. Miller knew she'd be swabbing it with Lysol the minute he stepped out the door.

Miller raised it his ear. Waited.

"Hello," a familiar voice said. "Do you have further compromised merchandise to report? Hello? Who is this? Please identify yourself."

"Hello, Leon," Miller said to his old boss.

"Who is this?"

"Christopher Miller."

"How did you get this number?"

"I'll tell you when I see you. I'm coming down on the next shuttle." Miller looked at Magruder, who nodded. "And, I'm bringing a few friends."

"What friends?"

"NYPD."

"Special Agent Miller, I suggest you stay in Newark. The Office of Professional Responsibility is still reviewing your probation. If you insist on forcing them to consider even sterner measures . . ."

"You know what, Leon? I'm not worried about that. But maybe you should be."

50

Kyznetsoff dragged Slava's body across the cabin floor.

Scott heard the thumping sound again as the dead man was hauled out the door and pulled across the front porch. Now he heard a grunt followed by a thud. Kyznetsoff must've rolled the body off the porch, shoved it down to the frozen ground.

He came back into the cabin, moved to the bed. Scott heard him slide the pot underneath the bed frame.

"Try not to shit too much while I'm gone," Kyznetsoff said. "I do not want my *dacha* to stink when I return to kill you."

The Russian made certain all four pairs of handcuffs were securely fastened to the bed frame: two on Scott's wrists, two on his ankles.

"You were stupid to try to escape. Did you really think you could run away from me? That I would not hunt you down? It is like that song I hear on the radio. Mariah Carey. All I want for Christmas is you, Scott."

Scott couldn't say anything in response: his mouth was stuffed with a tennis ball sealed in place by a roll's worth of electrical tape. He could only move his head about a half-inch in any direction because Kyznetsoff had strapped him into a black-leather mask. The mask had a metal ring attached to its back. The ring was secured to the bedsprings with a lock.

"You like your mask? I buy for you many weeks ago in sex shop. Greenwich Village."

Kyznetsoff knelt beside the bed and twisted two sets of red and black wires to the twin posts of a motorcycle battery. Next he took one pair of wires and attached them to a cell phone.

"This is my remote trigger. I can make a phone call and blow you up whenever I feel like it. I have also jury-rigged another trigger, Scott. One you will activate should you try anything stupid. Can you see where I placed this trigger?"

Scott tried to raise his head, couldn't.

"Of course not! I have hidden it very cleverly. But, let me assure you. Should you remove your weight from this metal frame, the trigger will sense this motion and blow you into tiny pieces. I may never be able to scrub the walls clean."

Kyznetsoff connected the other pair of wires to alligator clips attached to what looked like a plastic-wrapped brick, which he shoved under the bed.

"So, Scott—you are shit out of luck. But do not worry—I will be back before you have a chance to dehydrate or starve to death. Where is the fun in that, eh?"

He shook his cell phone in Scott's face.

"Or, who knows? Maybe I will just call you on my way to New Jersey."

51

Miller felt strangely liberated.

He could run the Wilkinson investigation the way he knew it should be run because he no longer had to fear Leon Owens.

"Owens is going down," Miller said to Detective Magruder as they drove out to LaGuardia to catch the next shuttle down to D.C.

"Says who besides you?" Magruder asked.

"My buddy at Langley. Seems some other guys in Virginia have been eyeballing Leon Owens for a while now."

"Is that so? Well, Norbert and me got our eyes on you."

Detective Norbert wasn't traveling to Washington with Miller and Magruder. He had gone back to the 61st Precinct to glare at somebody else.

"So," Magruder asked, "what *were* you doing in Brooklyn this morning?"

"Working a missing persons case."

"Something involving Lucky Seven Limos?"

"Yeah. I need to find one of their drivers."

"This guy have a name?"

"Kyznetsoff. Nicolai Kyznetsoff. You know him?"

"Doesn't ring a bell. I'll put someone on it. See if they come up with anything. Of course, my full cooperation is contingent upon you showing me something besides the Lincoln Memorial once we get down to D.C."

"Okay. Okay. No problem."

"Meanwhile, want to fill me in?"

"Five years back," said Miller, "Leon Owens was running a major sting operation—the Big Bust."

"Who'd he collar? Somebody huge?"

"Nobody. His bust *went* bust. Big time. He had this task force of fifty agents and they dug up a ton of dirt on a bunch of bad actors running hot jewelry through the back rooms of this high-end jewelry store. Place called Chronos."

"Sure. 'The Home of Exceptionally Fine Jewelry.' That's what their ads say, am I right?"

"Yeah."

"The home of exceptionally high prices is more like it," said Magruder. "Rolexes. Tag Heuers. I seen this one watch—ten grand. Like I want to strap a down payment for a house around my freaking wrist."

"Chronos also carries a nice selection of diamonds," Miller said. "You check those out?"

"Yeah. My wife had her eye on this one ring but wasn't crazy about the stones. The slick weasel behind the counter says they can custom build it for her, she can pick out her own rocks."

"Yes," said Miller. "They always seem to have a wide and varied selection of precious stones. Diamonds, rubies, emeralds. Some of those stones, however, might be 'gently used.' The Bureau suspected Chronos was playing laundry maid for lowlifes—mobsters, tax cheats, maybe even terrorists, anyone with hot rocks to unload."

"And your man Owens headed up the investigation?" Magruder was starting to figure out what Miller had worked out back in Elena Bizanko's apartment.

"We all assumed he'd shut Chronos down cold. But, it never happened. First, what should have been a slam dunk dragged on forever. Then, one day, out of the blue, Leon Owens called the whole thing off—closed up shop without ever making a single arrest or even filing one indictment."

"So, you got to figure he cut some kind of deal with Chronos," said Magruder. "Offered to sell them his own federal criminal protection program."

"Exactly. I also suspect they're returning the favor by feeding him information."

Magruder nodded. "So maybe the crooks at Chronos tell your pal Leon that they just got some interesting new merchandise in the back room—Russian diamonds with numbers lasered into them that match the numbers on a watchlist Owens is floating around after he hears from his buddy Bizanko?"

"Bingo," said Miller.

"So, tell me this—why is the guy using your name in his set up? Why are *you* listed as the emergency contact?"

"I guess so anybody nosing around this thing will think I had something to do with it."

"Like me and Norbert?'

"Yeah."

"Why? What'd you ever do to him?"

"Leon Owens was the AIC on that thing in West Virginia. Didn't get the credit he thought he deserved. Blames me for stealing his thunder."

"That was way back in 1989, am I right?"

"What can I tell you—the man knows how to hold a grudge."

They pulled into the daily parking lot near the Delta Shuttle at LaGuardia.

"You think Owens is even gonna be there when we show up?" Magruder asked. "He might run. The bad guys usually do that, you know. They hightail it out of town."

"My buddy P. J.'s keeping an eye on him."

"Who's this P. J.?"

"Powers John Ward."

"Powers?"

"He's from Tennessee. They still name kids stuff like that down there. He used to be with the Bureau."

"Okay. Yeah. We're talking about West Virginia again, right? He was the sharpshooter. I read about him when I read about you."

"We were both a lot younger back then."

"P. J. took out the bad guys from, what? Like a mile away or whatever?"

Miller nodded.

"He still that good?"

"Maybe better. P. J. can split a golf ball in half from a hundred yards out."

"And he's the one keeping an eye on Owens?"

"He is, as they say, 'currently in command of the target.'"

"What's he gonna do? Split Owens's skull in half?"
Miller smiled. "Only if he has to."

52

The next shuttle was scheduled for 12:30 P.M. and would get into Reagan National at 1:15.

Magruder helped himself to the free coffee in the waiting area and rifled through the racks of free magazines, trying to find something he wouldn't mind reading. He settled for *Modern Motor Boating* because it had a lot of pictures.

Miller used his time to make calls to his office in Newark.

First, he told his boss, Charlie Lofgren, what he was up to. With Lofgren's blessing, Miller expanded his investigation into the Wilkinson disappearance and added members to his support team. He now had about a dozen special agents at his disposal and they were all searching for any information related to one Nicolai Kyznetsoff.

"I also need someone to run an Internet search," Miller told the coordinating agent, the one who'd run the show while he was out of town. "We're looking for a party girl with a smiley-face bikini. Brunette. Skinny. With breasts that don't really fit behind that yellow grin. Possibly a pro lap dancer."

"Okay."

"Contact Mrs. Wilkinson. She can e-mail you photos."

"Yes, sir."

"Then have someone check the porn sites."

"Right."

"See if you can make a match, maybe find this girl in an ad for a strip club or an escort service—some operation within a half-day driving distance of LaGuardia."

"No problem," the agent said.

Miller had a feeling it would be pretty easy to find volunteers for this particular assignment—provided, of course, the coordinating agent didn't just tackle it himself.

53

The J. Edgar Hoover FBI Building at the corner of Tenth Street and Pennsylvania Avenue looked like a hulking concrete honeycomb designed in some sort of neo-Fascist style of architecture.

Hoover, himself, called it the ugliest building he had ever seen.

There were concrete barriers lining the sidewalks to deter truck bombers, serious metal detectors in the lobby, and no jolly holiday decorations anywhere—probably because nobody made concrete Christmas trees.

Miller showed his credentials to the security personnel, then he and Magruder went upstairs to see if Executive Assistant Director Leon Owens was in his office.

"Yes," his secretary said, "but he's busy."

"So are we," Miller shot back.

"Well, I'm sorry, gentlemen," the woman said. "You may have wasted your time coming down today."

"No they didn't," said P. J. Ward as he strode into the anteroom carrying a sealed envelope. "Sorry, I'm late, Chris. Confirmation from Moscow took a little longer than expected." He flashed his credentials at the woman guarding the gate. "Owens still in there, hon?"

"I'm sorry, but—"

"Ma'am?" said P. J., his accent as thick as overcooked grits. "I tell you what—I'm gonna take that as a 'yes.'" He turned to Miller. "Saint Chris—I've got your back."

"You gentlemen cannot simply barge in on—"

However, they did.

Miller gave the thick mahogany door a swift shove. It flew open. Magruder and P. J. followed him into the office.

Owens sat behind a big desk. He was on the phone and waved at his visitors to come in, come in, find a seat, make themselves comfortable. He even gestured at a silver carafe of coffee sitting on a tray with delicate china cups and saucers. Owens's gestures were grandly magnanimous, as befitted a man with nothing to hide.

"I'll only be a minute," he mouthed, cupping his hand over the phone.

The three visitors didn't sit or pour coffee. They waited for Owens to hang up.

"Yes, sir, Mr. Vice President," Owens said. "Happy I could be of assistance. If you need anything further . . . right . . . you, too."

He nested the handset in its blinking base. When he leaned back into his chair, Miller noticed how nicely padded and comfortable it looked, especially compared to the lumpy job he had back in his cubicle.

Owens tugged on his shirt cuffs, smoothed the sleeves of his suit coat, used his palm to iron out any wrinkles.

"Christopher," he said with a slight head nod.

P. J. shoved his credentials into Owens's face.

"Powers John Ward, sir. I work out of Langley."

"I know who you are, Agent Ward," Owens said smugly. "The other 'hero' from the hills of West Virginia. I believe you reported to me at the time."

"Yes, sir."

"So—what brings you across the Potomac this afternoon?"

"You, sir."

"Me?"

"That's right."

"Really? Whom have you been talking to? Not Special Agent Miller, I hope. That would be a mistake."

Miller didn't take the bait.

Owens leaned back in his chair. Locked his focus on Magruder.

"And you?"

"Detective Thomas Magruder. NYPD Brooklyn."

"A little out of your jurisdiction aren't you?"

Magruder shrugged. "Go figure."

Owens shook his head. "Another big mistake."

"No, sir," said P. J. "I reckon you're the one who's been makin' all the mistakes around here. The three of us are just trying to keep track of 'em. Starting with your involvement over in Moscow."

"I trust you're referring to my relationship with Alexei Bizanko? You're with the CIA these days?"

"Yes, sir."

"Then you must know I have been cultivating a top source deep within the Russian ruling elite." He tapped his telephone to remind everybody the level of important person he chatted with on a regular basis. "It is a matter of vital national importance. Part of the global war on terror."

Owens now linked his hands together to make a church steeple under his nose. He wrinkled that same nose to demonstrate his growing frustration with having to explain lofty matters of state to the three morons currently gathered in his office.

"We here in this office," he said, "are protecting the interests of Alexei Bizanko, who, in turn, provides our nation with a great deal of extremely useful information. In fact, I was just now passing on his latest intel to the White House. I must say, the vice president seemed quite grateful to receive the information."

"You made this contact with Minister Bizanko on your own initiative, sir?" P. J. asked.

"That's confidential. Classified information. I'm not at liberty to discuss the history of our arrangement."

"All right. I'll ask you something else: why'd you shut down the Chronos sting?"

"I began to see how that asset could be better leveraged."

Miller stepped forward. "Why'd you use my name?"

"Simple code. Easy for an elderly woman to memorize. 'C.M.' Christopher Miller. Compromised Merchandise."

"I tell you what, Mr. Owens," said P. J. "You have the right to tell your story any which way you like. I, of course, might have enjoyed it even more if Alexei Bizanko hadn't just decided to let our people over in

Moscow know how much you skim off the top of every diamond you help him smuggle out."

He opened up the envelope he'd been carrying. Placed a report on Owens's desk. Handed copies to Miller and Magruder.

Magruder whistled when he read it.

Owens didn't even look down at the stapled pages. Instead, he stifled a yawn. Looked bored. Miller had to hand it to him. The guy had balls.

"You know what, Leon?" Miller said.

"What, Christopher?"

"I am sincerely sorry my name got in all the papers instead of yours. But when this thing goes public, trust me—you'll receive more coverage than I ever did. You might even make the cover of *Newsweek*."

Owens, apparently, had had enough. "We're done here," he said.

Miller nodded. "You're right. We are." He tapped his copy of the report from Moscow. "You know the real reason we flew down here today?"

Owens shrugged. Gestured toward Magruder. "To show your new friend from Brooklyn the Air and Space Museum?"

"No, sir." He stepped closer to the desk. "We just wanted you to realize that, when this thing is over, we know where to find you."

54

Melissa Wilkinson went into Scott's bathroom to retrieve his comb and toothbrush for the two FBI agents in the living room.

Tyler, sound asleep in his crib, was unaware that his mother needed to locate a good sample of his father's DNA for the patiently waiting pair.

The FBI had found a limousine abandoned in an oil tank field in northern New Jersey. They had also discovered some significant hair strands on its crinkled leather couch. Apparently, whoever had been riding in the limousine had stretched out comfortably. The same person had also enjoyed a glass of expensive champagne. Dom Pérignon.

She used a washcloth to pick up Scott's bathroom cup. The maid hadn't cleaned in here since Scott disappeared, so she hoped the cup might have his fingerprints on it, fingerprints the FBI could use to match the ones they'd found all over the champagne bottle.

Melissa had first learned about the limo when Special Agent Miller called to let her know two of his colleagues would be stopping by the house.

"Have you found Scott's body?" Melissa had asked, fearing the worst.

Miller told her how the company that leased the oil tank facility had discovered the abandoned vehicle parked behind one of its equipment sheds. The local police had gone out to investigate, found nothing in the trunk or glove compartment to identify the owner, took down the vehicle identification number, and posted the information on the FBI's national crime database. The police suspected it had been stolen, used for a joyride, and then dumped.

They had been wrong.

"According to records," Miller told Melissa, "the stretch was leased by the same man we've tentatively ID'd as the driver who picked up your husband at LaGuardia. If Scott's DNA matches what we found in the back seat, we'll know for certain that this was the vehicle he was riding in before he disappeared."

Then Special Agent Miller had let the other shoe drop.

"There's one more item of interest regarding the limousine," he had said.

"What?"

"It was found parked across the street from this club. A strip joint, Mrs. Wilkinson. I suspect it's the same nightclub captured in those e-mail photographs. I'm going out there tomorrow morning. I'll keep you posted on what we learn. We're making headway, Mrs. Wilkinson. We're going to bring your husband home."

Melissa finished gathering Scott's things from the bathroom. She caught her reflection in the mirror. For the first time in days, she thought about makeup. She wanted to look good for Scott when he came home.

Because, thanks to Agent Miller, she was starting to believe it really might happen.

55

At 11:45 A.M. on December twentieth, with all the lights turned on, Johnny C's Carousel Club looked like what it was: a Sheetrock and drop-ceiling box.

Christopher Miller sat on a bar stool staring at the smudged bronze pole at center stage. He thought about his own daughter, thought about what he'd like to do to the men who tucked dollar bills into the bikini bottoms of other people's little girls.

He didn't like being here any better than the girls he'd ordered the management to get here by noon. This was about as early as any of them had been awake in years. Three sat in a booth, smoking cigarettes and sipping coffee out of Dunkin' Donuts cups. All wore sweat clothes as baggy as their eyes. Their hair stuck out at strange angles—the result of too much hair spray styled by lumpy pillows.

Miller was thinking a lot about hair this morning.

He had pushed the lab and they'd already run their initial DNA tests: it was definitely a strand of Scott Wilkinson's hair taken from the back seat of the limo. Now Miller hoped the dancers would tell him something about the man with whom Scott had been here.

The front door swung open. Blinding winter light made the cloud of cigarette smoke turn blue. The girls at the little table squinted. Sunlight seemed to affect them the way it does vampires. Or, at least, it wasn't their natural environment.

"Jesus! What's with all the fucking fluorescents?" the new girl said as she teetered through the door. "You fucking blind or something, Louie?"

This was the one Miller had been waiting for. She looked twenty-three but could be sixteen underneath last night's caked-on makeup. She wore a powder-blue ski jacket, tight jeans, and stiletto high heels. Miller figured it was the only kind of shoes she kept in her closet.

"That her?" Miller asked.

"Yeah. That's Ashley," the man named Louie said to Miller. Louie was the club's bouncer.

Miller stood up from his bar stool.

"Sorry about the bright lights," he said. "That was my idea. Makes it easier for me to take notes."

"Girls?" Louie called out. "Agent Miller here's from the FBI. You might want to watch your fucking mouths."

Ashley took off her sunglasses. "Is there coffee?"

"Yeah." Miller pointed to a Dunkin' Donuts shopping bag sitting on small circular table. "I brought donuts, too."

The girl rooted around in the bag and came out with a tumbler-sized cup and a cruller.

"So who's this dude you're lookin' for? One of those Arab terrorists?"

Miller gave her a photo.

"Jesus. This picture really sucks. You can't see shit. Just my ass, which is no way as fat as it looks right there."

Miller showed her another one. It showed off her smiley-face bikini.

"Okay. That's better. The guy looks like he's passed out underneath us, doesn't he?"

"He was here Friday night," Louie said as he wiped away some of the sticky circles decorating the bar. "Remember? I got you and Amber that special last-minute gig in the VIP lounge?"

"Oh, yeah." She tapped her fingernail on the photo. "That's Amber there. She looks good in a garter belt."

"Amber's in Florida," Louie said to Miller. "Took her kid to her grandmother's place for the holidays."

"I remember this guy, now," said Ashley.

"You do?" said Miller.

"Yep. A real stiff. Well, everything except his, you know, his little fishing buddy. I thought he might be dead. Like it was some kind of *Weekend at Bernie's* type deal. Either that or he was definitely overmedicated with something besides Viagra. He just sat there while me and Amber did the whole girl-on-girl thing for him. Most guys explode the second we start that one."

"Was this man alone?"

"No. He had a friend."

"Tell me about the friend."

Ashley shrugged. "I dunno. He wasn't from New Jersey, that's for sure. Had this accent, only I can't tell one accent from another. Could've been foreign. He had on these black military fatigues—with pockets all up and down the pants."

"That's the one I was telling you about," the bouncer named Louie said. "The Russki limo driver."

"He drove a limo? Then where'd he get all that money? He had like this major wad of cash. Kept peeling off fifties and hundreds and stuffing them in my panties."

Miller pulled out another photograph. This one had come in via fax with the personnel file from Lucky Seven Limousines. Nicolai Kyznetsoff.

"Yeah. That's him."

"When did they leave?"

"After we posed for the pictures," Ashley said.

"What time?"

"I dunno. Late."

"It was like two or three in the morning," said Louie. "Before the bachelor party let out."

"I'll want the names of everybody at that bachelor party. Those gentlemen may have seen or heard something." Miller refocused on Ashley. "Did the guy with the accent say where they were going?"

"Nope. He gave us an extra hundred bucks, snapped some more shots, and said he had to go. So I told to come back sometime and catch our 'legs and eggs' show."

"What's that?"

"Sundays and holidays we do a breakfast show. We're doing one Christmas morning."

Miller's cell phone chirruped.

"This is Miller."

"Yeah. This is Magruder. You still working your case?"

"Yeah. I took myself off probation."

"Good, good. Whaddya say we work together on this thing a little longer?"

"I'll take all the help I can get."

"Yeah. Me, too. You think your buddy in D.C. could track down some biographical material for us?"

"What's up?"

"We've just been talking to some people. Checking out this Kyznetsoff like you asked."

Miller moved to a far corner of the bar, away from the girls.

"What'd you find out?" he asked.

"That you're not the only one looking for him. Some of the locals are after him too. My snitches say a major player out here named Vasily is asking everybody and their cousin if they know anything about Kyznetsoff. Word is, Vasily is miffed. Big time."

"So why is Vasily looking for Kyznetsoff?"

"I'm assuming it has to do with these damn diamonds. Vasily sent out his top dog to hunt the man down."

"That guy Slava you told me about?"

"Yeah. Better known as the 'Butcher of Brighton Beach.'"

"Where did he go looking for Kyznetsoff?"

"Nobody can say. Slava never came home either."

56

Maksim Demichev's Town Car still looked filthy.

He was parked in the holding area at JFK airport, waiting for his next fare. He stood next to the car, smoking another cigarette, having opened his third pack for the day. He had been smoking four or five packs a day ever since he sat down with Slava and the Butcher had shown him photographs of what he had done to Kostya.

Maksim still had nightmares about them.

And now, Slava was missing. Maksim heard it everywhere. Even the little old women, the babushkas, were talking about it. Slava was missing and Vasily was mad. Furious.

No one else had come to see Maksim, not yet, but they would, probably soon. The other two men who had been with Slava that day would tell Vasily about the meeting on the boardwalk, that Maksim was the one who had told Slava where he might find Kyznetsoff.

But Maksim knew Vasily wasn't the only one searching for Kyznetsoff.

Maksim had been in the Lucky Seven offices when the FBI agent had shown up to ask questions. In fact, he still carried the black man's business card. Christopher

Miller. Newark Field Office. Maksim kept the card hidden in his wallet—just in case.

Just in case Vasily blames me for Slava's death.

His cell phone rang.

Maksim hoped it was Julie the dispatcher calling with a special job, maybe a run out to Long Island, maybe New Jersey. Anything to take his mind off all this.

Maksim reached into the car and found his phone lying on the beaded seat cushion.

"*Da?* Hello?"

"Hello, Maksim Petrovich Demichev," a voice said cheerfully. "How are you, my dear, old friend?"

Maksim's hand shook so fiercely, he couldn't pull a fresh cigarette out of his pack.

"Hello, Nicolai."

"So. You told Slava where to find me?"

"No," Maksim lied.

"No?"

"No. I swear. I did no such thing."

"Do not lie. You are the only one who knows of my *dacha*."

"No, Nicolai. I swear."

"You swear? On what is it that you swear?"

"All that I hold sacred."

"And what is that, comrade?"

"I . . . I . . ."

"Your children? Perhaps your grandchildren? *Horoshow.* Fine. I know where they live," Kyznetsoff said matter of factly. "I know where they all live."

"I tell you, Nicolai. When Slava came to me—"

"So—you did talk to Slava?"

"Yes. I couldn't help it. He killed Kostya! Showed me photos . . . like a slaughtered hog."

"Tell me, Maksim—do you remember how to hunt the wild turkey?"

"Wild . . . turkey?"

"Do you not remember what I teach you when, together, we hike into the woods?"

"I . . . I did not go hunting with you, Nicolai. I stayed in the cabin. I cooked your breakfast."

"Would you like to learn the secret to hunting turkey, my friend?"

Maksim exhaled. Perhaps Kyznetsoff was going to forgive him. He was talking as if the two of them might once again go into the countryside together. Perhaps he understood how badly Slava had frightened him, why he had talked about Kyznetsoff's cabin.

"Please, my friend," Maksim said eagerly. "Tell me about the turkeys."

"*Horoshow*. Very good. Lesson one. You must hike into the forest very, very early, before first light. This is when the turkeys are most likely to be strutting about."

"*Da*."

"Two: you must wear much camouflage so that you blend in with all the trees, so you disappear."

"*Da*."

"Three, you sit. You sit very, very still. The turkey has incredible eyesight—better than you or I or any human, and this turkey can see any small movement you make. So, you must sit perfectly still, hidden in the shadows of the leaves, never moving, understand?"

"Yes. I understand."

"You sit. And you wait. Then, you sit and you wait some more. You make turkey noises. You blow into the little turkey caller. You lure the stupid bird into your sights. You wait. The stupid fucking turkey? Without even knowing it, he will wander into your field of fire. And when he does? Do you know what you do?"

Maksim could taste the tar and nicotine dripping off his teeth.

"You kill him?"

"Bravo, Maksim. Very good. Now you know how you will die."

57

Kyznetsoff hung up the pay phone.

He looked around. He was alone here in a garage that belonged to a taxi company. He needed to remain alert. Someone might come in.

He had to think.

For the first time since he had killed those kids and taken the diamonds, his ability to turn them into hard currency had been compromised. Too many people knew what he was doing. It would be hard to find vendors, legitimate or otherwise, willing to turn his stones into cash.

It was Christopher Miller's fault.

First Wilkinson, now Miller.

These greedy Americans bent on destroying him, making his life more difficult. It was *too* much. His desire to teach Scott Wilkinson a lesson, to make him truly understand who it was he had treated so disrespectfully, was always going to be a costly operation. He had known this and embraced the challenge. Finding the money had been simple, really, for a man of his skills and cunning. But now there were new obstacles and he needed to address them.

He analyzed the situation and made a decision to change tactics, the way a field commander always must. The pleasurable process of revenging himself on Scott Wilkinson must become, at least temporarily, a secondary objective. His primary goal now must be a quick and efficient means to replenish his stash of money.

It came to him. Quickly. Brilliantly. The way it always did.

He searched in his shirt pocket for one of his prepaid calling cards, then punched in a phone number memorized months ago.

It took four rings for her to answer.

"Hello?"

"Mrs. Wilkinson?" Kyznetsoff's voice was a husky whisper.

"Yes?"

"May I call you Missy?"

"Who are you?"

"Please pay close attention. If you wish to see your husband alive again, pick up a pen and paper and write down my instructions exactly as I dictate them to you."

"You have Scott? Is he okay?"

"He will be much better when you quit asking questions and do as you are told."

"Can I talk to him? Is he there with you?"

"Did I not tell you to be quiet?"

"I—"

"Shut up and listen, or you will regret it. Do you hear me?"

Melissa kept quiet.

"You have the pen?"

"Yes."

"You are a very good girl. Very pretty, too."

She did not respond. She was learning fast.

"How much is your house worth?"

"What?"

"Your house. You heard me. How much was it worth when you had it appraised last May?" Kyznetsoff already knew the answer. The Northridge Realty Office told him when he inquired about a house "just like the one at 44 Canterbury Lane" last June.

"Scott said . . . two."

"Two what?"

"Million dollars."

"*Horoshow*. You will pay me *three* million dollars in unmarked American money. You will take this money in a duffel bag to a location of my choosing. You will leave it where I tell you to leave it and then you will drive away. When I pick up the money, when I am certain it is unmarked and that no FBI motherfuckers are watching me or tracking me or in any way pissing me off, I will send Scott home. Do you understand, Missy?"

"Yes."

"Good. You see? This is easy. If you do as I say, Scott will be home for Christmas."

"Thank you. That's all I want."

"*Horoshow*. I am Grandfather Frost and I will bring you what you want and you will have the merriest Christmas ever."

"I understand."

"Just remember—you are to talk to no one. I will call again with further instructions. No police, no FBI. If you talk to them, Scott dies. I expect the money by tomorrow."

"Tomorrow?"

"Is this a problem?"

"No, no . . . it's just that . . ."

"What?"

"Three million dollars is a lot of money."

"So?"

"You're only giving me one day."

"This is not my problem. It is yours."

Kyznetsoff slammed down the phone.

What choice would she have? The house was her biggest asset. He would be three million dollars richer and Missy Wilkinson would be looking inside packing cartons for her baby food jars. Maybe she and the baby would live in a cardboard wardrobe box set up on the sidewalk. He couldn't guarantee that she and her child would be homeless in the new year. However, he was certain she would be husbandless and destitute and about as miserable as he could dare dream.

Kyznetsoff almost wished he believed in Christmas because this was turning out to be the best one ever.

"Hey, Boris?" The balding Arab owner of the cab company came into the garage. "I thought you wanted to make some money."

"Yes, sir," Kyznetsoff said, feigning embarrassment. "I needed to call my wife. She worries about me working the nights."

His companion nodded to let Kyznetsoff know he understood.

"I sincerely appreciate you coming on board, Boris," the man said. "We are always busy this close to the holidays and need all the help we can get. Have you met some of the other drivers?"

"No. Not yet."

The owner draped his arm around Kyznetsoff's shoulder as if they had been friends for ages. "Come. I will introduce you around. The men can give you some pointers. Tell you which neighborhoods you might wish to avoid."

"Thank you, sir. This I would be appreciating much." Kyznetsoff was troweling on his accent, trying to sound as foreign and stupid as all the other drivers must who worked the night shift in Jersey City.

"Rizwan?" The owner waved at a man coming into the garage carrying a small plastic bowl. "Come meet Boris. He is new."

The newcomer wiped his hands on his pants leg.

"Rizwan Raja, this is Boris Smirnoff. Just like the vodka, right, Boris?"

"Yes, boss."

"Rizwan's people come from Pakistan." The Arab pointed at the other man's Tupperware. "That is why his dinner always smells so good."

The Pakistani held out his hand. Kyznetsoff took it.

"I am pleased to make your acquaintance."

"Likewise."

"Boris's wife is a little nervous," the owner said with a wink to Rizwan. "She thinks perhaps we still have a cab killer on the loose. Am I right, Boris?"

Kyznetsoff pretended to blush, like a husband with a

silly, overly protective woman constantly on his case. "Yes. But I tell her—the criminal was caught. That FBI man who works here last year under the covers was very courageous, yes?"

"Yes. Indeed. He caught the young devil all by himself. He was very brave."

"He is a good fellow," Rizwan added. "I have met him many times."

"No!" Kyznetsoff acted impressed. "You actually know him? You mean when he was working here you saw him often?

"He really wasn't here very long, when he was catching the killer. Just the one night. I know him outside work. Our daughters attend the same school."

"Really?" Kyznetsoff sounded extremely interested.

This time, he wasn't pretending.

58

The Critical Incident Response Group task force working the Wilkinson kidnapping case held its first official meeting at seven A.M. on December twenty-first in the conference room of the FBI Field Office in Newark, New Jersey.

Melissa had disobeyed her anonymous caller. She had told the FBI everything.

"I asked Mrs. Wilkinson to join us this morning," Miller said to the team assembled around the conference table. "She's outside. Waiting."

Coffee cups, laptops and file folders were scattered around the table. This team, hand-picked by Miller, had actually started working hours earlier, even before the sun was up.

When Saint Christopher asked for help, he got it.

"Last night," Miller said, "Mrs. Wilkinson and I reconstructed the phone conversation as best we could. You should have the transcript there in your folders. This is your chance to ask for any further clarification. We need to move quickly, that's the most important thing to know."

Time was never your friend in a kidnapping.

Time always seemed to work for the other side.

"Okay. I'm going to step out and ask Mrs. Wilkinson to join us. Just remember—keep the questions specific, relevant, and pertinent. What she's going through isn't easy."

Melissa Wilkinson took questions for half an hour. Most had to do with the language her caller used, what she called "the foreign-sounding" words.

"I'm sorry. But he didn't say much. Not really. Just enough to make me take him seriously if I want Scott home safely. You think he means it and I'll get him back if I do what he says?"

Miller didn't reply, but he was careful to nod sympathetically.

"There was that strange stuff about Frost," Missy added. "Grandfather Frost."

Magruder raised a finger to indicate he'd handle that one if Miller wanted him to.

"Detective Magruder?"

"That's the Russian Santa Claus. It fits."

"What does he mean?" Melissa asked Miller.

"The man the strippers recognized? His name is Nicolai Kyznetsoff. He's a Russian who used to drive for Lucky Seven Limousines."

Melissa gasped. "Then he's come to our house! He's been to our home. Scott uses Lucky Seven all the time!"

"We're already on it. Checking their records." Miller scanned the table. "Anything else? Anybody?"

"Could you tell where he was calling you from?" asked a member of the team. "Did you hear anything besides his voice?"

"No," Melissa said.

"Any traffic noises in the background? Fire engines? Sirens? Or maybe seagulls—like near the shore."

"No. I didn't hear anything except his voice. He was practically whispering, like he didn't want anybody to hear what he was saying."

"Anything else?"

Melissa shook her head. "No. I don't think so. I'm sorry."

"You've been very helpful," said Miller.

She pretended to believe him. Next time, she vowed, she wouldn't be caught off guard. She'd pay closer attention. She'd notice more. She'd listen for those background noises.

"I should probably go home." Melissa stood up from the table. "Tyler is with his grandmother."

"Burrows? Reed? Take Mrs. Wilkinson home. Stay with her. Get yourselves set up. If another call comes through, you know what to do."

"Thank you," said Melissa. "Thank you all."

For the first time since she had heard the kidnapper's voice on the phone, she let a tear trickle down her cheek.

There had better be another call.

59

Members of Miller's team were working with Melissa's father in the effort to produce the cash the kidnapper had demanded.

Other agents drove into Manhattan to talk to Scott Wilkinson's employers, the people at PP&W Advertising. They learned that, earlier in the week, the CEO had received an anonymous phone call suggesting Scott Wilkinson was attempting to peddle proprietary information to PP&W's competition. The caller had sounded Russian.

"Why would Kyznetsoff make that call?" Miller asked, back in the war room in Newark.

Keith Johnson, who worked a lot of white-collar corporate cases, took a shot at answering: "It makes the company a lot less interested in sending out a search party to find Wilkinson if they think the guy's a traitor."

Miller checked his watch. Then he turned to the agent working as a liaison with the New Jersey State Police. "How we doing up at the oil tanks? Any luck finding workable tire-tread prints?"

"No. Too many vehicles in and out of the gravel lot to pin anything down."

"We need to try harder. We've got to come up with something to help us ID Kyznetsoff's current vehicle."

"May not do us much good, Chris. The guy seems to switch cars every time he changes his socks."

The door opened and an agent walked in, handing Miller a piece of paper.

"This just came off the fax," she said.

Miller read it quickly and sighed heavily. He looked around the room. He wouldn't sugarcoat it.

"Okay. Here's what we're up against," he told them.

They listened intently as he paraphrased some of the most relevant information from the sheet of paper.

"Nicolai Kyznetsoff, our guy, is ex–Spetsgruppa Vympel. That's a special forces unit of the old Red Army that was run by the KGB." He scanned the summary of the group's military history. "From the look of it, it was pretty much a rogue operation."

He looked around the conference table before continuing.

"What they were 'special' for included reconnaissance behind enemy lines, sabotage and assassinations, kidnappings."

He paused again.

"It gets worse. Not only was Kyznetsoff trained by this unit, he was also kicked out of it. His handlers wound up committing him to some sort of an asylum, apparently because he enjoyed his work too much. It's one thing to be a highly trained killing machine and another to be a loose cannon who uses a commissary fork to blind his commanding officer."

None of the team said anything, waiting for Miller to

continue. He had to admire their restraint. They were FBI agents, after all, and this report seemed to call, instead, for a response team of James Bonds.

"So they put Kyznetsoff in some kind of psycho ward—can't have been too pleasant or very therapeutic, considering this was during the final days of the Soviet state—and he wound up back on the streets, just like all the other prisoners and psychopaths, once the U.S.S.R. collapsed."

One of the agents, detailed from Atlanta and very polite, now raised his hand. "Sir, I've read about this Spetsgruppa Vympel. They were improvisational killers. Shovels, knives, rusty nails, broken glass—yes, even a fork from the mess hall. Anything they could put their hands on they could turn into a weapon. Now, some of these implements can be seriously harmful even in the hands of ordinary civilians. But you hand them to a carefully trained and enthusiastic operative, we're talking about deeply lethal."

Miller nodded. Next he called on one of the other team members who had her pen raised. Marcie Adler was from the Manhattan field office and could be counted on for her sense of humor.

"Okay," she said, "that does it. From now on, I'm giving bigger tips to every cabbie who happens to have a foreign accent. In other words, every taxi and Town Car driver in the city. Who knew? These guys are all the Terminator in disguise."

That broke some of the tension in the room. Some.

A cell phone sounded. Everyone reached for their pockets or belts.

Miller put his hand up.

"It's mine."

He pushed "talk."

"This is Miller."

"Hello. My name is Maksim Petrovich Demichev."

"Who?"

"We meet one day in Brooklyn. You give me your business card. We meet at Lucky Seven Limousines but I no speak no English. Remember?"

"Okay."

"Tell me, Special Agent Miller—are you still looking for Nicolai Kyznetsoff?"

"Yes, sir."

"Good. Good."

"Do you know where he is?"

"*Da.* I mean, yes."

60

Miller circled his hand over his head.

Everyone in the room went quiet.

"Yes," Miller said loudly, so everyone would know he had something solid, "we're still looking for Mr. Kyznetsoff."

"Okay. He call me yesterday."

"He did?"

"*Da*. He say he is going to kill me."

"Why? Why does he want to kill you?"

"Because I told some people where they might find him, and I think now they did find him but Nicolai killed these same people before they could kill him."

"Where? Where is he?"

"His *dacha*. His country home."

"Do you know where this dacha is located?"

"Yes. It is near Browndale."

"Browndale?" said Miller. "Where's that?"

"Pennsylvania."

Miller swung his eyes around the room as he slowly repeated the information. "Browndale, Pennsylvania. That's where Kyznetsoff is currently located?"

Five agents hustled out of the room, heading to their

desks and computers and telephones to find out everything they could about Browndale and the tactical
options available there.

"You are certain he's still there?"

"I think so. *Da*. I think he killed Slava there."

Miller looked at Detective Magruder.

"He killed someone named Slava?"

The Brooklyn cop was on his feet.

"*Da*."

"Okay." Miller kept his voice level, friendly. "Do you
know how we can find this house?"

"Yes. I drive him one weekend. We go there to hunt."

Miller now understood his suspect would most likely
be heavily armed.

"So where is it?" Miller couldn't help showing
impatience.

"Is cabin," Maksim said. "Is shitty little cabin. I
will draw for you a map. Would you like to see such a
thing?"

"Absolutely. Are you located near a fax machine?"

"No. I am at home. In my kitchen."

"Stay right there, Mr. Demichev. We'll send over
some people to get you." Magruder nodded, pulled out
his own cell phone. "They'll pick you up in . . ."

Magruder flashed five fingers.

". . . five minutes. They'll escort you to the Sixty-first
Precinct police station and help you send us this map."

"*Horoshow*. Very good. I will wait here in my kitchen
for the police men."

Miller now prepared to hand the phone to Magruder.
"I am going to pass this telephone to a colleague from

the New York City Police Department so you can tell him exactly where you are currently located, okay?"

"Okay. *Horoshow.*"

Miller passed his phone. Magruder listened and wrote down the information.

"We're on our way," Magruder said when he had everything he needed.

Miller knew: this could be their dumb, lucky break. A Christmas gift dropped in their laps from out of the blue. The miracle on whatever-number street Maksim Demichev lived on out in Brooklyn.

61

Maksim hung up the telephone.

He was dressed in his heavy winter coat and black beaver hat that made him look like a retired Cossack. His mittens were stuffed into his pockets. It was a cold day and he knew he would be venturing outside again soon.

He picked up the telephone, looked at the paper cup of coffee he had purchased earlier, pressed in the numbers printed on its side.

"International Delicatessen," said the surly girl who answered the phone. Maksim could hear that the shop was crowded, busy. "Hello? International Deli?" She sounded impatient.

"Yes, hello," Maksim said. "I am a good friend of Vasily."

"Who?"

"Vasily."

"There is no one named Vasily working here. You must have the wrong number."

"Please," said Maksim. "You must tell my friend Vasily that I know where Nicolai is."

"Who?"

"Nicolai!"

"Listen, old man—we are very busy," the girl grumbled in tart Russian. "I do not have the time to remember so many names. Vasily, Nicolai—"

"*Konchaj bazar!* Stop yapping and listen to me, young lady. Listen well! If Vasily hears how you do not write down my very important message, he will drag you downstairs and deal with you himself!"

The girl said nothing. Maksim heard cash registers ringing. Russian holiday music. Finally, the girl exhaled a tremendous sigh. "Hold on. I will find a pen."

"*Spasibo.* Thank you."

Maksim checked the kitchen clock. The police would be coming in three, maybe two minutes. He wished the girl would hurry. He heard a scratchy old record, children singing, "Sleep, Christmas tree, sleep," telling the tired tale of the old man who chopped down the Christmas tree in the forest to give children happiness and fun.

Stupid old man. Wasting his time. Maksim knew it was most important in this life to look out for yourself—not foolish children who wish to hang chocolate candies off a dead tree. And so he made his phone calls. Somebody, either the FBI or the New York City Police Department or Vasily, would certainly find Nicolai Kyznetsoff before Kyznetsoff came for Maksim Demichev.

"Okay," said the girl. "I have pen. What is your very important message?"

"I know where Nicolai is!"

"Nicolai." She enunciated every syllable. She was proving an extremely slow scribe.

"I have drawn a map and taped it underneath the first park bench to the right when you reach the board-walk . . ."

"What?"

"Write it down, silly girl! Hurry! Write down exactly what I say or I swear Vasily will hear of your insolence!"

"Map. Taped. Under. Bench. On right. Second bench."

"The first! You will be dead if you give Vasily the wrong information. It is the first bench. As you face the ocean, the first bench on your right."

"First. Bench. On right."

"Yes!"

Knuckles rapped on his door.

"Mr. Demichev?" boomed a voice from the other side.

The police. Maksim cupped his hand over the phone so the girl would not hear his name being called.

"I am coming," Maksim shouted at his door. "I am in the toilet."

"Are you Maksim Petrovich Demichev?" the voice yelled back.

"*Da*. Yes. Wait a minute . . ."

"This is the NYPD."

"Yes, yes. I tell you, one minute. I will be right with you. I must flush toilet." He put the phone back to his ear. "You will give Vasily my message?"

"Yes," said the girl. "Shall I tell Vasily who it was that called with such urgent message?"

"No. There is no need."

"As you wish, sir. May all your dreams come true in New Year."

"Thank you."

The girl giggled. "You are welcome, Maksim Petro-vich Demichev!"

62

"Please, my friend. Have more tea."

"You are most kind, Boris."

Nicolai Kyznetsoff sat in a booth at the foul-smelling diner with the Pakistani driver named Rizwan. At least the grease in the air helped cover up many of the strange odors oozing out of the man's skin.

"Perhaps you would enjoy another slice of the apple pie?" Kyznetsoff asked. "As I said—this is my treat."

"No, I will pay for my own lunch."

Kyznetsoff held up his hand. "Rizwan? Please. I insist."

"You are most kind."

"No," Kyznetsoff said, looking humble. "You are the kind one. I am new to the company. I wish to do well, for myself and for my family. Perhaps you can give me some pointers?"

"Indeed. No problem."

"How is the boss? Will he treat me fairly?" Kyznetsoff knew he needed to move slowly toward the true purpose of his interrogation.

"Mr. Awadallah is a very, very good man."

"And I will make very much money?"

"If you work hard, you shall be richly rewarded."

"I am most happy to hear this," Kyznetsoff said. "I need to make much money right away."

"Do you buy many Christmas gifts?" Rizwan asked.

"Yes. I have six children. And my wife's birthday? It is also December twenty-fifth."

"Christmas Day?"

"Yes, my friend. You are very lucky you are a Hindu."

"I am Muslim."

"Either way—no Christmas gifts to worry about, *da*?"

"Yes." Rizwan laughed.

Kyznetsoff waved to the waitress and she came over to the table. She was a shapely woman in her early twenties who knew how to walk toward a man: breasts held high, hips swaying just enough so you could imagine her silky thighs rubbing together beneath her skirt.

"Yes, sir? Can I bring you something else? More dessert, maybe?"

"Yes. We would like a plate of those cookies, the ones decorated for Christmas."

"Sure. Anything else?"

Kyznetsoff made his black eyes sparkle. "Speaking for myself, I would like your telephone number."

The girl reacted as Kyznetsoff suspected she might. The corner of her lips twitched up into a smile. She enjoyed the attention of male admirers.

"I can bring you the Christmas cookies."

"What about the telephone number?" Kyznetsoff leaned forward, touching her wrist.

Rizwan stared at him.

"I don't know," the waitress said playfully. "I don't give my phone number to every guy who comes in here for lunch."

"Good. Then I will have you all to myself."

"Let me go get those cookies."

"*Spasibo.*"

The waitress walked away, making certain to sway her bottom a little more than necessary because she knew he was watching.

"Are you not married?" Rizwan asked.

"Hmmm?"

"Are you not married?"

"Yes, my friend. I am married, but I am not dead." He said it to make Rizwan laugh. Instead, the man frowned.

"You are unfaithful to your wife?"

"I did not say this!" Kyznetsoff sounded offended. "I have shared my bed with the same woman for over twenty-five years! Can you claim the same?"

"No. I have only been married ten years."

"Who, then, are you to condemn me?"

"But the way you carried on with that woman . . ."

Kyznetsoff raised his shoulders, tilted his head, gave Rizwan a can't-help-myself look. "I am the hopeless romantic. When I see a pretty girl, I flirt, but—and this I swear—I never do anything more. Flirting is for the comely shop girls, the shapely waitresses. But love? Love is only for the wife and family. How do you think I come to have seven children?"

"You said you have six."

"And one on the way. A son this time, we pray. But, tell me, Rizwan—do you have any children?"

"Yes. I tell you this yesterday."

"Ah, yes. I remember now—you say your daughter goes to the same school as the brave man's daughter. The man who catches such a deadly enemy."

"Mr. Miller's daughter and my Zinah are in the same school."

The waitress brought a little plate of sugar cookies decorated with red and green sparkles.

"Here you go, sir."

Kyznetsoff ignored her—even though she had unsnapped an extra button on her blouse.

"Thank you," he said, without looking away from Rizwan. "You may go."

He heard the waitress mumble "asshole" as she walked away.

"The same school?" Kyznetsoff said to Rizwan. "If both you and the brave man send your children there, it must a be a good place for my children, too."

"Oh, it is the best. The Horace Abercrombie School. The children are very happy there. They learn their lessons. Never any discipline problems."

"They are strict?"

"Yes, but the girls also have their fun. Tonight, they will present their annual pageant."

"Your daughter is in it?"

Rizwan nodded. "Since it is more a holiday pageant, a winter carnival open to all expressions of faith, celebrating all religions, yes, she is."

"How wonderful," said Kyznetsoff.

"Yes. Her mother has made Zinah a crown and dress and she will perform a traditional Ramadan dance."

"Will you go see her?"

"I will be working the night shift but Mr. Awadallah will generously allow me to take off an hour or so at seven thirty to see Zinah in her costume, watch her dance."

Kyznetsoff nodded.

"You are a good man," he said. "A good father."

Rizwan looked pleased to hear this praise.

"Tell me something."

"Yes?"

"Will your FBI agent friend be at the celebration this evening?"

"Oh, yes. He comes to every school event. I am told he is semiretired and has much time to spend with his child."

"Semiretired? What does this mean?"

"There are changed circumstances at his job. They have cut back his workload and he no longer chases criminals the same way he did formerly. He tells me he has become 'too old for such foolishness.'"

"I see. How old is he, actually?"

"About your age. Fifty years, I would imagine."

Kyznetsoff recognized a cover story when he heard one. It was obvious that Miller, in fact, was on a top-secret assignment, one handed to him by someone high up in the State Department. Looking after Alexei Bizanko's diamonds. This "semiretired" nonsense was the fairy tale he used for friends and neighbors to explain his underutilization at his visible desk job and to conceal the true nature of his clandestine work.

"I would like very much, myself, to meet this Christopher Miller," Kyznetsoff said to Rizwan.

"To thank him, yes? For capturing the killer."

"*Da*," Kyznetsoff said. "I would very much like to thank him. In person."

63

Scott Wilkinson was thirsty.

He hadn't had anything to eat or drink for almost two days. Most of his time was spent in a drowsy stupor. His metabolism had slowed to conserve energy and vital resources. Thankfully, the starvation had silenced his bowels.

He stared up at the knotty pine ceiling again. He dared not move too abruptly for fear of setting off the explosives hidden underneath the bed.

It was cold and dark in the cabin. Twilight came early this close to Christmas and the crazy Russian had not left a single lightbulb burning. At least there was some heat. Not much. Above freezing, that was all he knew.

His mind wandered, stumbled. It needed lubrication. Water.

He worked his brain, tried to stop it from shutting down completely. He stared at the ceiling, computed whatever data he could: the number of nail holes in the pine boards. He factored statistics. Nail holes per board. Was the number consistent? Was there a statistical pattern to the natural sequencing of pine knots?

He was trying not to lose his mind.

Two of the pine knots overhead, coupled with the spiraling tree rings around them, conspired to make a constellation that looked like Santa Claus carrying a sack of toys on his back.

Christmas is coming, the goose is getting fat, won't you please put a penny in the old man's hat.

"Atomic bomb, atomic bomb." That's how they sang *O Tannenbaum* when he was a kid. Atomic bomb, atomic bomb.

Christmas carols. Christmas movies.

Scott replayed his favorites, note by note, scene by scene, whenever he was awake. *It's a Wonderful Life. A Christmas Carol*, the Alistair Sim version, that was the best. And the George C. Scott. That was a good one. Patton made a good Scrooge.

He wanted Tyler to see that movie. He wanted to be there when he did. He wanted his whole family cuddled up on the couch, everybody eating popcorn and sipping cocoa with miniature marshmallows bobbing along the surface, watching somebody famous be Scrooge before they all hung their stockings by the chimney with care in hopes that Saint Nicholas soon would be there. That would be a holly jolly Christmas. There's no place like home for the holidays.

Atomic bomb, atomic bomb.

Miracle on 34th Street.

He needed one of those. He needed it soon.

64

Angela met her father in the front hall.

"You're home early!" she said. It was three P.M.

"I wanted to see you in your costume."

"You like it, Daddy?

She was wearing a silver wig, a sparkling white robe, and cardboard angel wings wrapped in crinkled aluminum foil.

"It's beautiful, baby! Now, who are you supposed to be? Wait, don't tell me. You're Rudolph, right? Rudolph the Red-Nosed Reindeer."

"Daddy? I'm an angel."

"Well, I know that, sweetie. That's why we called you Angela when you were born. But that costume. Are you the sugar plum fairy? A ballerina?"

"Daddy? It's an *Angel* costume. I am playing an Angel in the pageant tonight, remember?"

"An angel, hunh?"

Natalie joined them in the front room. "It's what all the Motown singers are wearing this Christmas," she said. "I believe someone even knows all the choreography to 'Little Bright Star' by the Supremes."

Angela started rolling her arms, yanking on an imaginary bell rope. She chanted the lyrics like she was doing the itsy-bitsy spider: "Little church bells ringing out at Christmas time . . ."

"Don't forget to do the snowflakes," Miller said, raising his arms, wiggling his fingers, bringing the arms back down, showering snow. Angela did the same.

"You go, girl," Miller said, his smile bright for his daughter, his eyes darting over to meet Natalie's.

"All right, Angela. Let's not ruin your costume."

Angela kept singing, making an arms-outstretched star with her tiny body. "Little bright star . . ."

"Angel?" Miller said. "Listen to Mommy. You want to look good for the big show."

"Yes, Daddy."

"Take the costume off in your room, honey. Lay it across the bed, and I'll pack it up."

"Yes, Mommy."

"And I'm baking cookies for the snack table. You want to help?"

"Can I pour on the sprinkles?"

"Only after you change out of your pretty costume."

"Yes, Mommy."

Angela raced up the staircase.

"No running in the house," Miller said.

Angela immediately slowed down, taking the steps one at a time, like she was a princess climbing her tower.

Both Miller and his wife closed their eyes and shook their heads. All children, of course, were cute—especially this close to Christmas. Their little girl, however, was undoubtedly the cutest.

"She's on her best behavior," Natalie said.

"Santa Claus is coming to town."

"Wish he showed up more often."

"Yeah. I hear that."

"What's up, old man?"

"We caught a major break. I need to gather up my gear. We're heading out at seventeen hundred hours."

"What's happening? Have you located Mr. Wilkinson?"

"We have a damn good lead. Might be able to bring him home tonight."

"Where you headed?"

"Northeast Pennsylvania. Up in the mountains. Small town called Browndale. Closest metro area is Scranton/Wilkes-Barre."

"You be careful, old man. Remember your vows."

"Yes, doc." Miller leaned in, kissed his wife. "I love you, you know that, right?"

"Do you think I'd put up with this nonsense if you didn't?"

"No, ma'am."

"Go grab your gear. I'll tell Angela there's an emergency."

Miller felt the familiar guilt pangs. "We haven't had one for a whole year."

"Yes. It was fun while it lasted. See if you can get put back on probation again after you finish this job. Now go do what needs to be done. I told Mrs. Wilkinson you were the best. Don't let me down."

Miller leaned in for one more kiss. He could never get enough.

"Come on, old man. Don't keep them waiting. You all have a helicopter on call?"

"Six of them," he confessed.

"You taking the whole army?"

"Just a division or two."

"Well, you better get a move on, honey."

Miller headed toward the basement door, stopped.

"You'll take the video camera, right?"

Natalie crossed her arms over her chest. "Don't worry. Your brilliant choreography will be immortalized for all time."

"All right. That's what I'm talking about."

He hummed a snatch of "Little Bright Star" and hurried down the steps to grab his tactical vest and duty belt. They were stuffed in a footlocker and hadn't seen daylight in twelve months.

Miller knew he was going to reek of mothballs.

65

They had set up a drop zone in a dairy farmer's field about two and a half miles from Kyznetsoff's cabin.

Fortunately, when the six military choppers swooped down and stirred up a cloud of dust and straw, all the cows were already in their barn.

Agents from the FBI field office in Scranton met the strike force at the farm site with eight black SUVs, which the Go Team would use to cover the final 2.5 miles up to the hot zone. The Pennsylvania state police had already shut down Route 247, the main highway up and down Kyznetsoff's mountain. At the road-blocks, state troopers told interested and agitated motorists there was "a situation up ahead: jackknifed tractor trailer. It was carrying toxic chemicals." The road, lightly traveled in the first place, was deserted. The FBI owned it.

P. J. and his crew, a five-man SWAT team up from D.C., jumped out of their helicopters with weapon cases slung over their shoulders. Dressed in full battle armor, they fanned out and immediately set to work fixing night-vision scopes to the tops of their rifles.

Miller had brought along a pair of night-vision binoculars that matched his commando fatigues. He looked like a high-tech cat burglar.

"Dang, that's a nice vest," P. J. said when he saw Miller. Then he sniffed. "But it smells like my granny's closet. What's the plan, old man?"

Miller frowned at his longtime friend. "You gonna call me that in front of everybody else?"

"Negative. Just when it's us two."

"Cool. I can live with that."

Miller motioned for the Go Team, the vanguard that would be the first up to the cabin, to join him around the hood of a Chevy Suburban. The men jostled over, weapons and field accessories jangling off all parts of their bodies. Detective Magruder wasn't with the strike force. He was in Brooklyn, with Maksim Demichev, helping him remember more details about his one weekend in the country with Nicolai Kyznetsoff. That intelligence—translated into maps, sketches, and diagrams—had been forwarded to the assault team that was now assembling on the ground.

Miller unfolded a topographical map of the mountains, clicked on his headlamp.

"Guys? Listen up. According to our intel, Kyznetsoff's cabin is here." His finger landed on a square penciled-in over the lines demarcating the slope of the mountain. "We need to establish a perimeter. Here. Here. Over here. If he tries to run, we cut him off."

"With extreme prejudice, sir?" one of P. J.'s younger gunners asked.

P. J. had to chuckle. "Damn son, you watch too many movies."

"If you're asking, do we kill Mr. Kyznetsoff," said

Miller, "I certainly hope it doesn't come to that. However, rest assured, this man is a threat I do not take lightly. Neither should you. You are authorized to use any and all means necessary to stop him. Understood?"

"Yessir, sir," the young man said.

Miller could tell: the boy was eager to take somebody down. Miller wondered if he had ever been that young, ever that excited over the prospect of snuffing out another man's life. Doubtful. The Jesuits had taught him differently.

"We'll drive up this road, Route Two Forty-seven," Miller continued. "We'll take the vehicles to this point, this big curve in the road. We can park there and remain unseen by any lookouts Kyznetsoff may have posted outside his cabin. We hop out, pack up our gear and hump the final half mile—spreading out to our perimeter positions. You see something, say something. Keep channel five clear and open for command and control communications. If we cannot extract Mr. Wilkinson without incident, we will abort. If fire teams need to communicate internally, team leaders should designate a subchannel."

The men adjusted knobs on the Motorolas clipped to their web belts. There were four fire teams, each consisting of five men cloaked in thick Kevlar vests and strapped into black ballistic helmets. Two other teams would remain with the vehicles, ready to go mobile should it prove necessary. They could roll into the cabin's driveway to assist in any firefight, or they could cut off Kyznetsoff, should he somehow make it to his own vehicle and attempt an escape. A team of Scranton field agents, augmented by the state police SWAT team, were set up on the far side of the mountain, prepared to perform the same duties should Kyznetsoff attempt a run in that direction.

Miller spread out a diagram of the cabin and its immediate surroundings next to the topo map. "Detective Magruder of the NYPD has been working with our informant. They pieced together this sketch. The cabin's front door faces south. There is no rear door, only windows on the north side of the building, which is parallel to the highway. Those rear windows are big enough for a man to crawl out, and remain potential points of egress."

Miller placed a photograph next to the diagram: a five-by-seven snapshot of Kyznetsoff holding up a freshly killed turkey in front of the cabin. "This is our primary target."

"You think he has accomplices?" one of the riflemen asked.

"I think it's always a possibility in these situations. Therefore, we will not initiate any aggressive measures until we have a better idea of what we're up against."

Heads nodded around the map.

"So," P. J. said, "I reckon we play it safe and don't start charging up San Juan Hill."

"Not tonight. This guy was KGB. Soviet Special Forces. He's probably got booby traps and land mines all around his cozy little cabin. We move quickly, but we move carefully. We go charging in, San Juan Hill might explode underneath us."

66

A half hour later, Miller, P. J., and four other team members had silently crept through the forest and a soggy carpet of old snow to the designated rock outcropping.

They could see the little cabin looming like a shoe box set against the spindly silhouettes of trees. The sky was bright with stars. Miller thought about Angela, stretching out her arms, doing her dance.

There were no lights on inside the cabin. No smoke wafting out of the chimney. No cars parked in the driveway. No sounds except the trickle of the icy creek behind them.

"Looks like nobody's home," P. J. whispered.

"So it would seem."

Miller snapped on his night vision goggles, scanned the front of the cabin. His head moved slowly—taking in all he could, searching for any telling details.

"What's that?" he said.

"Where?" P. J. responded in a tight whisper. The time for playful bantering was over. They were in attack mode. Focused.

"Base of the steps. On my right."

P. J. swung his rifle to the point Miller indicated,

adjusted the power zoom on his German-made scope. Miller knew P. J. could probably pick off an ant with that thing, if any ants were out crawling around in the dark in December.

"Looks like a body," said P. J.

"Yeah."

"Male. Leather jacket. Severe head trauma."

"You think it's Wilkinson?" Miller whispered, not expecting an answer.

P. J. turned to a man wearing headphones connected to a nylon backpack stuffed with sound-enhancing equipment. "What've you got, Vincente?"

"I mostly hear quiet, sir. Inside, I pick up some ticking. Clicks. An electric baseboard heater."

"You sure it's a heater?" asked Miller. "Not some kind of time bomb?"

"A bomb would have a different sound signature, sir."

P. J. chuckled. Nothing like know-how.

"I'm also picking up the hum of a refrigerator. . . some steady breathing."

"How many sets of lungs?" P. J. asked.

"Sounds like one. Shallow. Staggered. Someone asleep."

"George-o?" P. J. moved on to his infrared man. "Can you confirm what Vince is hearing?"

"Affirmative. Heat sensor shows one body. To the left of the larger window. The body is not moving."

"What do you mean?" Miller asked. "A dead body?"

"No, sir. Heat pattern is inconsistent with death. This body is warm but motionless."

"Damn," Miller grumbled.

"Your call, Chris," said P. J. "We going in?"

"Could be Kyznetsoff taking a nap," Miller said. "Worn out after a long day of killing folks."

"Or?" P. J. prompted.

"Or, it could be Wilkinson. Immobilized."

"Yeah. Which way you want to play it?"

"Get on the radio. Lock down the perimeter. Keep it tight. I'm going in."

"I'm going in with you," said P. J.

Miller motioned for him to stay where he was.

"I need you covering my back."

"Same old same-old?"

"Yeah."

Miller started up the hill toward the cabin, careful to look down before taking each step forward. Land mines. Booby traps.

Neither one was on his Christmas list this year.

67

Nicolai Kyznetsoff finally found a parking space in the three-tiered garage wrapped around the Portside Centre Mall.

Kyznetsoff's shopping list was short. One item. Maybe two.

Even the mall's garage was decorated for the holidays. He walked past cement columns wrapped with sparkling garlands. He heard tinny Christmas music blaring out of unseen speakers. The saccharine tunes competed with the clicking of speed bumps as frustrated shoppers cruised the garage, searching for a place to park.

Kyznetsoff reached the sliding doors and stepped into a tinseled wonderland.

The mall was enormous—rising three stories to a vaulted glass ceiling. Glittering decorations twinkled in all the shops ringing the vast atrium.

In the center of the mall, near the glass elevators, he saw Santa's sleigh. The jolly fat man sat up front on a bench seat. A red velour sack the size of a pickup truck filled the cargo bed behind him and was stuffed with unwrapped toys to be distributed to needy children in local hospitals. Kyznetsoff sneered at the chintzy charity. Drop off one crappy toy, a cheap chessboard, or last year's unwanted doll, and assuage enough guilt to go buy your own children fifteen shiny new ones.

Sniveling brats were lined up behind velvet ropes, squirming while they waited their turn to sit on the fat man's lap and have their picture snapped.

The young elf manning the Polaroid wore a short, fur-trimmed skirt that swung out from her hips like a bell, exposing most of her slender, green legs. She had marvelous, muscular thighs. Kyznetsoff thought about making her his Snow Maiden for the night. Unfortunately, she was too busy dealing with the screaming children. He moved on.

Past MaggieMoo's Ice Cream and Treatery. Aldo Shoes. Chronos, where the elegantly scripted sign in the window read: "We Buy and Sell Fine Jewelry."

Not mine, Kyznetsoff thought. Not any more.

Not since Christopher Miller fucked me over.

Kyznetsoff turned around. There it was: The Singing Christmas Tree he had read about in the mall brochure at his motel. A towering pyramid of boxed-in risers, its peak reaching the second-story level of shops. No choir was currently singing from its perches, but tomorrow the tree would be filled with eager amateurs from local churches and high schools, all regaling shoppers with the same old, tired carols.

He glanced at his watch. It was time to locate the key item he needed for the final phase of his plan.

A woman waddled past carrying two enormous shopping bags from a store called "Christmas Creations."

"Ho, ho, ho!" Kyznetsoff called out with a wink and smile. "I see somebody is in the holiday spirit."

The woman smiled back. "You bet! I wish every day was Christmas!"

"Me, too!" Kyznetsoff gushed. "I collect porcelain Santas and keep them out all year long!"

"Really? That's what I do! With my houses. Do you collect the Snow Village Houses?"

"Of course!"

"Then you have got to go upstairs to Christmas Creations! They have everything!"

That meant they would have the necessary item.

Kyznetsoff played dumb. "They're on the second floor?"

"No, the third," said the woman. "Right next to Spenser Gifts. Take that escalator, it's on your right when you get to the top."

"Thank you, ma'am. Have a Merry Christmas!"

"You, too!"

"Oh, I plan to!"

The holliest, jolliest ever.

68

"Sorry, sir," the state trooper said to the driver of the passenger van. "This road is closed. Jackknifed tractor-trailer."

"Really?"

"Yes, sir. The driver had trouble negotiating a hairpin curve up there, ended up in the ditch. Rocks ruptured his tanks and we could have a toxic chemical spill. We'll know more in a few hours."

"But I need to go home."

"You live in one of the cabins up this way? We could help you arrange alternative accommodations."

"No," the driver said. "I live in Browndale. On the other side of the mountain."

"Sure. Now I know it's a detour, but you could turn around here, go back down to Route 6, you know, back to the blinker?"

"Sure."

"Hang a right and head west on Six, catch Two Forty-seven where it hits Carbondale, double-back."

"Yes. Of course. This I know. I do this all the time. Good idea. Thank you, officer."

The driver pulled up on his transmission lever. The state trooper moved into the road, signaled to him that he had plenty of room to back up, cut his wheels, and negotiate the U-turn.

"Thank you, officer!" The driver smiled and waved to the trooper as he pulled away. The trooper waved back and gave the cooperative citizen a quick two-finger salute off the brim of his hat.

The van hummed down the highway, headed south toward the intersection with Route 6.

"Fucking trucks," the driver said over his shoulder to the four passengers huddled in the darkened seats. "Blocking the highway. We will have to take the dirt road up the backside of the mountain. We can reach his *dacha* this way."

"You are certain of this dirt road?" a gruff voice asked.

"Definitely. It is on the map. The county map. Is dotted line."

"What means this dotted line?"

"Is shitty little road nobody uses anymore except dumb fucks like us!"

His comrades grunted.

"Is probably nothing but a dirt road with tire ruts and big rocks every two meters."

"Like driving in the middle of Moscow," one of the men in back joked.

"And you think this van will make it up such a road?" asked the gruff voice.

"Relax, Vasily. I have faith in Japanese-built four-wheel drive. If this was American-made piece-of-shit minivan, then I would worry. I would piss into my panties like a little girl."

The van hit a pothole.

"Hang on," the driver said. "We will take right turn at cemetery. Next to old church."

"Is that where the crazy *mudack* buried Slava? This cemetery?"

"I do not know, Vasily."

"Well, then," said Vasily, "we will have to ask him. Right before I chop off his fucking balls."

69

It took ten minutes for Miller to transverse the one hundred feet from the creek bank to the front of the cabin.

He moved like a nervous stork. Raising a leg, scoping out the ground where he wanted to place it, lowering the leg gingerly, feeling with his toes, hoping he didn't lose them when he placed his full weight on his heel, taking it one step at a time.

He reached a poured concrete pad at the base of a short staircase. He saw the man's body lying in a crumpled heap. There was a pearl-handled straight razor stuck in the back of his neck like an axe in a stump. Miller hunkered down, saw the bullet craters blown into the back of the man's skull.

"Damn." He said it to himself.

His radio was muted. He couldn't risk making any sounds this close to the cabin. He fished his laser pointer out of a cloth loop on the front of his vest. Still kneeling, he shone the light up the steps, looked for fish line, trip wires, and improvised bomb triggers. The steps were clear.

He checked out the path he would need to take across the porch planks to the front door. Clear. He could move a little more freely now: it was doubtful

Kyznetsoff would have booby-trapped the cabin's interior where he might have tripped the triggers himself.

The floorboards creaked as he slowly made his way toward the door. He noticed it was open. Just about a half-inch. Did Kyznetsoff forget to lock it when he left? Or was he setting a trap? Was he crouched on the other side, weapon locked and loaded, waiting to ambush any intruders?

Miller reached for his Glock M22, nestled in the paddle holster at the small of his back. He pulled it out, slipped off the safety, held it with both hands in front of him.

He was going in.

He turned to his left. Nodded. He knew P. J. was monitoring his every move. Up in the woods, he saw the momentary glint of glass as riflescopes were maneuvered into firing position. The snipers were lining up their shots. The door. The two windows. Miller knew P. J. would also be radioing out commands, setting up the sharpshooters situated behind the cabin. Within seconds, every window would be covered.

"On my count," he said to himself. The ritualistic chant made it all feel a little more routine. "Three, two, one . . ."

He flexed his leg, kicked the door open and immediately rolled to its left. He hit the deck, ducked the barrage of bullets he expected to come whizzing out the door.

No shots were fired.

He clamped a gunlight onto the top of his Glock, flicked on its halogen.

"This is the FBI!" he screamed as he stepped through the open door and assumed a squat-thrust firing position. "FBI! Drop your weapons!"

No response.

He swung the light left. Saw an empty kitchen. Dirty dishes stacked in the sink. To the right. The bright circle swept across the wall, the TV, a closet, a gun rack, a recliner. He kept sweeping, moving the light right, over to his side, down to the floor.

A flash reflected back. The light hit the sharp corner of a steel bed frame. Miller moved the light slowly, crawled it up an inch or two at a time until he discovered the toe of a wingtip rimmed with mud. He jerked the light up to the head of the bed.

Scott Wilkinson.

The man's eyes were wild. Frantic. He seemed to quiver, like he wanted to shake his head, wanted to warn Miller of some danger, but he couldn't because the head was trapped inside some sort of leather mask.

Miller moved toward the bed.

"Mmmmfff!"

Miller froze.

"Bbbbmmmmfff."

Wilkinson was trying to warn him about . . . something.

Miller stood still, studied the situation. Wilkinson was gagged, lying spread-eagled. His black hood was anchored to the bed frame. Handcuffs tightly held his wrists and ankles. His pinstriped suit was filthy. Soiled. Blotted by circles of sweat and other bodily fluids.

Miller moved his gunlight around, trying to see what Wilkinson wanted to warn him about.

"Bbbmmmfff!"

"Okay, Scott. Hang on. Give me a second here."

The light flared off something gold. Copper. The twisted ends of two wires. One red, one black.

Detonator wires.

"Okay, Scott. I see it."

Miller reached for the handy-talkie clipped to his belt. He twisted its power switch and brought it up to his lips, his eyes never leaving the detonator wires tied off to the metal bed frame. "I'm clear," he said into the radio. As soon the words left his mouth, he heard troops charging up the hill. "We have Wilkinson," he called out. "Repeat, we have Wilkinson. Send a medic. Stat!"

Miller lowered his radio, focused on the wires, tried to trace them. "Hang on, Scott. We'll get you out of this mess as soon as we can."

"Chris?" P. J. was first through the front door.

"Improvised Explosive Device. Rigged to the bed frame."

"Affirmative." P. J. saw it, too.

"Hit the lights. Switch should be on the wall by the door."

"On it."

Miller squinted when the ceiling light came on, gave his eyes a second to adjust.

"Any of your guys good with this sort of thing?" he asked P. J.

"Vincente. He knows what to look for."

"Send him in."

"Vincente? We got an IED."

"On it, sir." Vincente lumbered into the cabin. His heavy bootfalls made the floor rumble.

"Easy," P. J. said. "Take it slow."

Miller only hoped the man's hands were a little more delicate than his feet.

70

"Play-Doh."

"Do what?"

"It's Play-Doh, sir."

Miller and P. J. crawled under the bed to see what Vincente had seen.

"You sure about the Play-Doh, son?" asked Miller.

"Yes, sir. My kid has tons of the stuff. It has that smell, you know?"

"Yeah."

"I was able to unwrap the aluminum foil without touching the wires. Our perp molded the Play-Doh into a brick to look like the real deal. C-4."

"What about that cell phone?"

"He rigged it up to look like a remote trigger."

"Well—is it?"

"Doubtful. Besides—battery's dead."

"You sure, son?" Miller had to ask one more time.

"Definitely. This is Play-Doh. And that's a fake trigger."

"Okay. Do it."

The young man yanked out the two wires. Miller closed his eyes as if that would somehow protect him when the bomb blew up and brought the whole cabin raining down on top of him.

Nothing exploded.

"Play-Doh," said P. J. He must have opened his eyes first.

The three men scooted out from under the bed.

"Scott? My name is Christopher Miller."

Wilkinson's eyes widened underneath the holes of the leather mask.

"I am with the FBI." Miller spoke fast. Clipped. He wanted to free Scott and get the hell out. "We're taking you home to Melissa and Tyler. Everything's going to be okay. Where's the medic?"

"Here, sir."

"He needs fluids. He's dehydrated."

"I'll set up an IV drip. Air Medical Assets are on the way. Life Flight will rush him down to Geisinger Hospital in Wilkes-Barre."

The Rapid Deployment Logistics team had done its job.

"Let's cut him free," Miller said. "P. J.—see if you can work that thing off his head. We'll undo the wrist and ankle restraints. Hang on, Scott. You're almost home."

71

Natalie Miller and another mom sat behind the long table set up in the hallway outside the cafeteria.

Spread out before them were foil-wrapped baking trays of brownies and muffins, mounds of donuts, paper plates of Christmas cookies under plastic wrap, and baggies stuffed with fudge. The other mom nibbled on a chocolate chip cookie. Natalie bit into a sugar cookie cut and frosted to look like Santa.

"Mmmm."

She reached into her purse and found another quarter, which she dutifully placed inside the bake sale moneybox.

"How many is that?" the other mom asked.

"Ten. I'm my own best customer."

"Me, too." Her friend licked melted chocolate off her fingertips. "I put five dollars in the till when I got here. Now I'm eating up my credit."

"How much do you have left?"

"I think I owe another five." She found her purse, pulled out a five-dollar bill, handed it to Natalie.

A boy dressed like a giant dreidel wobbled down the hall, his small head peeping out from a hole cut into the top of a cardboard box decorated with white paper and blue Hebrew letters.

He mumbled as he walked past. "Dreidel, dreidel, dreidel. I made it out of clay . . ."

"Guess he's still memorizing his lines," Natalie said.

"His mother brought rugelach. Did you try it?"

"No."

"Chocolate and cinnamon and tons of butter. I'm thinking about converting."

A cold gust of wind swept down the hall.

"Sorry if we are late."

"You're fine," said Natalie. "Show hasn't started yet."

A child wearing a tiara with twelve points sticking up like flaming birthday candles came running up the hall.

"You look beautiful, Zinah," Natalie said. "But you better not run in the hall, honey. You might trip on your robe."

The little girl slowed down. "Sorry, Mrs. Miller."

"Are you excited?"

"Oh, yes. Very much so."

Her beaming parents came up the corridor behind her, her dad clutching a video camera.

"Did you make that costume yourself?" Natalie asked.

"My mom helped."

"Care for a cookie, Mr. and Mrs. Raja?"

"Oh, yes," said Rizwan. "Please. An entire bag of them. I will be working the late shift tonight."

Natalie put his money in the box. "Don't get crumbs all over your cab," she joked and handed him a stack of napkins.

"I promise: the cookies will remain in the front seat with me at all times. Is Christopher here this evening?"

"No," Natalie said. "He's working tonight."

"Really?" Rizwan seemed surprised. "I thought he was semiretired."

"So did he. His bosses thought different. They sent him out of town on a business trip."

"I see. Well, do not worry." He tapped his camcorder. "I will videotape Angela's performance as well as Zinah's!"

"Thank you."

The music teacher in charge of the program walked purposefully past the cookie tables and darted into a classroom. When the door opened, Natalie could hear happy squeals from the overexcited kids.

"Five minutes, everyone," the teacher said. "Reindeer? You're on first. Angels? You're up after the reindeer."

More squeals.

"Mommy?" Angela stuck her head out of the door and waved frantically. "Mommy?"

"What's the matter, honey?"

"My halo won't stay on!"

"Did you use those hairpins?"

"It won't stay on!"

"Okay, honey. Hang on. I'm coming."

"Cell phones off, please," the music teacher announced as she ushered kids wearing reindeer headbands and lipstick-red noses into the hall.

"Just like Broadway, hunh?" Natalie dug into her purse to find her phone.

"Mommy?"

"Hang on! I'm coming, honey." She switched off her phone, locked up the moneybox, grabbed one more cookie, and headed into the classroom to deal with the halo crisis.

Usually, when her husband was in the field, Natalie Miller kept her phone turned on. Usually, if she went someplace where she was supposed to turn it off, she switched the ringer to the vibrate mode.

Tonight, however, she forgot.

Tonight, she had a halo emergency.

72

In the cabin, the medic worked an IV line into Scott Wilkinson's arm.

Miller was dialing his cell phone.

"Mrs. Wilkinson? This is Christopher Miller. We have your husband. He's going to be fine."

On the other end of the phone call, there was silence. Finally, Melissa said, "Thank you." It was over.

"We're airlifting him to a hospital in Wilkes-Barre, Pennsylvania."

"I'm on my way . . . Wilkes-Barre . . . how do I get there?"

"Mrs. Wilkinson?"

"What? Is something wrong? Is Scott hurt?"

"He's going to be fine."

"What is it then?"

"The kidnapper isn't here."

"So?"

"We still need to catch him."

"Why? If Scott's going to be okay . . ."

"Mrs. Wilkinson? Listen to me: I have to catch this man before he does this to someone else's husband, some other baby's father."

A pause. Miller pressed his point.

"I need your help."

"Me? I can't do anything about—"

"The kidnapper will call you again. I suspect he isn't here right now because he has positioned himself closer to you in order to expedite the pickup of his money."

P. J. motioned to Miller to hurry. He wanted to remove the wounded man from the cabin. Miller nodded. He only needed a minute more.

"The kidnapper is here in New Jersey?"

"We think so. He doesn't know we've rescued your husband."

"I'll tell him! And then I'll tell him he can go straight to hell!"

"No. When he calls, you need to act frightened. Terrified. You need to sound exactly like you sounded the first time he called. Can you do that?"

"I want to see Scott!"

"And you will. Soon. I promise."

Another pause. Miller prayed he had made his point.

"What do I need to do?"

Good.

"Take the call. Act afraid. Listen to all his instructions. The man wants to make certain he doesn't get caught so he'll make things much more complicated than they need to be."

"What if I can't remember everything?"

"The agents there will remember for you."

"Okay."

"We're gonna get this guy, Mrs. Wilkinson. But, like I said, we can't do it without your help."

"After he calls, can I come see Scott?"

"Soon. Not right away."

"What? Why not?"

"You'll most likely be the one making the delivery."

"Me? Why me? I can't—"

"They typically ask a family member to do the drop-off. But we'll have you covered."

"Agent Miller?"

"Yes, ma'am?"

"You know how you said you needed me to act like I was still scared?"

"Yes?"

"I don't think I need to act anymore."

Miller closed up his phone and moved to the bed.

Scott's eyes were heavy, his breathing shallow. The medic had shot him up with serious painkillers. Miller knew the man was only half here. Scott groaned.

"Mr. Wilkinson?" Miller said. "My name is Christopher Miller. We are going to take you home."

Scott scrunched up his face in pain. "You're Christopher Miller?" he rasped.

"That's right. I'm with the Federal Bureau of Investigation and—"

"You want his diamonds."

"Come again?"

"Kyznetsoff." Scott coughed out the word.

"Chris?" the medic cautioned. "This guy really shouldn't be doing any kind of debrief right now. We need to put him on the bird. Immediately, if not sooner."

Scott shook his head. Held up his hand. He wanted to talk. He just needed to find some strength and breath.

Miller crouched down so he'd be closer to the man's face.

"What is it, Scott?"

"He said . . ." Scott paused, took in a long, rattling breath. ". . . you would be dealt with."

"Me?"

"Christopher Miller." Another pause. Another desperate breath. "Diamonds. Russia." More air. More pain. "Slava told him . . ."

Scott's eyes fluttered shut. He was out of gas.

Miller stood up.

"Damn," he said.

"What?" asked P. J. "What's wrong?"

"That son of a bitch."

"Who?"

"Owens. Using my name to cover his ass. Now Kyznetsoff thinks I want his diamonds."

"Sir?" The medic was ready to evacuate the wounded. Now.

"Yeah. Okay. Let's roll."

"Vincente?" P. J. said to his man closest to the door. "Take the point."

The agent opened the front door.

Something popped.

Gunshots. More.

"Down!" Miller hollered.

Vincente stood frozen—his hands braced against the doorframe. Another flurry of gunshots. He flopped backward.

There was a circle of blood where his left eye used to be.

73

Nicolai Kyznetsoff pressed in the numbers from a fresh calling card.

When the tones chimed, he pressed in the phone number.

She answered on the fourth ring.

"Hello?"

"Hello, Missy."

"Who is this?"

"Do not ask such stupid questions. Not if you wish to see your husband alive."

Melissa hesitated. Kyznetsoff could hear her studied attempt to steady her breathing, regain her composure. Good. She understood who she was dealing with. She would pay him his three million.

"I have your money," she said.

"Good. All of it?"

"Yes."

A car drove past. Kyznetsoff covered the mouthpiece.

"Hello?" Melissa sounded panicked. "Are you still there? What happened? Hello?"

He waited, enjoying her panic.

"Are you still there?"

"Yes. Of course I am still here. I had to go kick Scott in his face because his wife asks so many stupid questions."

"No. Don't . . . please . . . don't hurt Scott . . ."

"Listen to me. Listen very carefully."

"Yes, sir."

"You are to put the three million dollars inside a duffel bag."

"Okay."

"You will take the duffel bag to the mall."

"Which mall?"

"Do you annoy your husband this way? Perhaps Scott would be happier if I killed him so he didn't have to listen to you ask so many fucking questions!"

"No, I'm sorry . . . I'm scared."

"You should be scared. That is proper. Now listen."

"Yes, sir."

"Write this down. Do exactly as I say. Bring the money to the Portside Centre Mall. It is near Jersey City. Do you know where it is located?"

"Yes. I mean, I can find it."

"Tomorrow at noon you will come to this mall and take the money to Santa Claus. You will place your duffel bag in the back of his sleigh with the pile of toys people donate for the tots."

"Okay."

"You will not inform the police or the FBI that you are doing so."

"Yes, sir."

"You will not try anything cute or clever. No dye-packs hidden in the money. No tracking devices. You will simply put the money in the sleigh and walk away."

"Okay."

"And remember, Missy, at noon tomorrow the mall will be very crowded. I will watch everything you do and I will be heavily armed. If I suspect that the police or the FBI have followed you, I will begin to shoot people. I will not stop until they are all dead. I am bringing to the mall my Kinkov. Are you familiar with this weapon?"

"No."

"It is very much like an AK-47. Only lighter. Easier to conceal. It fires thirty rounds very, very quickly and I am an extremely rapid reloader. I will have several clips of ammunition and I will be wearing a bulletproof vest. Do you understand what I am saying to you?"

"Yes, sir. I think so."

"You think so? Allow me to clarify. If you do not follow my instructions exactly as I have given them to you, you will have innocent blood on your hands. Many of those dead will be children waiting in line to see Santa Claus. Do you understand? It is Christmas, a happy time, not a time for the massacre of little ones. Or babies like Tyler. You must do, in every detail, just what I ask. No more, no less.

"Yes, sir."

"*Horoshow*. Now then, there is one more thing you must remember."

"Okay."

"The most important thing."

"Okay."

"If anything happens to me, if I do not return to my hideout by the appointed hour, my associates are under strict orders to kill Scott. Who are they, you ask? They are butchers. Monsters. When you find Scott's body, you will not recognize his face because they will have removed it."

"You won't have to do that. I promise. I'll do anything, everything, just like you said."

"Noon. Tomorrow. Santa's sleigh. The Portside Centre Mall. You drop off the bag, you turn around, you walk out the door, you go home."

"And when do I see Scott?"

"Are you asking me another question?"

"Wait! You have to answer this one. If I do everything you asked, if I pay you three million dollars, I have a right to know when the hell I get to see my husband, goddammit!"

Kyznetsoff grinned. The dumb blonde had balls.

"You will see your husband later."

"How much later?"

"That depends on how well you do as you are told."

He slammed the phone into its cradle. It was fun toying with her. But a bitter wind had come whipping up the street to remind him of his prior commitment.

He pulled his gloves out of the pockets of his elegant, double-breasted trench coat, the black one he had purchased at Brooks Brothers in the mall. The classic commuter's coat made him look like a distinguished businessman, another loving father come to see his children dress up as elves and reindeer and angels. He wiggled his hands to stretch the glove leather tight against his fingers. He wanted to make sure they were nimble, particularly his trigger finger.

The Kinkov automatic was hidden beneath the flaps of his coat, ready to be flipped out should that prove necessary.

Kyznetsoff stepped away from the pay phone and crossed the street. There was a Town Car parked near the curb. The driver had his seat tilted back so he could grab a quick nap while waiting for some rich asshole and his children inside. Kyznetsoff walked up the sidewalk to the sweeping stone steps leading into the Horace Abercrombie School.

A colorful poster on the front door told him the "PTA Annual Holiday Festival" was scheduled this evening at 7:30 P.M., just like Rizwan, his new buddy, had said it would be.

Soon it would be time for Kyznetsoff to face the enemy.

Christopher Miller.

74

Miller crawled across the cabin floor to the wounded man in the doorway.

Vincente's legs were trembling. Twitching. The heel of his boot kept bouncing up and down, drumming against the plywood floor. Blood was gushing out of his face where his eye used to be.

"Hang on," Miller said. "P. J.?"

P. J. had his rifle raised. "On me. Three, two, one. Go!"

P. J. swiveled left and laid down covering fire out the open door, spraying bullets at anybody stupid enough to be standing up in front of the cabin. Miller crouched beneath the line of fire, scrambled into the doorway, grabbed Vincente's vest, and dragged him clear of the opening, over toward the bed frame.

"Clear!" Miller hollered. P. J. leaped against the wall on the far side of the doorjamb. His rifle muzzle sizzled and smelled of burning oil.

Miller pulled Vincente to the medic, who tore open a sterile gauze pack and started working, tried to stanch the blood flowing out of the head wound. Vincente's whole body was trembling as if he were being electrocuted. Another volley of gunfire came rattling up from the forest. Windowpanes were smashed. Chunks of wood bounced out of the walls. Bursts of bullets thumped into the split log siding out front.

"Down!"

All the agents inside the cabin were squatting, hugging the walls, duckwalking into position around the windows. The barrage went on for another thirty seconds. More glass shattered. Kitchen cabinets were riddled, the refrigerator dented. Then, as quickly as it began, the firestorm ended.

"Damage assessment?" P. J. barked.

"Vincente's in real bad shape, sir," the medic said as he ripped open more bandages and pressed them down on the injured man's head to sop up the blood.

"Anyone else? Anyone hit?"

No one responded.

Miller turned to Scott Wilkinson, who had been strapped into his gurney before the attack began. The man looked zonked out, his head lolling sideways.

"Scott?"

"Mmmmfff?"

"Scott?" Miller kept at him. "Did Kyznetsoff have accomplices? Was there anybody up here working this thing with him?"

"No."

"Okay, Scott. Thanks. Take it easy. We're gonna get you out of here."

Scott drifted off.

Miller moved to the left side of the door. P. J. was crouched across from him on the right. The door was wide open.

"You still got men out back?" Miller asked.

"Affirmative. One team came through the windows." He motioned toward the five men clustered near the far front window. "Another exterior team is prowling the perimeter. I have them holding position."

"What about the mobile units? Down on the road?"

"Standing by. As are the choppers, in case we need air support."

"Why didn't the roadblocks stop these bastards?"

"Must've come through the forest. Maybe an old logging road."

"Okay. Okay." Miller rubbed his cheeks until they squeezed together over his lips. It helped him think. "You ever feel like Davy Crockett at the Alamo?"

"Just once," said P. J. "Right about now."

"I register five bogeys," said the CIA man named George-o. He had screwed together enough attachments to jury-rig an infrared periscope and was underneath a window using it. "Three to the right, two to the left. Both teams are on the move. Coming up the hill. Approaching the cabin. Stand by. Left team is stopping, right team is doing the same."

"Left team must be the leader," said Miller.

"Affirmative." P. J. agreed. "Can we target them?"

"At my ten," George-o whispered.

"Roger that." P. J. brought his sniper scope up to his eye, mentally envisioned his firing coordinates, got set to swing into action.

"Nicolai?" a voice shouted.

Miller held up his hand. P. J. stood down.

"Nicolai Ivanov Kyznetsoff? *Kak dela*? *Poide"m popizdim.*"

"I wish we had a translator," Miller muttered.

"George-o?"

"He's asking somebody named Nicolai how things are going. Wants to chat."

"Christopher Miller, meet George Dzianowski."

"Russian?"

"Ukrainian."

"Nicolai?" the voice outside called again. "*Poide"m popizdim.*"

"He repeats that he wants to chat," George-o reported. "But my little green screen shows all five intruders have their weapons raised and ready, trained on the doorway."

"Nicolai? *Ty mne van'ku ne val'aj. Ja Vasily.*"

"Anything we need to know?" Miller asked.

"Not really. More of the same. First, he said something like, 'Don't pretend you can't hear me.' And then, basically, he said, 'it's me, Vasily.'"

"Vasily," said Miller, suddenly understanding.

"You know him?" asked P. J.

"We've never met. But rumor has it he runs the Russian mob out in Brooklyn. Did these five bring backup?"

"Negative," said George-o. "None that I can pick up."

"Guys?" It was the medic. He sounded somber. Exhausted. "We lost Vincente."

The cabin went quiet. No one said a word. Miller heard the baseboard heaters clicking, the refrigerator humming: just like Vincente had said he heard when they were all clustered outside.

P. J. slid down the wall until he was seated on the floor. He slapped in a fresh cartridge of ammo. "Gentlemen? Lock and load. I want full night-vision gear. Scopes and goggles. George-o? Relay targeting data, calibrate any shifts when the battlefield goes dynamic."

"Will do. They're on the move, sir."

"Distance?"

"Fifty yards and closing. Bogies on my ten and on my three."

"You ready to take them out?" Miller asked.

"With a vengeance." P. J. pulled out his radio. "Beta team? Split and flank. Fan out around the sides of the cabin, move up the hill, box them in, cut off their rear."

"Roger," crackled back an emotionless voice.

"Charlie team? Hold your position on the road. Lock it down."

"On it."

"Delta? I want you racing up the road, making all sorts of noise. Tear into the top of the driveway. But be prepared to lay down massive responding fire because these bastards are going to swing around and start shooting at you the second you pull in. It'll be hotter than a fresh-fucked fox in a forest fire. Copy?"

"Will do."

"When the bogies respond to Delta, we take them down. Understood?"

"Got it," crackled back the radio.

"Wait for Delta. Delta? Let's roll."

"On it."

P. J. put down his radio. "George-o?"

"Left now at eight. Right moving toward two."

"Let them come in a little closer," P. J. said. "We have the advantage, gentlemen. We launch on George-o's command."

All around him, Miller heard gun bolts being slid

back, gear jangling as the combatants made their final adjustments.

"Chris?"

"Yeah?"

"You see those switches? In the wall, above your head?"

"Yeah. Okay."

"How much you wanna bet one of them lights up the whole front yard? Halogen flood lamps if we're lucky. On the go, flick the switches. All of them. Let's see if we can light up these sons of bitches and blind 'em."

"Got you."

"After you hit the switch, swing to the door. Lay down covering fire left. I'll go right. But Chris? Stay low, hug the damn floor."

"I'll pretend I'm a doormat."

Rifles were raised. Men moved into their final positions around what was left of the windows.

"Stand by," said George-o.

Miller heard an engine roaring in the distance.

Delta team.

"On my mark." George-o had the bad guys lined up. "Left is at nine, moving toward steps. Right is at two, holding position."

Tires squealed. A car horn blared.

"Go!"

Muzzles cracked through glass. Miller flipped up the light switches. Above him, some kind of ceiling fan started spinning. In front of him, the forest lit up stark white. Targets stood frozen like deer caught in a highway full of headlights.

P. J.'s men took their shots.

A dozen automatic weapons chattered and screamed: from the windows, from the forest, out the front door. Bullets thunked into trees and unprotected flesh.

It was all over in less than thirty seconds.

The five Russians never even returned fire; they just toppled over and collapsed into the slush and mud.

P. J.'s flanking teams converged on the dead men from the east and west.

"Clear!" the leader shouted.

"Do you need the medic?" Miller shouted down the hill.

"Negative. They're all KIA."

Meaning the mobsters were all dead. Killed in action. Miller figured they asked for it. Came up here looking for trouble, found it. Detective Magruder would probably be glad to hear the news: Don Vasily was dead.

Miller's phone chirped. He snapped open its clamshell.

"This is Miller."

He listened then passed the word on to his team: Scott Wilkinson's kidnapper had just made contact with Melissa. The ransom drop was on. Tomorrow. Noon. The Portside Centre shopping mall.

"He chose the most public place he could think of," Miller said to P. J. "He's definitely trying to make it difficult for us to take him out during the drop. We'll have to track him down. Collar him later, some place safer."

"You know this mall?" asked P. J. "The Portside Centre?"

"Sure. It's near Jersey City. Natalie goes there whenever . . ."

Miller stopped.

"What?" asked P. J.

"The Wilkinsons live in Northridge. Kyznetsoff's setting this thing up for Jersey City. That's *my* home town. You think that's just some sort of coincidence or you think he's still pissed off at me about the damn diamonds?"

"Shit." P. J. understood.

Miller reopened his cell phone.

He needed to call Natalie.

75

Kyznetsoff waltzed through the front doors of the Horace Abercrombie School.

The security guard, an old man in a military-style white shirt, sat behind a folding card table in the lobby. The geezer had a paunch that draped over his utility belt and was armed with only a walkie-talkie.

"May I help you sir?" the guard asked

In the distance, Kyznetsoff heard children singing about the reindeer with the red nose.

"Yes. Sorry. I'm running a little late."

The guard leaned back in his folding chair, studied Kyznetsoff. Assessed his threat level. Nicolai could tell: the trench coat was working wonders.

"You Shari's dad?" the old man asked.

"That's right." Kyznetsoff put on his best simulation of a charming smile. "Did I miss the whole show?"

The guard used his thumb to gesture over his shoulder.

"No, but you better hurry on in."

"Thank you."

He strode down the hall, followed the music, made his way into the cafeteria.

Thirty or forty small children dressed in various costumes stood in rows on risers at the rear of a makeshift stage. Six boys and girls with construction-paper antlers and bright red noses were lined up near the lip of the stage singing.

Kyznetsoff scrutinized the room.

The cafeteria was packed with beaming parents so thrilled to see their children trained to behave like idiots. Prancing on their feet, pretending to be flying reindeer. He checked out the other children, the ones waiting their turn on the risers. Which child belonged to Miller? The boy dressed up like a Jew-toy? No. Rizwan the cab driver had said Miller had a *girl* who went to the same school as his daughter so it couldn't be that one. The sugar plum fairy ballerinas, perhaps? The angels with the gold-tinsel halos bobbing up and down on their heads? He needed more intelligence.

He looked to the parents at the rear of the room and spied Rizwan, a video camera glued to his face.

Kyznetsoff set off to greet him.

The audience was applauding. The reindeer bowed. They held their arms up in front of their chests and dangled their wrists like begging dogs so they could pretend to the end that they were prancing, dancing reindeer.

"Rizwan!" he said in a tight whisper.

"Boris?"

"Hello, my friend."

"What are you doing here?"

The audience kept clapping. The two men spoke in hushed tones.

"I wished once more to hear little children sing the carols." He dropped his eyes, as if revisiting some haunting sadness. "There will be no children in my home this Christmas."

"I thought you had six?"

"Excuse me?"

"At lunch, you said you had six children and one on the way."

"Yes. This is true."

A mother turned around to shush him.

Kyznetsoff smiled at her. Turned back to Rizwan. "But, you see, my wife wants to take the children to their grandmother's house, and I promised the boss I would work Christmas Eve and Christmas Day because I need the money to buy them all many presents."

Rizwan adjusted some knobs on his video camera. "Listen, my friend, I would love to hear more. However, I must now videotape Angela Miller. She and her group perform next."

Kyznetsoff spun around. Scanned the stage. The reindeer were marching out of the room into the hallway.

A group of little girls, all five or six years old, daintily stepped down from the risers and took center stage. They wore fluffy wigs, shiny halos, and white robes with cardboard wings jutting out the back. One girl, a black child, came forward. She, apparently, was the star. The others formed a line behind her.

"Is her father not here?" Kyznetsoff asked.

"He is out of town. Business trip. Excuse me."

Rizwan brought the camera up to his eye.

"Which little girl is Angela?"

"Shhh! Boris, please. I am recording sound as well as picture."

Kyznetsoff kept his impatience in check and backed away. Rizwan swiveled toward the stage.

A woman now placed a portable stereo player on the stage.

"And now, ladies and gentlemen," the woman said, "it is my *supreme* pleasure to introduce Angela Miller and her Singing, Swinging Angels!"

The girl up front. Huh! What do you know, he thought. The easiest target happened to be Miller's daughter.

The woman depressed a button on the CD player. The costumed angels rocked up and down on their heels and started spinning their arms around each other like eggbeaters.

"Little bright star keep shining," the recorded singers harmonized on the CD. The little girls moved their lips to mimic the words.

Angela Miller pretended to rock a baby in her arms.

"When he was born long ago on Christmas night . . ."

Kyznetsoff needed to think. Improvise. Adapt.

"Above his head a little star was shining bright . . ."

Christopher Miller was not here.

"The wise men followed that light above . . ."

His daughter, however, was.

"Little bright star lead us today to his love."

Yes! Angela could be Kyznetsoff's little bright star.

Leading her father, the not-so-wise man, to his death.

76

"Dammit." Miller slapped his cell shut.

"Voicemail again?"

"Yeah. Natalie never shuts down her phone, not when I'm working a job."

Miller and P. J. were back at the loading zone in the cow pasture. The helicopters had their rotors spinning and engines roaring. They were ready for liftoff. Miller saw Scott Wilkinson being loaded onto a MedEvac chopper for the short hop over to the hospital. He also saw a black vinyl bag. Six men with grim faces handled it. Victor Vincente's body would be riding with Scott. The hospital also had a morgue.

"We've alerted the local police in Jersey City," P. J. said. "You know a Tony Cimino down there?"

"Yeah."

"He says not to worry. He's all over it. And he contacted Newark. The FBI is sending a response team to secure your home. I don't think Kyznetsoff will try anything until he gets his hands on the ransom money."

"The school," Miller said. "The Horace Abercrombie School. Downtown. We need to send somebody over there."

"Okay," said P. J. "I'm on it."

A helmeted chopper pilot trotted towards them. He screamed to be heard over the thunder of the thumping blades. "Gentlemen? I'm ready to move out."

Miller nodded. "Okay. Let's roll. Come on, P. J. We need to hustle."

P. J. held up a finger. He needed one more second. He brought the walkie-talkie close to his lips and practically screamed into it.

"The Horace Abercrombie School . . . Jersey City . . . I need them there ten minutes ago, copy?"

Miller couldn't hear the response, but P. J. gave him a thumbs-up.

"They're on their way."

"Can we beat them there?" Miller asked the pilot.

"Where to?"

"Grade school. Jersey City."

"This school have some place for me to put down?"

"Parking lot and playground."

"That'll work."

The three men ducked beneath the rotor wash and dashed toward the chopper.

Miller wished the helicopter was a jet. The Concorde. Maybe an F-16. Something supersonic.

His girls needed their old man.

77

Angela and her backup singers took their bows and rushed off the stage.

Kyznetsoff slipped out the back door and into the hallway. He could see the children jumping up and down, their cardboard wings flapping. They were devouring cookies, chattering with their mouths full of crumbs.

Kyznetsoff approached the mother pouring fruit punch into paper Christmas cups.

"Excuse me," he said, sounding as officious as he could. "Ma'am?"

"Yes?"

"I'm Agent Johnson. FBI?"

He flashed her his wallet. There was nothing in it but some fake credit cards but he flashed it so authoritatively the woman had to think he was legit. Kyznetsoff had studied many American movies and television shows. He knew how to play this part. The trench coat, once again, helped.

"Is there some problem?" the woman asked, setting down the juice carton.

"Yes, ma'am. I need to remove Christopher Miller's daughter to a more secure location."

"Oh, dear. Is something wrong?"

"Yes, ma'am. There's been an incident."

"Does her mother know?"

"Excuse me?"

"Mrs. Miller? Does she know?"

"Does she know what?" said a beautiful black woman in a tight-fitting holiday sweater.

"This man says there's been an incident with Chris. He says he with the FBI."

The black woman strode up to Kyznetsoff. He couldn't help but notice she had shapely legs.

"What kind of incident?" she asked.

"We have a situation."

"What kind of situation?"

"A bad one."

"Did Chris get burned?"

"No. The fire was brought under control."

"What?"

"He sustained no bodily injuries."

Christopher Miller's wife stared at him, placing her slender hands on her hips. Nice hips, too. Not wide. Shapely, suggesting a well-formed bottom.

"Okay," she said, "who the hell are you?"

"Agent Johnson," the other woman said, trying to be helpful. "He showed me his badge."

"Is that so?" Mrs. Miller stuck out her chest, moved closer. Kyznetsoff stared at her big breasts as they strained against the sweater. "Well, 'Agent Johnson,' when I asked did Chris get burned, I meant did somebody blow his cover, not did he somehow set himself on fire. And you'd know that if you'd spent even one second anywhere near an FBI office, so maybe you better show that badge of yours to me."

Kyznetsoff reached into his trench coat, made like he was going for his ID in an inner pocket.

Instead, he pulled out the AK-47.

The other woman screamed. Jumped back. Knocked the juice carton off the table.

The children heard the commotion, saw the gun. They started screaming, too.

Inside the cafeteria, the boy singing about his dreidel stopped. Kyznetsoff heard chairs being pushed back, metal legs screeching against linoleum floor. People rushed to the doorways to see what was going on out in the hall.

When they saw the man in the trench coat aiming his machine gun at Natalie Miller, they all ran back into the cafeteria. Women screamed. Kyznetsoff heard men trying to sound brave. "Someone call nine-one-one!" one man yelled, apparently afraid to dial the number himself.

Angela's mother moved toward her.

"Don't do anything stupid," Kyznetsoff said. "Stay where you are standing or I will splatter your daughter's brains all over the wall. These other children, too."

"Okay," Natalie said, holding up her hands in surrender. "Just try to chill—"

"Chill?"

"Take it easy. There's no need for you to hurt anybody. Just tell us what you want."

Kyznetsoff congratulated himself.

"Your daughter."

He wet his lips.

"And you."

78

The helicopter pilot raised his visor, turned to face his passengers.

"Special Agent Miller?" he yelled.

"Yeah?"

The pilot tapped his ear. Pointed at Miller. Gestured to his copilot. Tapped his ears again.

The copilot understood. He plugged in a phone jack, reached into the back with a third headset, handed it to Miller.

Miller slipped the thick ear pads into place, adjusted the swivel microphone.

"This is Miller."

"Chris. Tony Cimino, Jersey City PD. We have a situation."

"At the school?"

"Yeah. A nine-one-one call just came in. Caller reports a man with a gun. The man has taken hostages."

"Who?"

"We don't know."

"Tony? Is it my family?"

"I repeat, we do not know. We are currently en route to the scene."

"Tony?"

"Chris, I swear—I don't know. I'll tell you more when we get there. Right now, you know what I know. Man with gun. Hostages."

"Hurry. Tell Natalie and Angela I'm on my way."

"Ten-four. I'll keep you posted. Hang in there, okay? We'll nail this bastard. I promise. Out."

Miller slid off the headphones.

He had never felt so helpless.

Where was Saint Christopher when his family actually needed him? Up in the clouds, unable to do anything about what was going on down below, unable to change or control the situation, unable to do diddly or squat. He was like Santa Claus on the Fourth of July: he might've been a big shot a while back but right now he was nobody worth knowing.

P. J. tapped Miller on the knee.

"Bad news?"

"The worst." Miller stretched out the headphones, pulled them back down over his ears, spoke into the microphone. "Pilot?"

"Yes, sir?"

"Did you hear all that?"

"Yes, sir."

"Is this bird capable of doing any better?"

"Yes, sir. I can definitely goose her."

"Do it."

The pilot nodded, pressed forward on his throttle. Miller felt the g-force thrust him back into his seat.

They were definitely moving faster.

But probably not fast enough.

79

Kyznetsoff tapped on the car window with the muzzle of his pistol.

The limo driver was still stretched out in the Lincoln, still napping.

Kyznetsoff tapped again. Harder.

The driver woke up.

"Out!" Kyznetsoff ordered. In his right hand he held the AK-47, which he kept trained on Mrs. Miller and her daughter. In his left, he gripped a Makarov pistol with an attached silencer. He aimed the pistol at the driver. "Out! Now! Move!"

The driver was wide awake.

He opened his door.

"I have no money." The scared little man stepped out of the car and into the street. He raised his arms up over his head. "I have no money."

"What a pity." Kyznetsoff pressed the tip of his pistol into the driver's forehead. "For you will die a very poor man." He squeezed the trigger. The pistol made a soft *thwick*. The man's skull exploded. He toppled sideways like a marionette that had just lost all its strings.

Kyznetsoff turned to face his hostages.

Mrs. Miller was covering her daughter's eyes, shielding her offspring from the ugliness of such a brutal world. Stupid bitch. He tucked the still-warm pistol into his pants.

"Get in," he ordered. "Get in the car!"

"Okay. Okay." Mrs. Miller answered. But she just stood there, shielding her daughter's eyes with her hands.

"Move!"

Kyznetsoff knew the woman was stalling, wasting his precious time, praying that the police would come screaming around the corner to rescue her.

"Get in the car!" He yanked open the rear door. "Get in now, or I will blow her head off, too!" He grabbed at the collar of the child's costume and snatched her up off the ground.

"Leave her alone!"

With one hand, Kyznetsoff heaved Angela into the back seat. With his other he wiggled his rifle barrel in front of her mother's face.

"Do you prefer joining your daughter in the car or the driver in the gutter? Your choice."

Mrs. Miller held up her hands, ducked down, and slipped into the rear seat. Kyznetsoff slammed the door shut behind her.

"Fucking bitch!" He kept the gun pointed at his passengers and checked out the vehicle's control panels.

The keys were in the ignition. The motor was idling because the soft, lazy driver was wasting gasoline to keep himself warm while waiting for his pickup.

Kyznetsoff jerked a lever and popped the driver's seat back into its upright position. He climbed in, power-locked the doors, and made certain all the windows were rolled up tight. He looked into the rearview mirror.

"If you try anything stupid, Mrs. Miller, I promise you—I will shoot your little angel first. Understood?"

She nodded. "Understood." The girl said nothing. She had a glassy, blank look on her face. Poor little thing. To witness such a trauma. To see a man's brains fly in chunks out the back of his head. Kyznetsoff chuckled. The little *chernye* may never speak again.

He jammed the transmission into drive and squealed away.

When he passed the front steps of the school, he saw Rizwan. The dirty Paki still had his video camera glued to his face, only now he was filming Kyznetsoff's getaway. The dickhead was attempting to be brave.

Kyznetsoff's foot hovered over the brake pedal. He was ready to stomp it, ready to roll down his window and riddle the stupid *zalupa* with a full clip from his AK-47.

But he heard sirens. Police.

He tromped down on the accelerator. He would deal with Rizwan later.

80

"We found the car," Tony Cimino said to Miller.

They were standing in the parking lot next to Horace Abercrombie Elementary.

"The Lincoln he drove out of here was abandoned outside the Econo Lodge on Tonnele Avenue. The guys found a piece of gold tinsel in the back seat. Your wife, she was with the Bureau, am I right?"

Miller nodded. "Yeah."

"Figures. She's doing good. Leaving us clues. Letting us know we found the right car."

When the police first arrived on the scene, the officers had concentrated on seeing to the dead limo driver and making certain the school was secure, that all the children and their parents were safely evacuated.

Then, Rizwan Raja had shown them his video. An all-points bulletin was immediately issued for a black Lincoln Town Car with Jersey tags, license number RK 45989. Rizwan had used his zoom to capture a close-up of the rear plate as the car sped away.

That car had now been found—but not the driver or his hostages. The police had shown Rizwan a photo of Nicolai Kyznetsoff sent over by the FBI. He identified the man in the photo as Boris Smirnoff, a Russian immigrant who had recently started work at the Jersey City Cab Company.

"Was Kyznetsoff staying at the motel where you found the Lincoln?" Miller asked.

"Yeah. We showed his picture to the desk clerk. She recognized him."

"Did they take down his license number when he registered?"

"No. He told them he caught a cab at the airport; didn't have a car."

P. J. ducked under a sagging ribbon of yellow crime-scene tape to join Miller and Cimino.

"We're setting up a command center," P. J. said. "Downtown at police headquarters. Your friends from the FBI are already there. I tell you what—that man Rizwan? He caught a good close-up of our doer on his video camera. We exported the image, cleaned it up some, and sent it out. We could issue an Amber alert. Splash this thing all over the radio. Put Kyznetsoff's face on TV. We can still make the eleven o'clock news."

"Hold off," Miller advised.

"Why?" asked Cimino. "We get John Q. Public helping us, we'll track down this dirtbag in no time."

"This dirtbag happens to be holding my family hostage. He is also KGB-trained, psychotic, heavily armed, and prone to unpredictable fits of violence when cornered."

"Understood," said P. J.

"Why's this nut job gunning for you, Chris?" asked Cimino.

"Long story. I'll tell you later."

"Special Agent Miller?" It was a young policewoman. She came over to the men with a serious expression crinkling her otherwise unlined face.

"Yes, ma'am?"

"I just heard from headquarters. There's been a development."

Miller's anger surged. "Did he hurt my family?" he demanded.

She remained calm. "We don't know, sir. However, someone just called Mrs. Melissa Wilkinson." The police officer checked her notes. "Nicolai Kyznetsoff wants to change the time of the ransom drop."

"Okay. Okay. Sorry I snapped at you."

"To be expected, sir. Considering." Miller could tell that this young woman was already a pro. He was glad to have her on his team.

"Yeah. Okay. This could be good. Kyznetsoff still wants his money. He's not going to do anything stupid until he picks up his three million dollars."

Cimino looked puzzled. "This same Russian guy? He's some kind of three-million-dollar kidnapper, too?"

"Like I said, it's a long story."

"Sounds more like a frigging novel."

"Yeah." Miller turned to the policewoman. "What's the change of plan?"

She checked her notes again. "The caller told Mrs. Wilkinson to put the duffel bag inside Santa's sleigh at the mall tomorrow morning at nine thirty A.M. Sharp."

"Used to be noon," said Miller, figuring Kyznetsoff was in a hurry to grab his money and hightail it out of town now that he knew everybody and their aunt would be on the road looking for him. "P. J.? We need to deploy a strike team up at his cabin. Kyznetsoff doesn't know yet that we rescued Scott Wilkinson. He could head back up there to deal with him."

"We'll contact the Pennsylvania State Police," said P. J. "We can coordinate through them."

"Okay," said Miller. "Let's stay where our feet are. Deal with what we can deal with." Miller said it to the others, but he was the one who really needed to hear it. "What time does the mall open?" he asked the policewoman.

"I'm not sure," she answered. "I think around ten . . ."

"So Kyznetsoff wants his money at nine thirty? Before the place is even open?"

"No," said Cimino. "Tomorrow is Fabulous Friday."

"What?"

"The mall opens early. The radio said seven A.M. You know the bit: big sales in every store, drastic last-minute markdowns, huge holiday savings."

"So, the place will be packed?"

"Mobbed," said Cimino. "Last year the bargain hunters started lining up at five, six A.M. We had to swing by a couple times to break up fistfights, women wrestling over the same sweater, knocking each other down to grab the last Kick Me Elmo."

"Tickle Me," said Miller, remembering how much Angela loved hers.

Cimino shrugged. "Whatever. Your guy must want a crowd around him."

"Yeah. We think so."

"Well—he's gonna get one."

81

Angela had still not said a word.

Not since the Russian shot the man right in front of her.

"Don't worry, baby," said Natalie. "Mommy's right here. I won't let anybody hurt you."

Angela only stared back blankly. Her eyes had lost their twinkle. Her chubby cheeks drooped, dragged her small, sunny smile down into a frown.

She was probably in shock.

"Stay quiet and stay warm, sugar." Natalie had already peeled off her heavy sweater and draped it across Angela's shoulders. Now she reached over, tucked it in tighter. "Stay warm."

The Russian was outside the car, urinating against a graffitied wall. He was using one hand to steady his stream, the other to smoke a cigarette. The AK-47 was lying on the ground near his feet. The pistol, the murder weapon, fired in a moment of mild irritation, was tucked under his belt.

Natalie considered running. Thought about making a mad, desperate dash. But it wouldn't work: Angela weighed too much for her to carry while dodging automatic-weapon fire. And the child couldn't run because she was barely conscious. Angela had drifted off to someplace safer. Someplace where she didn't have to watch a man's head explode.

"Daddy will come for us, honey. You know he will. Just hang on. Okay? Mommy's here. Daddy's coming."

If he can find us.

Natalie and Angela were locked inside the back of a 1988 Chevy Caprice. It looked like all the other secondhand clunkers still cruising the Jersey Turnpike. This was the third car they had been shuffled into that night.

It seemed to Natalie that the Russian had stashed vehicles in various locations around Jersey City as part of an elaborately plotted escape plan. He wasn't going around town stealing cars; he was picking up automobiles he had previously parked. Natalie knew this because, after the man had forced them out of a minivan and into the Caprice, he had gone around to the rear of the car and opened its trunk. He seemed pleased to find whatever it was he was looking for, whatever he had stored back there earlier.

The man had stopped one other time, to make a phone call, and then he drove them here, out to this abandoned stretch of Jersey City: a lifeless ghetto of forgotten warehouses and bombed-out–looking factories situated beside some old freight train sidings.

Nobody came out here anymore, nobody except the gangs and crack addicts who spray-painted tags on the stained walls and collapsing coal chutes.

The Russian finished his business. He extinguished his Marlboro by flicking it into the puddle of urine pooling at the base of the wall.

He turned and stared at the car.

Then he walked over to it and jerked open the door.
He lowered his hand to the crotch of his pants.

"You are one foxy lady," he said. "Very foxy. Tell me,
foxy lady, does Christopher Miller fuck you good?"

Natalie turned to Angela.

"Don't listen to this man, sweetie. He's a liar. Everything he says is a lie." Angela stared blankly, her eyes
glazed. She was focused on somewhere far away.

When Natalie turned back around, their captor was
leaning inside and had his face almost touching hers. He
flicked his tongue in and out, as if to lick her with it.

"I could fuck you better," he said.

Natalie didn't say anything. She didn't flinch.

"I could fuck you and your little girl could watch."

The Russian man grinned. He sucked a fleck of
tobacco between his teeth.

Natalie kept cool—her face chiseled in stone.

"Would you like that?"

Natalie slowly crossed her arms over her chest and
stared at the man staring at her, made her eyes turn icier
than his.

Then she mirrored his sly smile—gave him back his
own mocking grin.

It seemed to piss him off.

"Your husband? He tried to fuck me! He tried to
steal my diamonds! Did he promise you a big, fat ring
this Christmas? Is that what Grandfather Frost has in
his bag for you, bitch? Did you know Christopher
Miller was working with Alexei Bizanko? Smuggling
uncut diamonds out of Russia? Did you know this?
Your husband—he may be FBI, but he is a crook!"

Natalie said nothing. She held her stare, allowed her grin to slide into a bored sneer.

"Ah, fuck you!" The man backed away from the car, the AK-47 held limply alongside his thigh. "Tomorrow," he said. "Tomorrow, I will deal with you both. I would kill you now, but I must wait, foxy lady. You must help me run a little errand at the mall. After that? We shall see."

The man turned his back on the car. He cupped his hands against the wind and hunched over to light up another cigarette. Natalie watched the glow illuminate his angry face and, confident the Russian was concentrating on his cigarette, not her, she finally let the revulsion shiver out of her body. The man disgusted her—scared her—but she'd never let him see it. It would only make things worse.

She knew psychopaths lacked guilt or remorse. They did not feel empathy. They lived only for themselves. In fact, this man thrived on making others feel miserable. He was like the feral cat who toys with a mouse it has already caught—hoping fear will somehow make the mouse secrete terror enzymes to make its meat even tastier.

If you showed fear, pleaded for your life, begged for mercy, if you showed the psychopath how scared you truly were, you were only giving him what he craved.

Dr. Natalie Miller would give this man nothing.

"Hang on," she whispered to Angela. "Daddy's on his way. Saint Chris is coming."

82

At six A.M. on Friday, December twenty-second, Christopher Miller was at Melissa and Scott Wilkinson's house.

"When can I see him?" she asked.

"As soon as you leave the mall. We'll have a chopper standing by to take you right out to the hospital."

"We talked last night. He was already feeling better."

"That's wonderful," said Miller, forcing a smile. He had not told her about his own family. He figured if she knew about Natalie and Angela, she might freak out, might not be able to face Kyznetsoff, should he decide to show up at the drop site. "Glad you two talked."

Two field techs were finishing work on the duffel bag. They zipped it shut.

"It's loaded," one of them said. "We've sewn three miniature GPS transmitters into the lining of the bag. Two on the sides, one on the bottom. We only need one, but the redundancy insures trackability should we experience any type of technical hitch."

"And," the other tech chimed in, "we tossed in a couple dye packs for good measure."

That piqued Melissa's curiosity. "What's a dye pack?"

"A stack of bills that explodes when he opens it," Miller explained. "Stains the money a bright red." He turned to the techs. "Take them out of the bag."

"How come?" asked the tech.

"Take them out."

"Well, if Scott's safe," Melissa said, trying to be helpful, "you might want to use every trick in the book to catch this creep."

"I want nothing that's going to upset this guy. Nothing but the transmitters," Miller explained. "And I want those hidden better than my kid's Christmas presents. Understood?"

"Yes, sir," the tech said. "Sorry."

Miller nodded.

Now all he had to do was make certain Angela got home to open those presents.

83

"We have fifty FBI and about three dozen local police in place," Marcie Adler, the New York–based agent running logistics, explained.

"A lot of these guys were already starting their Christmas vacations, but they signed on when they heard what was up. You know Myers? He was at the airport and sent his family down to Disney World without him." She took a short pause. "Of course, who could blame him?"

Miller nodded. "Tell everybody I appreciate it."

Miller was being briefed by Adler while en route to the Portside Centre Mall, traveling with part of the team in a van with blacked-out windows. He kept reminding himself: stay where your feet are. Deal with those things you can actually do something about.

Yes, he was sick with worry about Natalie and Angela, worried that they had spent almost twelve hours in the company of a killer. But Natalie was sharp. Highly trained. Able to think on her feet better than anyone he'd ever seen. And she'd fight like a lioness to save her baby girl. Miller had to hope that Kyznetsoff was so eager for his payday that picking up the ransom had become his primary objective. Maybe he only intended to use Natalie and Angela as bargaining chips to facilitate his escape. Maybe he'd send everybody scurrying off to find *them* while he slipped out the back door and hit the highway.

Maybe he'd use them as some kind of shield.

If he did, if Kyznetsoff brought Angela and Natalie into the mall with him, his friend P. J. was a good enough sniper to take the man down. Nail him in front of Santa and all those kids. Please let it not come to that. He could only pray that Kyznetsoff would flee with his money and the transmitters and lead his pursuers straight to his hideout.

"We've coordinated with mall security," Adler continued. "All available personnel will be on-line with us and all cameras will be trained on the Santa sleigh area."

"Good."

"You'll be in the security office coordinating."

"Okay."

"We have plainclothes folks working every level."

"Good."

"We have cars in the parking lot, a SWAT team standing by in the garage."

Miller didn't respond.

"We're in good shape, Saint Chris."

Now he nodded. "Thanks, Marcie. Where's P. J."

"Already at the mall. Choir practice."

"Come again?"

"He'll be with the Saint Luke's Choir. Stationed just below the top tier of The Singing Christmas Tree."

Miller liked the sound of that.

He knew P. J. would be taking his sniper rifle up there with him.

He could hide it under his choir robe.

84

At 9:20 A.M., the Portside Centre Mall was already packed.

The announcement of last-minute Christmas sales had done its job. It looked like the whole state had decided to drive to Jersey City to snap up the bargains being offered.

Parking, however, was no problem for Melissa Wilkinson.

She had been instructed to park in a yellow-striped, no-parking zone on the first level of the three-tier garage, right in front of the sliding-glass entrance closest to Santa Land in the atrium.

"You okay, Mrs. Wilkinson?" a voice asked from the small handy-talkie sitting in the passenger seat.

"Yes," Melissa said. "A little nervous, but fine."

"You see the bell ringer? On the other side of the sliding doors?"

Melissa saw a man in a Santa hat standing next to a red Salvation Army money pot.

"Yes. I see him."

"He's one of ours. We have people spread out all over the building, so don't worry, okay?"

"Okay."

"All right. Grab the duffel and head in. I'll talk to you again when you come out."

"Okay."

Melissa got out of her car. She had driven the hatchback because with all the passenger seats folded down, the big bag fit in the back. The money was very heavy. Fortunately, somebody at the FBI had been smart enough to purchase a rolling bag, the kind hockey players use to haul their equipment around the rink. It was huge but had wheels and a handle so she could maneuver it.

Melissa walked around to open the hatchback.

She heard the guttural rumbling of an old car in need of a new muffler. She glanced up and saw a blue clunker cruise past: somebody still searching for a parking spot, probably making their fourth or fifth loop and, most likely, cursing her out for parking so illegally. She didn't blame the family in the clunker—they didn't know her real reason for parking so close to the door. And if they asked? She couldn't tell them. The police and FBI told her not to speak to anyone. Get in, get out, go see Scott.

That was her mission this morning.

She grunted and the bag dropped to the ground. It nearly smashed her foot.

Melissa would be glad when this was over.

She tugged on the handle and headed into the mall.

85

Melissa heard the strains of live Christmas carols coming from the direction she was headed in.

As she reached the atrium, she saw a church choir up in The Singing Christmas Tree. They were proclaiming "Joy to the World." All the choristers wore red robes and green holly-wreath crowns on top of their heads, just like the Ghost of Christmas Past in that movie Scott loved to watch every year.

Just beyond the glass elevators, the Santa area was visible. His sleigh was parked on bright red carpeting beneath a giant arch supported by four gold columns, and the sleigh was so huge any reindeer would need steroids to make it fly. The cargo area was stacked high with unwrapped Christmas gifts being collected as part of the annual Toys for Tots drive. Baby dolls. Chess and checker sets. Plush stuffed bears. Bright red Elmos.

Melissa had brought one more present to add to the mountain: three million dollars in a duffel bag.

She rolled the carrier across the slick floor. To reach the sleigh, she had to weave around a gaggle of teenagers and squeeze past families and sidestep old people nibbling frosted pretzels, searching futilely for some place to sit down.

"Excuse me."

She cut through the long line snaking toward Santa. There had to be at least a hundred kids. It spilled out of the fenced-off switchbacks and wound its way halfway across the atrium, all the way down toward Sears. A hardworking elf in green tights snapped digital photographs of children sitting on Santa's lap. Another sat in a booth, ready to sell digital printouts in keepsake paper frames.

Melissa wondered if they were both young FBI agents.

She reached the rear of the sleigh, tilted the rolling duffel bag up on its wheels, leaned it against the strut of a curved runner. She wasn't strong enough to hoist the bag up and over and into the toy bin so she just left it sitting there.

She turned and walked away.

She figured the Russian must be somewhere in the crowd watching her. She wanted to find him, wanted to tell him to go to hell, to punch him in the face, to knee him in the groin.

Instead, she kept walking.

86

"The money's in play," said the agent sitting beside Miller in the mall's security office.

Black-and-white video monitors were lined up along one wall. Miller had seen Melissa Wilkinson drive in, park, enter the mall, make her way across the atrium, maneuver the rolling bag through the crowds, and position the duffel against the sleigh. Then, as instructed, she had turned and walked away.

On one of the cameras, he spotted P. J. up in The Singing Christmas Tree. What a good friend he was. Getting the interagency clearances so he could be here, looking ridiculous in a red velvet robe and holly headgear. And singing along, to boot.

"Mrs. Wilkinson has left the building," crackled a voice over Miller's Handie-Talkie. "She is in her car. Two unmarked vehicles will escort her. She is now clear of the garage."

"Time check?" Miller asked.

"Nine thirty-five, sir," came the reply.

"Good," said Miller. "We're on schedule. Jumping through all his damn hoops. Tell the chopper to stand by. Have Mrs. Wilkinson escorted to the airfield."

"Copy that. Will do."

Within the hour, Melissa would be in Pennsylvania, hugging and kissing her husband. Her job here was done.

Miller had the feeling his was just about to start.

87

Kyznetsoff parked in a no-parking zone close to the door.

It was the same space he'd seen Missy Wilkinson use the last time he looped around the parking structure. The police were obviously monitoring this entrance to the mall. He didn't mind. He had a plan.

He also had insurance.

He found the strings on either side of the white beard, hooked them up over his ears, smoothed out the curling strands around his lips. The Santa suit (and its accessories) that he had bought at the Christmas Creations store in this same mall was a costume worthy of the real Grandfather Frost, a professional-grade garment.

He checked the ammunition clip on the AK-47, to be concealed in the toy sack slung across his back. He had cut out a firing hole in the bag should he need to swing it up into action. He rechecked the military knives holstered into his big black boots, felt the extra ammo clips and Makarov pistol Velcro'd into the stomach padding beneath the wide belt buckle.

Santa was locked and loaded.

He plucked the white-cotton–trimmed Santa hat off the front seat and tugged it down over his curly wig.

He looked up into the rearview mirror.

The wide-eyed little girl in the back seat was staring at him.

"Angela?" he said. "Where is your costume? Where is your halo?"

The girl said nothing. Her face remained dead.

"Mrs. Miller? Where is her Christmas costume?"

"She's still wearing it."

"*Da*. She has on the robe and the wings, but where is the halo?"

"It's broken. It tore apart when you shoved us into the car. Outside the school."

"Bullshit. Put it on her head. Now. Or I will make her a real angel. I will send her straight to heaven with a bullet up her nose. Do you understand, Mrs. Miller?"

"Yes," she replied calmly. "I understand."

Natalie found the crinkled gold tinsel lying on the gritty floor in the back seat. She stretched out the wire, crimped its ends together again and formed a smaller circle. While her mother worked on the halo, Angela continued to stare, without seeing, straight ahead.

Natalie gently placed the halo on her daughter's head.

"Just like a little princess wearing her crown," Kyznetsoff said, the words muffled behind his Santa Claus beard. "Ho! Ho! Ho!"

The little girl's stare fixed on him

He winked at her.

"You better not pout, Angela," he said. "Santa Claus has come to town."

88

The agent operating the video control panel zoomed a camera in on the driver of the dark blue car parked in the no-parking zone.

"Is that him, sir?" he asked.

"We should assume so," Miller answered. "All units, be advised: suspect is wearing a disguise. He has costumed himself as Santa Claus. Red hat, beard, the works." He squinted at the screen. "Can you zoom in there tighter? Is anybody in the back seat?"

"We'll see, sir."

Nicolai Kyznetsoff faded into a pixilated hodgepodge as the camera lens miraculously achieved a close up of the rear seat.

Miller held his breath.

The lens now pulled back slowly until he could make out two shadows in the back seat. One silhouette was taller than the other.

"Okay," Miller sighed.

He snapped open his microphone. "Ladies and gentlemen, our kidnapper seems to be carrying precious cargo. More specifically, my wife and daughter. So listen up—be extra careful out there. Steer clear of that vehicle. Give the man a wide berth and let Santa Claus come to us. Let him make entry and pick up his money. When he is away from the vehicle, we will initiate our rescue."

"Hold up, Chris." This from Cimino, who had just stepped into the Security Command Center. "We need to make sure he hasn't rigged the car with explosives or something. It would fit his M.O."

Oh, God. What if that were true? It made sense.

No way was Kyznetsoff going to let Natalie and Angela simply walk away while he went inside to collect his cash. Maybe this time he'd rigged up a real bomb, not a hunk of Play-Doh.

"He's likely to have some sort of booby trap hooked up to the car doors," Cimino continued. "Something to keep them in place until he gets back."

"What about your bomb guys?"

"Five minutes away."

"Not here yet?"

"No. Five minutes. When we put together our response package, nobody was thinking he'd blow up his getaway car."

"Okay. I get it. Let's do what we can do now."

"Four more minutes."

"Okay. Good. Four minutes." Miller made another announcement to the full team. "Ladies and gentlemen, the bomb squad is on the way. Until they arrive, stay away from that vehicle. Repeat: stay clear of the blue Caprice. We have reason to suspect it is wired with explosives. Once Santa is on the move, lock down any civilian foot traffic in that general vicinity. Close down all garage entrances on that side of the mall. I want nobody in, out, or anywhere near that vehicle until we know for sure it's safe. *Nobody*."

Not even Saint Christopher.

No hugging Natalie and Angela, who he knew were being so brave, until the all-clear was given.

Now he knew how Melissa must've felt when he told her she wouldn't be able to see her husband until her job was done.

89

Santa Claus stepped out of his car.

Popping open the trunk, he bent over and fiddled with some wires. When he was finished, he opened the passenger side door. Balancing the gun bag over his shoulder, he moved it into place so both his hands were free.

"Okay, you lucky little girl," he said to Angela. "It is time to go pick up presents with Grandfather Frost."

He reached into the back seat, grabbed her arm.

"What the hell do you think you're doing?" Natalie protested. "Leave my daughter alone!"

"*Poslushay ty, mudack!*" he snarled at her. "Listen to me, you stupid bitch. You do not tell me what to do. You stay here and you wait for me to return."

"Leave her alone!"

Kyznetsoff was delighted to see his glacially cool passenger so deliciously afraid. All night long, she had seemed so emotionless. Fearless. Now she was trembling.

He yanked on Angela's arm, dragged her out of the car.

"Don't!" Natalie screamed.

Kyznetsoff roared with laughter. Angela remained blankly silent.

"Take me!" her mother pleaded. "I'll go inside with you! I'll be your hostage! Leave Angela here! Take me! Please? *Take me!*"

"You? You I will take later. *Da.* I will take you and take you and take you. You will be dealt with, Mrs. Miller. You and the Wilkinsons and everyone else who tried to fuck with me. You will all be dealt with. And, if you try to run away, if you are gone when I come back with my money, I will kill your daughter!"

Kyznetsoff hoisted Angela up over his head and placed her on his shoulders. The girl remained lethargic, like a limp sock puppet, her limbs dangling loosely around his neck as he carried her toward the glass doors leading into the mall.

"Bring her back!" Natalie screamed from the car. "My baby! Bring me back my baby!"

Kyznetsoff spun around.

One hand steadied the little girl's two feet against his chest.

The other gripped the trigger of the AK-47 and aimed the cloaked rifle up at Angela.

Now Natalie finally got it. She sank back into her seat, held up her hands. She'd stop yelling. She'd wait quietly in the car. Enough.

Kyznetsoff was pleased. He pulled a remote control out of his pocket and aimed it at the rear of the Caprice. The remote chirruped.

"Ho, ho, ho!"

He was going inside to pick up his Christmas loot and nobody could stop him. Not even the stupid cop so poorly disguised as a Salvation Army bell ringer on the other side of the door.

They couldn't touch him.

Kyznetsoff was wearing a Kevlar vest underneath his Santa suit.

And the child, riding along, up on his shoulders, would deter any sniper bold enough to think he could take Kyznetsoff down with a clean headshot.

Not today.

Today he had insurance—a guardian angel.

90

Miller leaped out of his chair.

"I'm going down there."

Cimino held up his hand. "Wait a second, Chris."

"The bastard's got Angela. He's bringing her in—"

"Because he guessed we'd have snipers."

Miller whipped around to face the monitors. The choir in the tree was singing.

"P. J.? Stand down! Do not take the shot. He's using Angela as a shield. Abort your mission. I'm coming down there."

Again, Cimino held up his hand.

On the screen, P. J. shuffled out of the tree.

"Out of my way, Tony."

"Wait, Chris."

"What?"

"You ever heard of a nineteen-eighty-whatever Caprice with remote door locks?"

"What?"

"I didn't get my first door remote until, like, 'ninety-two or something."

"Do you have a point?"

"Yeah."

"Make it."

"That baby's wired to blow. He just switched on the timer. Think about it."

Miller was thinking.

He glanced at the video wall. P. J. was out of the tree, moving toward the sleigh.

Miller bent over and snapped open his communications microphone. "P. J.? Everybody? Listen up. We need to allow the Russian to keep moving. Do not try to interfere with his actions or slow him down. He's on a tight schedule and if he's delayed, we anticipate all hell will break loose."

Down on the ground, P. J. immediately changed course and ambled over to the window of Victoria's Secret, where he became a tall choirboy checking out the lacy lingerie.

"We stick with our original plan," Miller said, calming himself. "We let him take the bag, return to his vehicle, and deactivate the bomb. We will then follow the GPS trackers. We will apprehend him in a more remote, safer location."

"The bomb boys are in the garage," Cimino whispered.

"Okay. Good. Thanks, Tony."

Miller looked at a different monitor. Santa was marching into the mall. Children began to notice him, started to swarm toward him, to drag their parents over to meet him, to giggle and squeal with delight. Kyznetsoff was prepared. He held out a long ribbon of plastic-wrapped candy canes, dangling it like a fishing lure. The children moved closer to grab at the candy. They formed a protective wall. Completing his defenses was his tower—Angela perched atop his shoulders.

Wading through the sea of children, Kyznetsoff, in fact, resembled Saint Christopher making his way across a raging river.

Only instead of carrying the Christ child on his back, he had Christopher Miller's only daughter.

91

"Merry Christmas, everybody," Kyznetsoff said with a rumbling chuckle. "Merry Christmas! Happy New Year! *Feliz Navidad!*"

"Are you the real Santa Claus?" one child asked, confused to see two Santas: one marching through the mall, the other sitting in his sleigh.

"I am Grandfather Frost!" He moved closer to the sleigh. "I have come from Russia to bring you presents! Who likes candy?"

The crowd of children squealed.

"Fetch!"

Kyznetsoff hurled his candy canes as far away as he could. He heard them crack and shatter when they hit the marble floor fifty feet away. Screeching children scurried after his flung treasure, just as he knew they would.

The children had served their purpose.

He reached the duffel bag, grabbed the handle, felt its weight. He knew it was loaded down with money but he didn't have time to unzip it and check. If they had shorted him, he would make them pay. He would, of course, kill Scott Wilkinson. And the little angel, too.

Mrs. Miller?

Unfortunately, she would already be dead.

He started walking, dragging the rolling bag behind him. He checked his watch.

Mrs. Miller would be dead in five minutes.

He kept walking. Away from the sleigh. Away from the doorway he had used when he entered the mall.

92

In the security office, Miller realized what Kyznetsoff was up to.

"He's not going out the same way he came in! Send in the bomb squad. Immediately! Haul Natalie out of that vehicle. Do it now!"

Cimino made the call.

Miller stood up.

"Where you headed, Chris?"

"You guys get Natalie. I'm going to go get Angela!"

He flicked the talkback switch on the console.

"P. J.?"

"Yeah?"

"Track Santa. Tail him."

"I'm on it."

"Everybody else? Concentrate on clearing out that parking lot near the Caprice. It could blow at any second."

"Is Natalie still inside?" asked P. J.

"Affirmative," Miller said.

"Suspect is heading west," P. J. reported. "Moving toward the exit opposite Macy's."

"He probably stashed another car in the garage over there," Miller said to Cimino. "Shut it down!"

"Will do!" Cimino yelled back.

He had to yell because Miller was already racing out the door.

93

Natalie saw seven men in what looked like full battle armor come sweeping out of the rear doors of a white van.

They surrounded the Caprice.

"Check the trunk!" ordered the team leader.

The SWAT team member with the most padding, the one who looked like a hockey goalie, moved around to the rear of the car and popped open the trunk.

"Four minutes," the goalie reported to the others.

"Doors wired?" asked the leader.

"Negative. Single charge. On a timer. Get her out! Stat!"

Doors were nearly ripped off hinges.

Natalie slid across the seat.

"Mrs. Miller?" A man grabbed her arm to help her out.

"He has my girl!" Natalie couldn't see the man's face because he had his visor down.

"We know," the man without a face said as he yanked her up off the ground. Another clutched her under her other arm. Natalie's toes were ten inches off the garage floor. The two men started running, carrying her between them. They hurried up a steep ramp toward a sliver of daylight. They wanted her out of the garage, out of the concrete cavern, and they wanted her out *now*.

"He has my daughter!" Natalie reminded them again as they ran.

"Our men are on it!" the leader said between gasps for breath as they raced up an asphalt lane lined with evergreens. "Oh, Jesus. Down!"

The men dropped Natalie in a brittle patch of frozen grass and covered her with their armored bodies.

"What's going on?" she demanded. She lay crushed beneath their padded bodies and it wasn't easy to speak.

"Johnny couldn't defuse it. The bomb will blow in twenty-nine, twenty-eight—"

"Did he get out? Is he clear?"

"Yes, ma'am."

"Johnny's clear," affirmed the other one helping to cover her. She could hear a faint scramble of voices leaking out of the earpiece in the soldier's helmet: a countdown. Urgent commands. Men screaming, "Down! Now! Go!"

And then the earth shook.

94

Kyznetsoff heard the explosion at the far end of the mall.

As he anticipated, it was immediately followed by panicked screams. What were seconds ago harried but happy holiday shoppers were now simply terrified creatures. Screaming, yelling, whining, pissing in their panties.

The police would be busy now. Too busy to chase after Grandfather Frost in his nondescript Honda minivan. They wouldn't be able to stop every vehicle fleeing the shopping mall parking lot, either. The respectable citizens of New Jersey would ram right over them; they would break down roadblocks and barrel through barricades. They would be merciless in their mad dash to save their own sorry asses from the terrorists on the loose in the mall. When a bomb blows, it's every man for himself. Kyznetsoff would slip away unnoticed.

It was a brilliant plan.

Nobody in the chaotic mob cared about a Santa Claus dragging a three-million-dollar duffel bag and carrying away someone else's child.

They were all much too busy.

Worrying about themselves.

He pushed open the glass door that led into the parking lot where his escape vehicle waited, where it had been stowed since yesterday.

Santa Claus had come to town.

Now it was time for him to leave.

95

The police officers and the mall security officers formed a human wall to hold back the swarm of shoppers attempting to exit into the garage opposite Macy's.

Miller and P. J. were at the doors.

P. J. was kneeling, screwing on his silencer.

Miller addressed the crowd: "There's another bomb over here!" he improvised. "Another car bomb! In this garage!"

The crowd screamed and ran away.

"Okay," said P. J. "That'll work."

96

Miller followed the blinking green dot on his handheld tracking device.

P. J. followed Miller.

The duffel bag with the GPS trackers was a hundred feet in front of them. So was the Russian.

They crouched behind a car, waited, moved forward. Car by car, they moved closer to their target. Both men stepped lightly, knowing any sound they made would reverberate off the low ceiling. P. J. was extra careful about his choir robe, keeping it bunched up around his knees.

Miller held up his hand.

He pointed at the screen of the tracking device.

The green dot wasn't moving.

They heard a van door slide open.

"Get in," a voice echoed off the concrete walls. The door slid shut.

P. J. tapped Miller's shoulder. He touched his chest, pointed right. Miller nodded. P. J. moved into position.

97

"Why so sad, little *chernye*?"

Kyznetsoff took off his sweaty Santa beard, tossed it into the back seat with Angela Miller.

"Do you miss your mommy? Well, since you are an angel, you can go see her up in heaven." He twisted around in his seat, slipped the key into the car's ignition.

His mouth was dry. The morning had proved physically draining, the costume hot.

He reached through the pocket slit in the Santa costume pants and found his military fatigues underneath. He snapped open the hip pouch and pulled out two pieces of cherry candy.

He leaned around to offer one to Angela.

"You want candy? Is Russian. Is good."

The van's rear window exploded.

98

As soon as P. J. took his shot, Miller went flying.

He ran like he had never run before. Not in high school, not in college, not in that open field in West Virginia, not in his nightmares.

He made it to the minivan, tore open the sliding door.

Angela was okay.

She was smiling at him.

"Mommy said you'd come," she said.

"That's right, baby."

"That man?" She pointed dismissively at the slumped body in the front seat. "He's not really Santa Claus. He's too mean."

"He sure is, sweetie. He sure is."

Miller cradled his daughter in his arms. Kissed her forehead. Kissed her chubby cheeks. Breathed in her smell, the smell only she was blessed with.

"Saint Chris?" P. J. hollered from his firing position behind a cement column. "I tell you what—I'll feel a whole bunch better when you two are out of there."

Miller scooped up his daughter.

"Come on, honey."

"Where's Mommy?"

"Inside, talking to the real Santa. Telling him what a good girl you've been."

"I kept real quiet—just like Mommy told me to."

"Good for you." Miller picked up his pace. Started trotting. Instinct told him to run. To break into the open field and run for the goal line.

He saw P. J. rest his rifle against the column.

Then Miller heard a snap.

"Shit!" he heard P. J. exclaim.

Miller felt something burning in the back of his right thigh. His legs crumbled. He fell forward but twisted sideways so he could land on his back and catch Angela on his chest.

He'd been shot again. The nightmare wasn't over.

99

"I've got him lined up!" P. J. yelled.

"Big fucking deal!" Kyznetsoff yelled back. "I have the girl lined up, and this is a fucking machine gun!"

"Drop it!" P. J. screamed.

"Fuck you! You drop it!"

Miller was flat on his back, wincing in pain. He was clutching Angela to his chest, trying to protect her.

"Nicolai Kyznetsoff?" Miller called out from his sprawled position, staring up at the concrete ceiling.

Kyznetsoff mimicked him. "Christopher Miller?"

"That's right. I'm Christopher Miller. We need to talk."

"About what?"

"Diamonds."

"You fucked me over, you dickhead."

"I see now that I made a mistake."

"Oh. You see now? Now that I will splatter your daughter like I splattered your wife?"

Angela's eyes went wide. Miller winked up at her. She winked back. She understood. Daddy was playing one of his silly games.

"Let my little girl walk away and we can talk."

"Talking bores me."

"I know where there are more diamonds."

"Bullshit."

"What?" Miller laughed. "You think Alexei Bizanko is the only dude I'm working with over there? You think I set this whole thing up for one client? There are others. Mind you, we don't use dolls all the time. In fact, you might want to check out a shipment of caviar tins coming into Brooklyn the first week of January. I guarantee it's better than beluga."

"Bullshit."

"Let the girl go and we can talk."

"Fine. Send her away with your marksman. The dickhead sniper who shot me in the chest. The *zalupa* who wasted his bullet denting my Kevlar vest. Send them both away."

"Go on, Angela," Miller whispered. "Run to Uncle P. J."

"No, Daddy."

"Unh, unh, unh. Listen to me. Run to Uncle P. J. Run fast, honey. As fast as you can. Go!"

Angela pushed up and off of Miller's chest and scampered over to P. J.

"Go!" Kyznetsoff said. "Take the girl and go!"

"Chris?"

"Move out, P. J. I've got my own back this time. I don't need you distracting Mr. Kyznetsoff while he and I talk business. You understand?"

"Understood."

"Then move out!"

"You heard your boss!" Kyznetsoff snarled. "Leave before I change my mind!"

"Come on, honey," said P. J.

Miller heard feet scuff across concrete, the whoosh and squeak of the automatic door leading back into the mall. They were gone.

It was just the two of them now.

Miller could hear heavy Santa boots clomping across the concrete, coming closer.

Then he heard the madman slide back the bolt on his AK-47.

100

Miller propped himself up on his elbows.

"I do not really need more diamonds," said Kyznetsoff as he stood over Miller. "I have three million dollars." He looked ridiculous—beardless but in a Santa suit, a machine gun jutting out from his hip.

Miller could see the hole where P. J.'s sniper round had torn through the red velvet coat. It was centered over the Russian's heart—though Miller wondered if Kyznetsoff really had one.

"Three million dollars! More money than Bizanko ever paid you!"

"Maybe. But you can't spend any of it unless you can drive it out of here first."

"Is no problem. Have you not heard? I am professional limousine driver."

"You'll also be extremely easy to spot driving down the road with that very large bullet hole in your rear window."

"This is true. This is why I am taking you with me, Christopher Miller."

"What?"

"*Nashla kosa na kamen*, as we say. Your scythe has hit a stone. You have met your match. You will be my new hostage. You can tell me all about these other diamonds hidden in the caviar tins while we drive out to my *dacha*. If we are followed, I will kill you just like I killed your wife. Do you want your only child to become an orphan?"

"No. Of course not."

"Then get up."

"Give me a second."

"Get up!"

Miller sat up, put his hand near his kidney. "Damn, man. You shot me, remember?" Miller rubbed his back and grimaced. "It hurts like hell."

"You are a *petuh*. Do you know what this means?"

"No." Miller grimaced as he worked his hand under his jacket to rub the pain away.

"A *petuh* is a man whom all the other men use as their woman. Do you understand now?"

"Yeah."

"You are my bitch. You will do whatever I say."

Miller heard a whiz-ping behind Kyznetsoff.

Kyznetsoff heard it, too. He whipped around to see where the noise came from.

That's when Miller pulled his Glock out of the paddle holster strapped against the small of his back.

Kyznetsoff whirled back around, his finger on the AK-47's trigger.

Miller fired first.

He brought the Russian down with two quick pops.

Both were head shots.

101

"We're getting too old for this shit," said P. J.

"Yeah," Miller agreed.

P. J. tore off another shred from his T-shirt and wrapped it around Miller's wounded thigh. He had already draped his choir robe over Kyznetsoff's dead body.

"That was code, right?" said P. J., tying off a knot.

"What was?"

"That thing about your back."

"Yeah."

"I thought so. When you said you had your 'own back this time' and I might 'distract' the man, I figured that meant you had your Glock strapped to your back like you always do but that you could use a minor diversionary tactic to help you take him down."

"You figured right."

"I'm glad."

"Yeah," said Miller. "Me, too."

P. J.'s holly wreath crown was tipped over one ear and sliding down toward his nose. He moved it back into place with a tired chuckle.

Natalie and Angela came running into the garage. Two medics were right behind them.

"Daddy!"

"Hey, sweetie."

Miller wrapped his arms around his daughter and squeezed her tight, maybe tighter than he had ever squeezed her before.

He looked up. Natalie looked down.

"Hey, old man."

"Hey, doc."

Natalie cocked an eyebrow, curled her lip into a frown. "So, what happened? You get shot again?"

"Yeah."

"Same leg as last time?"

"Nope. The other one."

"Finally got himself a matching set," P. J. cracked.

"And I guess he forgot all about his wedding vows," said Natalie. "Decided he needed to be a hero just one more time."

Miller looked up at his beautiful wife. Saw the salty stains on her cheeks from when she had been crying.

"Baby . . . I'm sorry."

"Sorry? Could you please be more specific?"

"I'm sorry I, you know—I'm sorry I did what I did."

"Why?" Natalie's frown melted into a smile. "Somebody sure as hell needed to do it."

Miller grinned back. Natalie knelt down and hugged her husband and daughter. Pulled her family closer.

Angela gave her father a wet, sloppy smooch on his nose.

"I love you!"

"And you know what, angel? I love you, too. I really do."

ACKNOWLEDGMENTS

I can never fully express my gratitude to Don Weise and everyone at Avalon for publishing *Tilt a Whirl*, *Mad Mouse*, and now *Slay Ride*. Will, Michele, Karen, Wendie, Linda, Jamie, and Betsy—thanks!

I'd also like to thank my agent, Eric Myers—because he read all three manuscripts first (well, right after my wife).

I would be nowhere without my editor Michele Slung. She always makes my words work so much better.

And to those whose names appear as characters in this story because they donated to charities—thank you and I hope you're happy with who you became.

By the way, none of them is named Nicolai Kyznetsoff.